J
F
HEN

Hendry, Frances.   97

Quest for a maid.

$14.95

DATE			

QUEST FOR A MAID

QUEST FOR A MAID

Frances Mary Hendry

FARRAR STRAUS GIROUX

NEW YORK

Text copyright © 1988 by Frances Mary Hendry
All rights reserved
Library of Congress catalog card number: 89-46396
First published in Great Britain by
Canongate Publishing Limited, Edinburgh, 1988
Printed in the United States of America
Designed by Martha Rago
First American edition, 1990

To Bill Wilson
in memory of the *Sea Minx*

CONTENTS

———◆———

Author's Note

———◆———

The basic facts on which this book is founded, that Alexander III of Scotland fell from a cliff and his granddaughter, called the Maid of Norway, died in Orkney on her way across the North Sea to be married to Prince Edward of England, are reported in all the history books. But few record that, ten years after, a woman turned up in Norway, at the funeral of King Eric, claiming to be his lost daughter . . .

This is a tale for young people, not a history, though I have tried to be as accurate about the feelings and events of the time as I could. Mr. Richard D. Oram, M.A. (Hons.), of the University of Saint Andrews Centre for Advanced Historical Studies, has done his hard-working best to keep me within sight of the facts. He is due the credit for what is correct in the book; what is mistaken is so in spite of him. For instance, Richard warned me there is no historical record of Sir Patrick Spens, known to so many British schoolchildren from the famous ballad of his last voyage, but I went ahead and brought him in anyway; he was too good a character to lose.

Another person I must thank most gratefully and heartily is Bill Wilson, who told me about boats, sailing, and storms and tried to share with me his great love of the sea in all its moods. His lovely boat, the *Sea Minx*, lies now on the bed of the North Sea half-way over to Norway. I hope this book may bring him happy memories, not sad ones.

I must apologise, though, to the shade of Fru Ingibiorg Erlingsdatter. For all I know, she was a most excellent person; but the False Margaret, as the girl claiming to be the Maid of Norway was called, blamed the lady, so I made Fru Ingibiorg one of the villains.

Apart from the famous people on the fringes of the story, everyone in it is imaginary, and as they say, any resemblance to any real person is purely coincidental.

Anyway, that's my story, and I'm sticking to it.

I hope you enjoy reading it as much as I enjoyed writing it.

When Alexander our King was dead
That Scotland held in love and le
Away was sons of ale and bread,
Of wine and wax, of gaming and glee.
Our gold was changit into lead.
Christ, born into Virginity,
Succour Scotland and remede
That stayed is in perplexity.

le—law, sons—plenty, remede—cure

QUEST FOR A MAID

DEATH OF A KING

◆

*W*hen I was nine years old, I hid under a table and heard my sister kill a king.

For two days I'd had terrible toothache. I hid it as long as I could, for Dad had no patience with whining, but last night I'd tossed and wriggled and groaned in my bed till, what with my stir and my next-up sister Birgget beside me snarling at me to lie quiet and let her sleep, we woke the bairns, and they woke the babies, and they woke the house. Dad was annoyed.

"What the devil's wrong with you, Meg?" he shouted at me, storming to the entrance of the women's room, just a blanket round him, hopping and swearing, for he'd not stopped to fit on his wooden foot. I was petrified. All the serving lasses and bairns were giggling on the benches and pallets all round the bower. "There's not a soul sleeping from Queensferry to Dunfermline itself, with all your whingeing, and there's some of us has to work the morn."

"Away, Dad," called my oldest sister, Inge, from behind

the blue curtains of her corner bed. "Leave the lassie alone. It's the teethache. She's not trying to waken us."

"I know that fine!" he snapped. "If I thought she was, I'd leather the hide off her backside, so I would. Try what you can do for her the morn, lass, for if she's the same the morn's night I'll lift some wee pincers from my tool-box and have that tooth right out."

I was so scared I lay trembling but quiet till the children settled, he snored again, and at last some scraps of sleep came to me, too.

In the morning it was as bad as ever. I could scarce see, let alone do my work, for the tearing, stabbing pain under my eye. Old Asa, my father's ancient nurse, sneered at me from her huddle by the long firepits for such a carry-on and it a milk tooth, but Inge was sympathetic. She was aye my favourite sister. As soon as the early work was well started, with the bannocks baking, the big simmering pots of breakfast oatmeal and dried apple stirred up, the orphan lambs that were my special task seen to, and Dad, yawning and scowling, away out with the men to the shipyard, she called me over.

"Come away and we'll see what we can find to ease you, my pet," she murmured, in her clear, musical voice, like a blackbird singing.

Birgget looked jealous at me as we left, and I hadn't the spirit to make a face at her, but I started to feel better even as Inge unlocked the door of her own storehouse. No one was let in there without Inge at her side. Seldom a man set foot in it at all. For it was not the common store, full—or at this time of year, the middle of March, half empty—of the bere, barley, and oatmeals, the dried and salt meats, fruit, beans, and fish, the honey, wax, larded eggs, wool, and the thousand other things that kept us fed, warm, and comfortable. It was the wee house, apart from all the rest, that Inge had had our father put up for her, to be her own private place, to keep all the herbs and spices and—and other things, that she used to make her spells. For Inge was a witch.

Everybody in Inverkeithing knew it, and nobody had anything but respect for her. It was a grand thing for a town— even a big Royal Burgh like ours—to have such a skilled person for its wise wife. Inge went to Mass every Sunday and at least once more a week, and gave money for the new church tower, and took the Host like the rest of us, and not a soul would dream of lifting an eyebrow. Old Father Michael himself was glad of her help, when his back pained him in the winter, and she rubbed in a warming oil for him. And if she dipped babes in Saint Erat's spring after they'd been baptised by Father Michael in the church, to put them right with the Good Folk as well as the Christ Lord, well, was that not a helpful thing, and who would complain?

And she was so lovely, so tall and slim and graceful, with the long, silvery hair flowing from under her maid's chaplet, and the long, slender hands that she creamed every night. All the burgh lads were in love with her, and would gladly have wed her; but she refused them all, kindly and graciously, so that they loved her more than ever. She was the fashion for every man in Fife; even the lords riding on the king's business between Edinburgh, Stirling, Saint Andrews, and Perth used to call to speak to her, ask advice and help in their wooing, drink a cup of her fine ale, and bring gifts for the reward of a smile.

It was one of those presents that first showed folk what she was, when she was about fourteen. She'd been spinning, using a pretty new spindle a local lad had given her. It had a wee man's head carved at the top and coloured, with a red pointy hat, and a black beard for the wool hook. When I tottered up, about two years old, and wanted it to play with, she let me hold it while she got some more rolags of carded wool; and I tripped and fell on it, breaking the shaft. Furious, as she seldom was, she hit out at me, slapping the top of my head. I cried, and got no sympathy from anyone but her, for she was the only one who knew that the green stone weight from the bottom of the spindle had been in her hand, and the slap had been harder than it seemed. Anyway, from then on, a white streak of hair grew among the light brown on my head, just where her hand had touched me: a mark of her power for everyone to see.

I'd not been inside her store often before. It was a kind of forbidden treasure-house for us all; a room about four paces by six, with bags and barrels stacked high. Bunches of herbs hung drying from the rafters under the heather thatch, and on shelves and hooks all round the wooden walls were more bags and packages, pots and jars, each with its different coloured thread, knot, or mark to identify it, that only Inge knew. There was a table against the far wall, split planks smoothed and neatly fitted together, pegged to two of the wall posts. A brown linen bundle filled most of the space underneath, with some bags jammed in above it.

I hesitated at the door, looking round and sniffing greedily. "Come away in, my pet," Inge murmured. She never spoke loud. Somehow she never needed to. "You'd like to learn what I have in here? Well, maybe some day."

It was aye "some day," I thought. As if she knew my thought, and perhaps she did, she laughed gently. "When?" I asked. "Why not now?"

"First we've your tooth to see to, haven't we?" She could aye find a way to put me off. I noted the bags as she checked them along the shelf. "Cumin, costmary, fennel seed, mummy, aye, here it is. Cloves. Sniff that, my lamb. Is that not a grand smell?"

It was indeed. A scent of glory, of kings and gold and angels soaring to heaven. She took a wee browny-black knob of wood out of the bag, which she set back on the shelf among the rest. "Now, my pet, you put that in your mouth and bite on it with the sore tooth, not too hard, while you say three Ave Marias and three Pater Nosters. And by then all the pain will be away."

Eagerly I seized the tiny chip and bit the piercing throb down on it. A strange hot taste burned my tongue, and I'd have spat it out if she'd not been watching, but I held on. As I repeated the prayers to myself under her amused eye, the burning feeling died to a spicy warmth that slowly melted away the agony to a pain, to an ache, to a dull twinge, to nothing at all. I smiled at her, and she smiled back. We nodded confidently to each other.

Birgget sniffed as we returned to the main hall, and she caught the scent. "Cloves!" she spat. "Cloves for a bairn's teethache! They're worth their weight in gold, so they are, not even silver! And it a milk tooth, just! Have you taken leave of your senses altogether, Inge?"

Inge just looked at her. Suddenly Birgget decided that the porridge was sticking to the pot, and needed stirring at once. Something like that often happened to people who spoke rudely to Inge. I was very proud of her. Old Asa snickered to herself by the fire.

"Now, pettie, you keep that clove safe in your pouch. Whenever the pain comes, just slip it back in again, and say the prayers like I told you. Maybe in a day or two you'll not need it." She raised her voice the least bit. "It was a gift, so we'll say no more about the cost, eh?" Birgget's back was furious. Inge never glanced towards her. "Minna, have you and Alis not finished carding that fleece yet? You'll need to move faster than that if you want your new kirtles this Beltane. Everyone else's gown gets made before yours, mind! Domna, what shade of blue do you want that new thread dyed?" And she moved off into the bower, the women's room built out at the far end of the house.

All day I kept my clove carefully to hand. I needed it five or six times, but each time it seemed to work just as well. I held it gently in my teeth as I collected the hen and goose eggs while their mothers were occupied with the scrapings of the breakfast pots—it was safer then—helped my third sister, Elsbet, who was a grand cook, mix herbs and set salt cod, dried beans, and onions to stew for that night's meal, and sat out with the rest, enjoying the thin March sun for an hour or two while we span. We all spent a lot of time spinning.

We came in when the rain started. I saw to the lambs again, and then Inge set me to begin knitting for my second sister Domna's next baby that was due soon. With six older sisters, four of them wed, eight servant girls, and about a dozen wives of Dad's workers that lived in rough, lean-to bothies scattered round the big hall, there always seemed to be a new baby about the place, and Dad insisted each one should have something made specially for it, not all hand-me-downs. I didn't enjoy knitting and was a poor hand at it, but babies can't complain, so that job was given to me. I aye did a wee vest—it was quick, and the mangled stitches would be hidden by shawls anyway.

At dinner that night, disaster struck me. The toothache came again. Happily I fished out my precious clove, popped it in my mouth, bit down.

And swallowed.

Over my gullet it went. Lost.

I coughed and spluttered, hawked and spat till Inge frowned at me, but it was no use. It was away. What could I do? Ask for another? If they really cost their weight in gold—and the way Birgget had been mumping at me all day they must do—present or not, if I asked for more, I'd never hear the end of it.

But my tooth was aching something fierce.

What should I do? What could I do? Ask Dad to get his pincers, and get rid of it for good and all? I was too scared. I aye hated being hurt. "A right coward," Asa aye sneered, "in spite of she running to join in the lads' games instead of to her spinning!" I could just hear her, in her twisted Norse-Scots. I went away out into the dark, to try to hide my pain and embarrassment.

I visited the great draught oxen in their stalls, resting after their hire to the cottars for the spring ploughing, and gave them a handful of new grass each. The pain stayed. I hung over the pigpens for a while. There was a litter of piglets only a day old, nuzzling noisily at their dam. The pain stayed. My wee lambies were doing fine, looking for more milk from me. The pain stayed. If anything, it grew worse.

At last I left the sprawling outbuildings and cuddled up with the fiercest guard dog, Wolf, in his hole in the last of the haystacks, to warm myself. He loved me, for I'd raised him when his dam wouldn't feed him—I somehow got all the orphans—but even his tongue on my cheek couldn't ease the pain. After an hour, I was crying sore. Could Dad hurt as bad? Maybe—

Suddenly Wolf growled and the other dogs barked, sensing strangers nearby, and when I stuck my head out of the rustling hay I heard horses and voices. In the patchy moonlight I made out half a dozen riders dismounting away over by the gate, and one crossing to the hall door. Somebody had come to see Inge; somebody important. It happened from time to time. A medicine, usually. Or a love potion. I hushed Wolf, lay in the hay, and watched.

The hall door opened twice, and Inge came out with the man who'd been sent for her. She crossed the yard to the group of people, and dipped knee deeply—so deep, it must be one of the court, I thought. Dad had got a sore head more than once for failing to stand aside for them in the road. Then, while the others started to water their horses at the well, one took Inge's arm and stumbled with her across the cobbles to her storehouse.

Inge opened the door, but then turned. I could just hear her say something about a lantern, and she returned briskly to the hall. The visitor crossed back towards the horsemen, calling something about keeping good watch.

It came to me that if I hurried, I could slip in and get a clove before Inge and the lord came back to the store. I knew exactly where the bag of cloves had been left. Though I wouldn't be able to see it, I could pick it out of a thousand by the smell. Then winkle one out, and away. It would only take a second or two; and Inge had to go up the hall, explain to Dad what had happened, cross to the long shelves, get a lantern, light its candle with a taper from the fire, close over the horn panel, and watch it to see it didn't blow out while she collected her visitor again. I'd be well away by the time she'd done all that. And my tooth was tearing at my jaw. Did I dare?

I must have been mad.

I hushed Wolf, tiptoed over, and slipped in the door no

bother, felt my way across to the back of the store, fumbled for the shelf, sniffed only four bags before the right one—and as I remembered, the string was still loose. I wriggled one clove out, put back the bag, and was luxuriously sliding the hot little chip into my mouth when my shadow spread over the shelf before me. A light—Inge was coming in! Lord help me if she found me in her secret place!

In less than three seconds I was biting my knuckles behind the bundles under the table, praying I'd not sneeze with the dust on them.

"Enter, lady, and nothing fear."

That wasn't Inge's voice. That was Asa. And "lady"! Not a man, then? It was most often the men who sought Inge out.

"Fear? What is to be feared?" She had a nasal court accent. "I ask only can you do it."

"It's a great risk you'd have us take, lady," said Inge. "Can you not just wait? If your man has the right, like you say—"

"Did I ask for your advice, woman?" the sharp voice snarled. "If he should have a child—a son—our chance would be gone. And with this new young wife, anything is possible, is it not? He is not yet old."

"Aye, a young wife can a man's strength renew," snickered Asa maliciously.

"But meddling with a king . . ." murmured Inge.

A king? What king? Not our King of Scots, Alexander? What was going on?

The lady was angered that Inge did not obey her without question, but she tried to hide it. Maybe she was afraid, too. "Who is ever to know? If you can but weaken him with your spells—I hear you can do great magics—"

"Magic?" Inge cut in quickly. "That's against the law and the Church, lady."

"You argue with me? I have proofs. Oh, yes. You wish to face the church courts for trafficking with the Devil? You know what would happen then, no?"

I could hear Asa draw in her breath hissing between her teeth. For though no one local would bother Inge, if one of the nobility chose to press charges of witchcraft she might end up drowned, or on the gallows.

Inge herself seemed less worried. "You say you have proof, lady?"

"Indeed. Not a month past, a man came to you for a cure for his wife, who had a melancholy upon her, and you sold to him advice and a magic potion."

"I remember him. A poor soul. I bade him love his woman better, and gave him a bottle o' brandy wine with a nutmeg in it to cheer her. No magic at all. Not much to hang me for, lady."

"But enough."

"Maybe so. But this that you'd have me do is far more."

"And you will be paid far more for it. Not in silver; in gold. And have no fear, you. If you do as I desire, is it likely, think you, I will tell anyone?"

"Is it likely, lady, you'd leave me alive when I might tell? There's more risk to this than you'll admit. But I do not fear you. I've seen my death, and it's not by rope or water, and not yet a good few year." The woman gasped at the gentle certainty in Inge's voice, as much as at the mystery of what she said. To see your own death! How terrifying! But Inge went on quietly, "No, lady, I'll not do it for fear o' any laws, nor for all the silver or gold you could give me."

Even as I gladdened at her refusal, something in what she said caught at my mind. The noblewoman noticed it, too.

"Then for what will you do it?"

Inge did not answer directly. She paced the clear space between the sacks and barrels for a minute, while we all hung silently on her words.

When at last she spoke, it didn't seem to be to the point. "Would you not say I'm bonny, lady?"

After a moment, the visitor nodded. I could just see between the bags how her eyes, red like a ferret's in the candlelight, turned to follow Inge moving gracefully up and down, up and down, and I gently widened my peep-hole under the cover of the table top. "My face, my hair, my smooth hands, my voice? My shape? All fit for more than a shipyard?" The woman nodded again, her sable-trimmed hood falling back. Her face was thin and yellowish under the fine linen barbette that hid her neck and hair, and her starched fillet was wilting with the damp of the night's misty rain. Inge was far the more beautiful. "And yet I'm still here. I have had offers, but only from men that I despise. Fools who obey other fools. Or else offers that would dishonour me. I'll have no such trash, lady. If you want the road to the crown cleared for your man, aye, I'll do it for you." The woman's eyes opened sharply, and she drew breath, but Inge did not pause. "But the price is power. Not power in a wee town, like a cock on a midden, nor in behind any man. Power in the court. Power where I can be seen to have it. Power men will honour, and love, and fear me for. You swear to do your best to get me what I want, and I'll do my best for you to get what your heart's set on."

I crouched in my corner, full of despair. Inge, my beloved Inge! I didn't understand all she said, but I knew she was offering to do something dreadful to the king. That was treason, and she'd be killed! Or if she succeeded, she'd go away. She didn't fully love me, or Dad, or any of us. We were the fools in the midden.

And yet, in spite of the betrayal, I loved her still. It was true, she was different. She was fairer, finer than the rest of us. It was only right she should go away from us if she could.

The other woman rose to her feet, her cloak gleaming redder than her eyes in the dim candle-light. "I swear you this, on my life," she said. "If you can make it possible for my husband to claim the throne—if you can do that—I will take you as one of my maids of honour. Not a servant—a companion. To come to court with me. What you may achieve then is in your hands. More I cannot do. Will this make you happy?"

For some reason, Inge paused. Then, as if defying an enemy, she tossed her head high and faced the other. "Happy? It's what I want. But be heart sure that the crown is what you want, lady. If it's cursed now, it will bring small happiness to its wearer in the future."

The woman smiled. "It never did. If it brings power, that will be enough for me—as for you."

"Then sit you, and stay still," said Inge. "Do you know where is the king this night?"

"This very night? In Edinburgh, at a Council meeting."

"And the queen?"

"Yolande? I left her at Kinghorn, at the king's house there. He's not expected to return tonight. It is too stormy."

"Aye? But I think he will, to his new young bride. Asa, give me a hand to pull out the fire there."

As I stiffened in under the table, cold with more than coldness, I watched and listened to my sister chanting over some bitter-smelling leaves singeing in a metal dish on the old brazier from the corner of the store. Asa crouched by the fire, feeding it with peats and sea coals, and keening quietly in a low whine that raised the hair on my neck. The lady sat on a bale at one side. Her hands were clasped between her knees, but still trembled.

Inge's voice never varied in loudness, but somehow, as she sang and sang, it deepened and grew more powerful. The smoke rose wisping from the leaves. It grew no warmer. After a time the candle in the lantern guttered and went out, and the only light came from the brazier, casting weird shadows up on the three faces, still and intent. The wrinkles on Asa's face were like black cracks in a cliff. The wind rose and rose, whuttering and wheeping round the thatch, and still Inge's monotonous singing went on and on.

She stopped suddenly. A new voice came from a far place and filled the hut. Somehow I knew no one outside could have heard it, though it was loud inside. I couldn't understand it, but Inge spoke, kneeling, and it answered, several times. Asa had stopped her chant, and as I peered out, nearly too scared to breathe, I saw that the deep, harsh voice was jerking from her throat as she knelt rigid by the brazier. Then there was a silence. A long silence. Not an empty silence, but one so full of horror that no words could express it.

At last, in a slow, tight voice, with long pauses, Inge spoke again. "He is coming home. They tried to hold him back, but he is coming. Over the ferry, in spite of the rain and the wind and the sea waves, safe, safe, for the ferryman is skilled, and wears a blessed sign. But the horse does not. He mounts. The horse is strong, wild with the wind. The others can scarce see in the rain. Darkness hides the path. Ride fast, Alexander, King of Scots. Outpace your guides, lose them in the dashes of rain. Your bride awaits you, bonny Yolande is wearying for you. Ride fast. The path is narrow by the sea cliff, not easy to follow in the gloom. The darkness hides the ground. And if your horse is startled, will it not turn aside in fear? Which way, King Alexander? To the land, or to the air? You have your chance, but what chance have you? Ride, King of Scots, ride fast, ride to your turning point. You are awaited."

We sat, still and silent, waiting, waiting. Suddenly she screamed, leaping to her feet and throwing her arms over her head. "Turn, King o' Scots! Turn!"

As I crouched there, the blackness before me seemed to open. I saw as if from a window in a dark room a man in a blue cloak, on a fine grey horse, galloping too fast for safety along a wet path on a cliff edge. Without warning, a woman in a green dress—Inge!—stood before him, waving her arms. The man shouted silently, and dragged at the rein. The great horse reared, twisted aside, and, coming down, found no earth below its hooves. It slipped slowly down out of my sight, eyes rolling, screaming in soundless terror. The man's cloak blew up as he crashed down the rocks to the sea crawling black below. Then there was darkness before me again, and Inge wailed once.

Her eyes were turned back in her head till they showed pure white. Asa barely caught her as she fell, toppling to the floor without a hand out to save herself, like a cut tree. She lay unbreathing, still as death.

And her hair and dress were wet. As if with rain.

Asa crooned to her as she rubbed at her chest and back. "Wake up, my darling, my dear, my great one. Wake now, wake now. Here iss your old Asa calling you. Wake up now." Nothing happened. She started to look anxious. The lady sat as if frozen, while Asa's voice rose, and her rubbing became harder, faster, frantic. I couldn't have moved if the whole place had burst into flames.

At last, after an age had crawled by, Inge's body softened and sagged as she lay in Asa's arms, and she started to breathe again. Her eyes opened. They were rolling still, but more normal, and her gasping breath began to steady.

The lady rose stiffly to her feet. "What was that?" she whispered. "I had thought of a poison, or—I never expected anything like—"

"You have what you wanted," Inge's voice murmured. She sounded exhausted. "Go away home. You'll learn the morn's morn."

"What?"

"He's dead. The king's dead. He was a good man, and a good king. May God forgive us what we've done this night."

"Forgive you! I did nothing!"

"Aye, did you. And you'll mind what else you've to do."

The lady hesitated at the door. Unwillingly, I thought, she nodded. "If it is true—"

"It's true."

"I shall do what I have said. To be a queen! My man to be a king!"

"No," whispered Inge. The woman turned sharply. "Not your man. Your son. An' there's many a woman in Scotland will curse the day he ever set his face to the crown."

The woman looked as if she was going to argue, but in a moment, seeing that Inge was nearly past speech, she merely shrugged. "Wife to a king—mother to a king. The one or the other. What matter?" She turned away. As the door opened, I heard her whisper to herself, "King! King Robert!" Then she was stumbling out across the stones, and the horses clattered away up the path.

Asa was rubbing Inge's neck, to loosen it, muttering encouragingly. After a few minutes, Inge could rise shakily, holding Asa for support, and sit on a sack. "It hass taken too much from you, my darling," the old wife said.

"Aye. But it'll not be to do that often, Asa," Inge replied.

"There's no more kings left. Nor peace, not for a hundred year! Oh, God! Oh, God! What I have seen! What have I done?" She rocked back and fore, clasping her knees, weeping.

"Ach, let it be, my sweet. It wass a great deed. Old Asa will see you to your bed. You will to your full reward come for this, be sure of it."

"My reward?" she whispered bitterly. "What should be my reward for killin' a king?"

Asa supported her out, half-carrying her across the yard. It was a far longer time than I wanted before I could make my cramped legs unfold and bear me away from that place of horror, but I forced myself out and hidden round the corner before the old wife returned to lock the door again. I couldn't go back into the hall. I was crying too hard. At last, sobbing wretchedly, I crawled back into the hay beside Wolf. Protected by his trusty love, hugging his warm, shaggy neck, I slowly sobbed and hiccuped myself to sleep.

THE DINNER

◆

*F*or days messengers were racing up and down the Roman Road like cockroaches, never stopping for a friendly chat at the alehouses as they sometimes used do. The king's body had been found at the foot of the cliffs by Pettycur, his neck broken, under his dead horse. Some folk couldn't credit it at all; after all, Alexander had been king for over thirty years, many a man's lifetime. One wife started shrieking that the end of the world was near, now the good king was dead, but Inge slapped her hard and told her not to be so hen-witted, and her shouting and sobs stopped. And no one else tried it, though for a moment it had looked to me as if half our household was starting a fit.

Inge herself went about the hall looking grey and drained. Dad and the men couldn't work at the slip for waiting on news, but hung round the house getting under everybody's feet till at last Inge lost her temper and chased them out. "For I'm sick to the back teeth with the whole jing-bang o' you! Go away and clutter up the High Street if you must, but clear to hell out o' my house!" I'd never heard her so loud and edgy, and Dad couldn't keep the surprise off his face as he picked up his bonnet and stumped out. And she threw the house into the spring-cleaning before we knew it.

Between changing the rushes, with a great scattering of rats, lime-washing the walls, and stinking out the house with boiling soap, we watched the nobles gather to Dunfermline for the king's funeral. We held a Mass for him in Saint Peter's ourselves, with every soul weeping for grief at the king's untimely death. Rumours chased each other for days, that the queen was pregnant, that the Black Comyn was dead, the de Brus had been crowned, or was in revolt, or a dozen daft tales; but Inge kept our folk too busy to pay much heed, what with washing and mending clothes and blankets and scouring every last inch, even the rafters. And the folk: we were all scrubbed scarlet, from Dad down to the yard lads. Inge's temper, if anything, grew worse.

I knew why. Her conscience was tearing her fiercely, and she couldn't say anything to anyone to comfort her—not even in confession to the priest. How could she? And how could I?

There was stiffness between us. It wasn't as if I was lying; not really. I aye flushed scarlet when I tried that, a clear giveaway that the lads jeered at me for. But I could keep my countenance now, by simply keeping clear of her. I was scared she'd ask why I couldn't speak to her with the usual ease, but she said nothing. Maybe she was too miserable herself to notice.

About a month later, when Dad led the men back in for dinner he had a guest with him. We were ready, for he'd waved to us as he and his man rode by down the muddy path to the slip. When Inge carried the guest cup up to the visitor, I insisted it was my turn to go with her to hold the water for his hands. It was, anyway. Birgget sulked.

He eyed Inge with clear admiration. "You're bonnier than ever, Inge, lass!" he boomed. "Rolf, you ugly devil, how did you ever get a bonny lassie like this? Tell me, Inge, my sweet, my bonny bird"—taking the ale-cup from her with one hand and slipping the other arm round her waist—"when will you wed me?"

"When your wife says I can, Patrick Spens, and not before!" She smiled, twisting smoothly out of his grip. He roared with laughter, not at all offended, tossed back the ale in one great gulp, and returned the cup with a silver penny in it. "And if you sink ale like that, she'll agree just to get rid of you!" she scolded him.

"Ach away, lassie!" He laughed. "I'll be your husband yet, before I make old bones!"

Suddenly her blue-grey eyes lost focus and turned quite dark. "No, you'll not," she said quietly.

"Not wed ye?"

"Not make old bones."

There was a stillness, as we all saw her eyes, and knew that what she said was true. Then Dad, trying to cover over the awkwardness, called for some ale himself, and in the bustle she turned away and the moment passed. Only I saw Master Spens watching Inge for a while as she moved round the great hall, with a new kind of grimness in his look.

I was too busy to pay much attention to the talk until at last the men were all served and the women could settle down with their husbands and relax, leaving just the lasses to keep the plates and horns filled. It was my privilege this night to attend our visitor, and hear all the news he brought. I had to grab what food I could between serving him, but if I watched, I did well—for the best dishes came to the top table first.

My family all sat in order round the tables on both sides of the long centre firepits, for Dad's house was built fairly like the old Viking hall he'd known in his youth. Dad and his guest had their high chairs at the top, with Inge, the woman of the house, between them. Then came my sisters Domna and Elsbet, Inach and Emma, with their husbands, and Birgget, whose platter I usually shared as I shared a bed at night. She was six years older than me, and betrothed to the Inverkeithing customar, old Master de Voylans, in charge of collecting the king's dues on goods through the port of Inverkeithing. It wasn't just for her prettiness he wanted to wed her; he was getting too old and dreamy now to keep a sharp watch on his clerks, and she'd do that for him, and enjoy it. I looked forward to her marriage near as much as she did.

Further down the tables sat all the men who worked for Dad, with their wives. They slept in cot-houses, turf bothies worse than Inge's store, thrown up quickly as a shelter for the cold nights, for they spent their days at the yard or the hall. Below the couples sat the unmarried men and boys, who slept in the hall, and the kitchen lasses, who crowded the bower floor and benches at night. They all brought in their own smells, of pigs or tar, dyes or canvas, onions or wood-shavings, to mix with the wood-smoke.

We fed well in Dad's hall, with seldom any shortage of fine hot stew to fill our bowls, and good ale, for my dad said no man could put in a good day's work on a rumbling belly. He had men coming from all over to buy apprenticeships with him for their sons, for he built the best ships on the East Coast of Scotland. That was why Master Spens was back again. He wanted a big new cog to replace a small old one, and they were well started on the long bargaining that would set its size, shape, and price.

"The *James an' Mary* not good enough now, eh?" Dad was grinning. "More stew? Meg—aye, grand, lass." I was already ladling out another good helping of mussels into the wood platter Master Spens shared with Inge. There was no meat, of course, for it was Lent. "How many ships is that now—four? Five? Aye, man, the Hansa had best watch out! You're that great with all your ships, wool out an' wine back—you'll be in with all the lords and ladies! When'll it be Sir Patrick, eh? Not that long, I'm thinking!"

"No, no, Rolf, no, no. I'm wanting no knighthood. Who would want it, an' be called on for war service, eh? No, burgess in Dunfermline'll do me fine."

"An' provost sometime, maybe?"

"We-ell, I wouldn't refuse if they picked me—"

"Dod, I'm right sure you wouldn't!" Dad and his guest both bellowed with laughter, their ale trickling down their beards, till all the benches stopped their chewing and chatter to laugh with them. Somehow these two were alike, though Dad was wider, fair-bearded, and red-faced, and Master Spens, five years younger, beech-brown in both hair and skin, for he spent much of his life aboard his ships. Some merchants just sat in their counting-houses and sent orders to their captains, but Master Spens enjoyed ordering a ship himself, and was the finest shipmaster, they said, in all the Northern Sea, even among the Hansa League pilots. The two big men liked and trusted each other, and each respected the other's mastery of his craft.

"But there's no great chance of it." Master Spens grinned. "And if things go as they may at the court, it could be a right good seat to be clear of."

"How's that, then?" asked Dad. We all listened avidly, for though we often had guests, few were as well informed of court and country as this one.

"Well, man, what'll happen now the king's dead? And

nought but a wee lass to come to the throne?" Master Spens's laughter had died quite away. "You don't think the great lords'll accept a wee bairn as queen? There's not one o' them that's like to take it peaceable-like. And which would the Provost o' Dunfermline support, eh? And what would happen to him if he picked the wrong one?"

"They swore loyalty to the lass not a year since," Dad argued, but Master Spens just sniffed.

"Swore? Of course they swore. They'd have had hard words and maybe harder blows from the king if they hadn't. They'd swear on their mother's hope o' heaven, but would that keep their fingers to themselves if they've the chance o' a crown? Never."

"You think there'll be fightin', then, Master Spens?" asked Inge. She was sitting by the guest, keeping an eye on the whole hall and his plate and horn in particular. She seemed unusually stiff, as if the answer mattered to her more than she wanted to show. It did, of course.

He knew her well, and answered straight as if to a man. "I wouldn't lie to you, Inge, lass. I think so, aye."

Some of the women moaned, but she nodded. "That's what I thought myself. I thank you for speaking truth to me, sir. Now I can plan ahead."

"Aye, it's aye better to know." Dad spoke soberly. "But could they not maybe keep their sworn oaths?"

"Aye, and pigs could fly," snorted Master Spens, shaking his head scornfully. "There's some would. Young Duncan, the Earl o' Fife here, maybe, he's a good lad, but there's others . . . The Comyns aren't likely to be at peace. Nor the de Brus. And there's that many with claims o' some kind."

"Aye," Dad agreed doubtfully.

My second sister, Domna, spoke from her seat by her man

round the corner of the tables. "I can't untangle them, sir."

Master Spens smiled at her. "Well—it's a long tally, dame."

"We've all night, man! See can you not sort it out for her," said Dad. He meant, sort it for him, but of course couldn't say so. He couldn't even remember all his grandchildren's names, though he could give you details of every peg in every strake he'd ever fitted in a ship's side. "Here, your horn's empty! Ale, lass!"

As I shamefacedly brought more ale, Birgget smirking at my slip, Master Spens stretched and settled more comfortably on his cushion. "Let me see, now—the king that's dead, Alexander the Three, married an English princess, sister to Edward that's the king there now, but his sons died. His daughter wed the King o' Norroway, and had a wee lass before she died, that they call the Maid o' Norroway. Or the Damsel o' Scotland, sometimes. Her that'll be queen, if she's ever crowned. Now, the king was an only child, and so was his dad; so it's right away back from his grandad's time the claim has to come.

"Now, grandad's young brother David had three daughters, that were our king's aunties. The eldest had a daughter wed a Balliol, and her son, John Balliol o' Galloway, has a claim. Myself, I'd say it's the best. In Scots law, anyway. He's not a bad fellow, him; honest enough . . . a bit soft, maybe . . . And he's well in with the English. His mother—was it? Or his grandam, one o' the two—founded a college for Scots lads in the great university at Oxenford, away south there. The King o' England, Edward, would likely support him, if his wee niece was out of it. And that's a strong hand to aid him, for Edward's the greatest fighter in all Christendom. And the Comyns are likely to support him, it could be, for young John Comyn, Badenoch's eldest, he's wed to Balliol's sister. Aye, he has a good claim, John de Balliol, and no lack o' friends.

"But David's second girl's son is the Brus, Lord o' Annandale, and old Robert's a hard man. He'll not sit still and watch a kingdom fly past him. He says he was picked out as heir by the king's own father, before this Alexander was born, and that sets him before all the rest by the old Celtic law, and it could be he's in the right o' it there. His son's wed to the Countess o' Carrick, Marjory. Fair hates the Balliols, that one. If she can stop them getting the crown she will. And she's a right vixen. More a man than her man. You've heard how they were wed? No? She was out hunting and met him riding along, and she liked the look o' him, so she told her men to grab him and dragged him off to her castle, and she'd not let him loose till he wed her. Aye, not a word o' a lie! They've sons, too, and that's aye a help—the line would be safe for years. The eldest, young Robert, he's a likely lad, they say. What is he—about twelve?"

My memory called up a whisper: "Mother to a king—King Robert." Inge's face showed only polite attention.

"And then," Master Spens went on, "there's old David's third girl's grandson as well, John Hastings. And then grandad had two sisters, and there's a great-grandson o' each o' them that's put his name down on the list, too. And all the men from the far side o' the blanket. There's more than a dozen o' them altogether."

He gave us details, but I missed most of it, for I had to go right down to the far ale-cask to refill his horn again. When I got back he was still on the subject. "No, it's a great pity there's just this wee lass to be heir to the crown. They say she's not that strong, neither—not that it'll make much difference. Either one o' them'll wed her, sick or well, or he'll just take the crown by force o' arms. No wee bairn in a far-away land's going to claim Scotland. She'd be like a wee mousie trying to get its bittie cheese away from a pack o' wildcats. They'll eat her in one gulp."

I felt a sudden pity for this poor little princess who'd have to come to a foreign land and be fought over by so many ruthless lords.

"But is there nobody at all for her?" said Dad. You could see the strain where he'd been thinking—it was never his hobby.

"Aye, man, all the churchmen and lawyers," said Master Spens. "They've set up this Council that they call the Guardians o' Scotland to rule the land till she's o' age to come here. They'll do their best, and some o' them's good men, but there's trouble already. What churchman could rule the Comyns? Or de Brus? They need a king's hand firm on them. There'll be bloodshed, sure as sunrise."

Suddenly there was a disturbance down at the far end of the long hall. Old Asa was having a fit. We could hear her screeching as the women closed round her to calm her. It sounded like, "Blood! Blood!"

"Don't fret, man," said Dad, as Master Spens frowned. "It's a daft old wife just, not right in her wits, that carries on like this from time to time. It's nothing. She'll be right as rain in a minute." And Master Spens sat back and made some joke.

But I glanced at Inge and saw her eyes blank and dark again. From nowhere a tiny coldness shivered up the back of my neck.

Master Spens returned to talk of his ship. He was keen to get it started. Dad was willing; every year he hunted through the forests round about, picking out, buying, and barking trees of the right size and shape for ship's timbers, so that they were standing dead and seasoning in the forest until they were needed. He could send my brother-in-law Jackie, Domna's man, and a gang of men straight out next day with the great ox-tugs to fell them and fetch them in. Dad said he'd be near ready to launch the knorr he was working on by the time the men got back, and the two ships could be worked on together, one finishing and fitting, one laying the keel.

I always enjoyed riding the trunks as they swayed along on the huge sledges, dipping and bumping like a boat on a rough sea, and asked Dad if I could go with Jackie, but he refused. I was irked; I wanted to get away from Inge. But there was nothing I could do about it—what Dad said, happened.

That settled, the talk circled again to the greatest thing in the land—the succession. Dad, with some pride, told Master Spens that he was from Norway, like the little princess.

"Aye, man?" said Master Spens. "I knew you were from Norroway, but I never heard just how you came here."

This was just what Dad had been angling for. Every so often, when he'd eaten and drunken better than usual, he'd tell us how he, a lad from Norway, had become a master shipwright in Scotland here. We never objected; let alone that Dad didn't take to being interrupted, it was as good as a harper any night—and never just the same twice running.

"Sit yourself back, then, and I'll tell you," he said with a sigh of satisfaction. And we all sat back as he said, belched, most of us, and settled to listen.

"You know how twenty year past, old Hakon, that was King Eric o' Norroway's grandad, he laid claim to all the islands on the West Coast o' Scotland—aye, and a fair bittie o' the mainland as well? Aye? Well, King Alexander—him that's but now dead—he was just a laddie, but he said this was his kingdom, and he'd suffer no other king in it. So Hakon gathered a great army, and came over wi' five hundred ships all stuffed full o' bonny fighters—and me and my dad as well.

"My dad it was that built King Hakon's very ship, and he sailed with the king as shipmaster. I wanted to come along, to join in my first battle an' become a man. And my dad, he saw I was that desperate to come that I'd have stowed away on board one o' the other ships if he'd refused me, so he let me come with him. I'd be—what—fifteen about.

"Well, we came down by the Orkneys, an' on down the West Coast, gathering more men from all the islands. But when we got to the Cumbraes, on the Clyde, a great gale blew up, and near the half o' the fleet was blown ashore at Largs, and a many good men drowned. And it was then King Alexander's men attacked us.

"Well, did I not fight that day? Me and my dad, we stood for hours right by King Hakon, fending off and fending off the Scotsmen's swords and spears, guarding each other's backs, and a man dead at every blow, till we were red from head to heel with blood, and a fair bit of it our own, and I could scarce lift my axe. But at the last, I leaned out a bit too far at one swing, and when I stood back a spear had slipped in past me and my dad was dead at my feet."

The next bit, how Dad was wounded in the foot during the retreat and couldn't reach the ships, changed for the braver every time. Sometimes it was a spearthrust, sometimes an arrow, or a sword from behind, while Dad fought off nine or a score Scotsmen. But one night when Inge was tired, and annoyed at Dad for keeping everybody up, she told me it was a runaway horse trod on his toes. I preferred Dad's versions.

He'd dragged himself up the hillside and hidden, starving, under a fallen tree, away from the men—and women—who crept down to the battlefield to kill the wounded, and rob the bodies. "For there was no soul in all Scotland would have had mercy on a Norseman those days. Seven days I hid, creeping out at night to drink from a wee runnel o' water. But the eighth morn, I looked at my foot, and saw it was turning black below the bandage and starting to stink. And I knew there was but one thing to do; for that was the sign my foot was going rotten, and if it was left on me, it would kill me as sure as any sword—but a deal harder."

Dad always stopped to drink here, while we sat spellbound. Master Spens's face screwed up in spine-scraping anticipation.

"I had to cut it off. Cut off my own foot. With the one blow—for I'd not have the strength or maybe the courage for a second. It was the hardest thing I ever did in my life. I tied my belt as tight as ever I could round my leg just below the knee. Then I gathered up my courage. I lifted my great axe, that I'd dragged with me even as I crawled away, and twisted sideways to get the best stroke at it. And then, with all my skill and strength, I swung the axe down, and I saw it strike where it should, just above the ankle. Ker-runch."

We all winced. He paused to drink again. Not a soul stirred. We knew the next line by heart. "Next thing I knew, I was bumping along face down between a roll o' furs and a shield, on the top o' a garron. And damned uncomfortable it was, but I was past complaining." We cheered.

His track down to the stream had been seen by a party of East Coasters returning home after the battle. They'd stalked him, and were about to leap out and kill him when they saw what he was at, and stood grinning among the trees to watch. Admiring his courage, their leader had decided that he'd take the lad home with him, as part prisoner, part slave. He tended Dad's wound, loaded him on a pony, and brought him back here, to Inverkeithing.

Dad was a strong, handsome youth, and as his leg healed and he made himself a peg-leg to get about on, passing girls started to turn and look after him. His captor, Master Preston, was a shipwright, and when he found Dad knew ships, too, he thought the more of him. The young man was soon allowed to eat and sleep in the house. And there he met Margaret Preston.

An only child, at sixteen she'd have been wed long since, but when she was little she'd fallen in the fire and her face and one hand had been badly burned. No man would court her, and the men that would wed her for her money she'd not have for pride's sake. But Dad was forced to find out the things that others never stayed to learn—her sweet temper, her fine cooking, her good business brain. And he was a good worker, and proud of his skill—he'd argue with Master Preston himself on a point of craftsmanship, and be proved right—and besides, he had the art of happiness. Within a year they were wed.

Soon after their first child, Inge, was born, a sweating sickness struck the town. It took Master Preston, and both Dad's wife and the new baby were very ill. Dad was in despair. Just as he was giving up hope, the door creaked open, and his old nurse from Norway, Asa, walked in, uncalled, unannounced. She dropped her small bundle and looked down at Dad, kneeling hopeless beside the sickbed.

"So. It was ordered to me to come, that I was needed. In good time I arrive," she announced. "Rolf, to your work go. I will to your wife and babe see." And she did. She nursed them well again, though it took her near two months, and Dad somehow never got round to asking who had told her to leave her home and make the dangerous journey to help him. She stayed on, learning enough Scots to get by, sleeping in a corner of the hall till Dad built on the bower, as nurse to every baby. Inge, though, was aye her favourite. She just lived for that girl, they said.

But when I was born, after a six-year break, and my mother died, she'd have nothing to do with me. They told me she even tried to smother me one night, but Inge woke and saved me, and faced her, clutching me protectively. "If this babe dies, Asa," she'd cried fiercely, "you can take yourself away back to Norroway. For I'll never speak word to you again." And Asa had wept, and given in; though she'd not touch me, and never had, she told Inge how to care for me, so that I lived and thrived.

Was it any wonder I loved Inge?

But that, of course, was not part of the tale my dad told. When he'd finished telling this night's version of the story, we gave the usual cheer, and Master Spens drank a toast to Dad's luck and courage. Dad bowed, pleased.

As the general talk started again, there was a thumping at the door. The nearest lad lifted the bar, and a barefoot cottar lad shuffled in, blinking under his matted hair in the light of the torches. Dad called him up to the top of the hall. There was a whale grounded in Saint David's Harbour, just the far side the Ness, he muttered, his accent so strong we could scarce understand him, staring at the floor and pulling shyly at his short leather tunic, his bare arms and legs shining red in the firelight. Was it true there was a reward for bringing the word?

Master Spens reacted faster than Dad. "Aye, is it, man!" he shouted approvingly, and the lad's face split in a huge gaptooth grin. "All whales belongs to the king, and you'll get a silver penny for the news!"

"But there is no king, Master Spens," objected Jackie.

"Makes no difference!" he cried cheerfully. "They all have to be reported to the sheriff. That'll be the earl himself, eh? Well, he's at Dunfermline tonight. I've to see him the morn. Here, lad, why did you not tell your own lord?" The lad said nothing. His grin turned to a sullen glower. "Who is he?"

"Macduff, o' Donibristle, sir," the laddie muttered.

Dad grunted. "Donibristle? No wonder you came here, son. A pinchpenny hog, him. Wouldn't give you a sniff o' any reward. Wouldn't give his mother the paring off his toe-nails. You were wise, son, unless he hears of it." He reared up and looked commandingly round the hall. "He's not to hear it from here, you hear?" Something odd in his words caught his attention, and he sat for a minute mumbling, "Hear—from here, you hear," to himself. He wasn't drunk. Not totally.

Master Spens grinned at him, and at the lad. "You've your wits about you, my laddie, eh? You can come back with me. Here, I'll need to be off. Beelzebub's bum, my head's fair splitting. What d'you put in your ale, Inge—vipers' heads? Andra, you dismal devil, where are you? Andra!" His sour-faced manservant stood up from his bench half-way down the hall. "Get your long nose out your ale an' fetch up the horses! I've to see the Earl o' Fife the morn, and if I'm late he'll not be best pleased with me!" As Andra left, Master Spens turned to Inge. "I must leave you, lassie. Much against my will, I do assure you. Are you certain sure you'll not wed me?"

She started at being addressed, and smiled up at him stiffly. "No, sir, I've told you."

"I am betrayed! There is another!" he howled dramatically, and clutched his head. "Ow, my head! You shouldn't let me do things like that, Inge! It's all your fault!"

"It aye is, sir," she replied quietly. He looked at her doubtfully for a moment, but Andra shouted to him that the horses were at the door, and he roused and started rolling down the hall with Dad, kissing every lass on the way. He was hoisted, with some difficulty, onto his beast, and they charged off at a canter up the path, the cottar laddie running beside Andra's horse, holding the stirrup.

A shout came back through the night: "I'll maybe see you the morn, Rolf!" Then the sounds faded, and we turned back into the warmth.

THE WHALE

◆

Next day, at first light, we all wrapped up warm. I persuaded Dad that Wolf needed the exercise, and should be unchained and let come too. He was fair delighted, and had a grand time meeting and beating old acquaintances as we trooped away round the East Ness to see the whale.

I'd never seen one before, and couldn't believe my eyes, but even Dad was impressed. It was the biggest he'd ever set eyes on. We sometimes got smaller pilot whales grounding, he said, but never one like this. The great fish was enormous, as big as any ship Dad had ever built—about thirty of Dad's paces long. Its tiny eye—tiny? The size of my hand—peered at us from the corner of its huge jaw, weeping slow, oily tears. It had grounded about half a mile up from the Ness, on an underwater ledge alongside a jutting point of rocks, its head towards the shallow muddy shore. Folk were splashing about this side of it, for it lay in three feet or so of water. The far side, sloping down into the bay, was too deep for wading out, but some hardy lads were swimming there.

There was a good crowd already, and the shore was like a fair. Folk kept arriving every minute, even over the ferry, and gypsies and pedlars coming from all round. They did a roaring trade in ribbons, pins, and other small goods, "for to put your lasses in mind o' the rare sight, lads!" I had no money, of course, but Dad bought me a honey sucket from an old wife, and I was as chirpy as a robin at Yule.

It was a damp April morning, with heavy showers blasting on a cold wind between wee blinks of sun, and the rest of the family grew chilled. Dad stood above the fish on the rocks and studied it for a good while, muttering about "a ship with lines like that would be the fastest in the world, but how much cargo would she carry?" The others met their friends, saluted Father Michael, the provost, and the bailies, talked and admired the fish for an hour or so, and then hurried back home to a hot bowl of broth or spiced ale to warm them, but I kept out of the way, didn't answer when they called me, and stayed.

I spent a happy morning with a gang of lads and lasses from the town, poking about round the huge fish—king of the fishes, Dad said—splashing about in the cold water on the shore side of it, jumping from rock to rock to get up to its side, and rubbing my hands over its wrinkled skin, like old leather. It was huge, towering over me like a grey-black hillock. Every now and again, it hooted through a hole on top of its head, with a huge roar of hot, smelly air, and there were strange rumbling noises from inside its belly. Its sad eye watched us as we wandered round it. The lads threw stones at it, but I didn't. I felt a bit sorry for it, stuck there like that.

I'd expected Wolf to bark at it, but he didn't seem interested at all. He ignored it, as if it was an upturned boat. Perhaps it had no land smells to interest him, and was too big for him to see clearly.

Johnnie Parker said it belonged to the king, but when there wasn't a king, it belonged to the local lord, the Earl of Fife. I told them what Master Spens had said the night before, and one of the men confirmed that the sheriff would be coming down to judge on it. "We can't touch it till then," he said. "But look at it! He'll never carry all that away. A train o' carts might manage, but not a troop o' sheriff's men!" And we all agreed. We settled that once the best bits had been taken for the king, the ordinary folk would be let take the rest.

That seemed to be the general idea. The cottar folk, the fishers, the monks, folk from miles round were all gathering with baskets and bags, barrels and firlots, for this was a chance of more meat than most of us would get in a month—and fresh meat, too, just when all we had salted away was turning rotten past spicing. There were more folk here than came to the Lammas Fair in August, it seemed like, singing and shouting, pointing and jostling, some just standing to stare. A wee wrestling match for the local lads set itself up at one end of the beach, a couple of cutpurses were chased, and two men had a real fight over a lass they both fancied. It was a great morning, waiting for the king's officials.

As time passed, some of the lads found a tree-trunk along the shore. They balanced it like a gangplank from the rocks up against the whale's side and climbed across the tree onto its back, running about on it and playing king of the castle on its head. I wasn't going to let them think I was scared, so I clambered up to join them. If Dad or any of my sisters had seen me, I'd have been for a leathering for sure, but only two of the serving lasses had been left, and they were both friends of mine; they'd not tell on me. I'd probably be well warmed for staying behind, but it was worth it. Wolf was busy making and renewing friendships all over the beach, and didn't miss me up on the fish.

It was queer up there—so high, and rough with barnacles, not slippery at all. The creature was enormous, the wide swell of the huge body with the waves swirling round it, like a smaller version of the Bass Rock. The lads dared each other to stand astride the hole where it breathed, and the one that got a blast of the hot stink up his rear when it blew out had to jump into the water on the far side, to wash, while his mates roared with glee. I didn't try it—not in a skirt. I was just—well, I just wouldn't, with so many folk there, even though the lads jeered at me. It wasn't that I was afraid of going in the water, although it was cold and quite deep on that side, and the tide coming in to make it deeper; I was a good strong swimmer. When Johnnie dared me, and some of them sniggered when I refused, I reminded them of the race we'd swum last summer from North Queensferry right round Inchgarvie rock and back, and I'd won. That silenced them.

While we played up there, the king's sheriff arrived, Duncan of Macduff, the twenty-year-old Earl of Fife, riding down with a score of soldiers and about thirty brightly dressed sightseers from Dunfermline. We all crowded to the bows, as you might say, of the whale, to cheer as the provost and bailies came hurrying back out to bow their welcome to him. Some cottar lads who'd climbed up called remarks about the provost's red stockings, and he shouted and waved to us to come down, but although most of us did, some, including me, didn't. We just stayed and watched.

Master Spens was there, with a wee boy about five years old perched on the saddle before him. I waved to him, and he pointed me out to the lad. I wondered if he'd like to come up, so I beckoned, showing him the tree-trunk. After a bit of hesitation the laddie nodded, and Master Spens rode out to the side of the whale and helped him up the first half of the trunk. One of the lads and I grasped his hands from the other end and pulled him, giggling all the time, the rest of the way.

As he reached us, he turned his face up to me, instead of watching where he put his feet, and smiled. I nearly fell over.

His hair was long and light brown like mine, in ringlets tighter than my own round a delicate heart-shaped face. He had great brown eyes, with long, curling lashes and arched eyebrows. And below his up-tilted little nose, his soft upper lip was split in a great pink gash up the centre, running right up under and into the left nostril, splitting those tiny pearly teeth into two half-smiles, hideous and sickening to see.

He had the worst harelip I'd ever seen.

I gasped. The lad beside me swore, and nearly shoved the wee laddie away in his eagerness to let go. The boy tottered, almost falling, and naturally I grabbed him harder to steady him. The big lad backed off, cursing, rubbing his hands on his tunic as if he'd touched something filthy, and the wee soul's eyes filled with sudden tears as his hands fluttered up in a pitiful attempt to hide his face. His head drooped, and he sniffled, trying to stop the tears running. Failing, he wiped his eyes and nose with his fine embroidered sleeve. He must be used to this reaction, but it still hurt him.

I couldn't stand it. I plumped down on the hide of the whale, that was queerly warm under me, gathered the wee lad into my arms to sit on my lap, wiped his face with a corner of my shawl, and talked and talked, to cheer him. I was vaguely aware of Master Spens watching awhile, and then turning his horse back to the shore again. I told the laddie about the whale, how it belonged to the king—I never thought that Master Spens must have told him all this already—and how it breathed. Just then it did so, with a gushing roar, and the boy jumped and turned to see. He looked up again, spread that dreadful mouth in what was meant to be a smile, and muttered something. I couldn't make it out, bent over him, and said, "What was that?" And into my ear, in a kind of cluttered, jumbled way, he told me that he'd been scared.

"No blame to you, pettie," I said. I was getting almost used to the sight of him by now. After all, his face wasn't his fault. "I was scared my own self the first time it did that. What's your name, my wee lamb?"

He stared at me for near a minute, his expression changing to a kind of unbelieving joy. The mumbling, shooshing voice said quite clearly to me that he wasn't a lamb, he was a lad. He was six years old, and his name was Davie Spens. Then the old eyes in the ruined child's face looked beyond me, and widened suddenly, and the hands rose to hide his mouth again.

I turned round. My own friends had gone down. All that were left were some cottar lads, all strangers to me, who had been scuffling among themselves on top of the whale. They were gathered together in a single shaggy group, staring at us and muttering. As I turned, they started to inch towards us, the ones at the back pushing the front ones. I could hear what they were saying: "Monster—dirty wee beastie—drooned at birth—mak' ye boke—ach, gyaggers—throw it awa'—root it oot—de'il's bairn—throw it aff!" And I, that had for a horrible second felt exactly that, was scalded with shame and fury.

I scrambled to my feet, nearly oversetting the wee lad, and turned on the big louts as I'd seen Elsbet turn on the kitchen lasses when they were unbearably clumsy. I screamed at them that they should be ashamed of themselves, acting like animals, rapscallions with neither decency nor humanity in them. I told them at the top of my voice just what I thought of them, their disgusting manners and filthy appearance, and the families unfortunate enough to have produced them. I described their vile homes, their likely futures, their possible but unlikely children. I had a good memory and a strong imagination and used both, quoting from my father in a rage and going on from there.

Those big lumps, six or seven of them, some near twice my size, backed off from my temper. I followed them, half aware of the laddie following, clinging to my skirt, and of the sound of shouting somewhere outside my mind behind me, until I had penned them right down at the tail end of the whale.

And then I made a mistake. I kept advancing.

They couldn't go back—they'd have fallen off. The tide had come right up round the great fish by now, and its back at the tail end was awash. As the front one recoiled from my fury, he shoved the rear one back into the water; he yelped and jumped forward again, knocking the one before him, who bumped the next—and before I knew what had happened their movement had charged them right past me, oversetting me as they rushed by and leapt for the teetering tree-trunk and the shore.

I rolled over, unhurt, surprised and rather pleased at the effectiveness of my attack, coughing with all the screeching I'd been doing, and sat up. Something was wrong. Something missing. What was it?

Then I heard a cry, and suddenly saw a wee hand slipping down the far side of the whale into the water. "Davie!" I yelled, but it was no use. He'd been knocked, or kicked, right off into the sea.

Hearing a roaring noise, I looked up and along the whale, and saw the whole crowd waving to me and shouting, and a couple spurring their rearing horses into the water. I couldn't think what they wanted, but anyway it would have to wait.

For the wee lad couldn't swim. I could see him struggling below me. Only three feet away—the tide had been making faster than I'd realised—but still out of my reach. I whipped off my shawl and tossed him an end, but as the waves carried him aside, it was just too short. Nobody else had seen him— or at least nobody was diving in to save him. I didn't know if I could pull him out, but if I didn't try, nobody would. A flash in my mind said, "With a face like that, he's better dead," and my disgust at the thought spurred me on. I dropped the shawl, hauled off my kirtle—me that had been so shy earlier—took a deep breath, ran down the slope of leather, and dived in, feeling as I did so the huge bulk of the whale rolling under me.

As I went down, my mind caught up with my ears, and I realised that the people had been calling to me to come back, the whale was going to float off the bank into the deeper water. Worry about it later. Where was that lad?

In the mucky water, full of sand and peat, seaweed and twigs, I could see very little, but I was lucky. One arm, flailing wildly, bumped something. It could have been a dead branch, or even the side of the whale, but I grabbed at it, whatever it was, and struck out for the air somewhere above me. The water was deep, deep enough to drown anyone. As my head broke the surface, I hauled up my catch and found it was a leg in a brown stocking.

Treading water as hard as I could, I twisted the lad round so that his head came up. Then I gripped his collar, and turned to make for the shore.

But where was the shore? As I peered round, coughing, my eyes streaming and stinging with salt, I could only see a choice between the huge cascading wall of the whale's side and the open sea. No land at all. My mind went quite blank. I didn't know what to do.

And the lad's head kept dipping under.

And the waves of the whale's churning rose and fell on me.

And I was cold and getting tired.

And my throat was choking, full of water, as the whale twisted and heaved to be free of the rocks at its belly, free of the people that had pestered it, free of its own immense weight, as the spring tides swept in from the Firth and lifted it farther and faster than anyone had dreamed, and it swirled me away in its struggle. My chest was burning as I gasped for breath and found only water. A roaring noise was bursting my ears. It suddenly came to me that I was drowning, and I thought, What a shame, when I can swim so well. A dark-red calm opened before me like a cavern. Just as I gratefully left the pain behind and slid into it, I felt a tug at my hair, and my last thought was: Sorry, you're too late . . .

And then I was coughing and choking again, over a rock by the shore, with a big hand rubbing my back up and down and a loud voice bellowing, "Wake up, you wee bitch, you dare die on me now and I'll kill you!" while I painfully sicked up sea water and dead leaves through my mouth and nose, and wished to God they'd just left me to die in peace.

Later, I was glad they hadn't. For when at last I lay turned right way up again, wrapped in somebody's cloak and breathing more or less regularly, with a ring of faces hovering over me between excitement and worry and gladness, the wee lad came round to my head, and that horrible mouth, that I didn't mind at all any more, gave me the sweetest kiss I'd ever had on my cheek, and that shambling voice told me how happy he was

I wasn't dead, and asked me to marry him. So I said aye, I'd marry him if he liked, and the whole world started to laugh.

I went to sleep.

When I woke, I was in my own bed at home. Alone. Pale sunshine was streaming in the cracks in the shutters—why weren't they open, so late in the day? I really ought to get up to them, but I was too tired. I just lay there, my mind empty.

My belly was empty, too—I was starving! This was more important than shutters. With considerable effort, I sat up, aching in my throat and chest, heaved my feet off the bed, and was just starting to slide out when the curtain swung by and Inge stepped in with a bowl of soup. She looked at me, one eyebrow raised, and without a word I collapsed back onto the bed. Shaking her head, she tucked the blanket round me again, spread up the feather quilt over it, and then sat down beside me to spoon the broth into my mouth.

For a moment I choked again, remembering, but under her unsympathetic eye I stopped and swallowed my soup without any fuss. She nodded briefly, smiled at last, kissed me, and left the room. I slept again.

When I next woke, it was dark, just the wee lamp lit in the bower, the maids snoring round me. I was desperate for the night jar by the door. I was very stiff. But again Inge was silently there, her arm round my shoulders to support me.

As I climbed back in the bed and collapsed on the woollen pillow, I said, "Where's Birgget?" Talking hurt.

"Ssh!" she whispered. "I put her in my bed."

"Oh." Then I thought. "But where are you—"

"I'll slip in beside you here. Just you sleep yourself better."

"I'm fine," I protested, cuddling up to her warmth, and fell asleep again.

Next day I felt all right if I didn't try to talk, and Inge let me up. I had to put on my good dress, as my other one had vanished with the whale.

"Do you know what happened there?" Inge asked me. "It was Master Spens and the cottar laddie that brought word o' the whale that pulled you out o' the water, but it's not them you owe your life to, for they couldn't see where to go for you. It was that daft dog."

"Wolf?" I croaked.

"Aye. All anyone could see was just foam," she said. "Master Spens and the lad—his name's Peem, Peem Jackson, I think—they went in seeking you up to their necks, for Master Spens's horse wouldn't carry him, with the rolling o' the whale in the water. But then it headed out to the Firth, and sudden-like Wolf swam past them into the waves. They couldn't see anything, but they just splashed after the dog, and then saw a glint o' your hair far down, and grabbed for it. They carried the pair o' you out together, you and wee Davie Spens. Your hands were gripped that tight in his tunic they couldn't separate you. And then that dog went fair demented."

"What did he do?" I whispered. Had he bitten the provost? Or worse, the earl?

"He wouldn't let a soul touch you! He'd got it in his daft head you were in danger, and it was his job to protect you. Not a soul could get near you. They were thinking they'd have to spear the dog to save your life."

"What happened?" I was in agony.

"One o' the fishers had his net with him, thank God, and threw it over the dog. If it hadn't been for that . . . Nobody wanted to, you see, but they had to get to you. And then Master Spens pummelled the water out o' his son, and then helped the other men with you—"

"I mind on that, a bit," I said, shivering.

She grinned. "Maybe you'd rather not, eh, pettie? But the wee lad recovered quicker than you."

"I mind on that, too." I remembered, and smiled, and then saw her watching me with a curious glint in her eye.

"How much do you mind on?"

"Ach—some bairn's joke," I muttered.

She smiled again. "He's not a bad wee lad, if it wasn't for his face," she mused. "If he could but speak—"

"He can so speak," I protested. "He was speaking to me."

Her mind, that had been half on the lasses setting the bower to rights, was suddenly now all directed on me. "He spoke to you? How? What did he say?"

I explained what had happened. "But . . ." she said, and then paused a minute, thinking to herself, while I rested. Then, in a different tone, she went on, "Did you like the laddie?"

"Why not?" I asked. "His face isn't that bad when you get used to it. And from what I could see, he's a nice enough wee lad."

"Aye," she said, her mind clearly distracted again. "M'm. I wonder . . . Aye."

"What became o' Peem?" I asked. "And the whale?"

She came back to herself and glared at me. "Peem ran away before we could find him to thank him—the daftie! We'll find him again. But that whale! It got away as well! There wasn't a soul had the sense to stick a spear in it before it was out o' reach!" I smiled, and she glared at me again. "What's with you? Snickering away there—anybody'd think you were glad it got away!"

"I am," I whispered.

She nearly gaped at me, and then smiled and shook her head. "Ach, you're too kind-hearted, lassie. You'd argue for the Devil himself if he looked sad at you. Just a right wee softie. Aye well, Master Spens is right pleased wi' you, pettie, so it's likely you'll not be in that much trouble for staying and losing your kirtle and shawl. We'll see when your dad comes in." And she went off to see to the house, leaving me with something new to think about, which was maybe what she meant to do.

Everyone talked round me that morning. It was very queer. "Would she like a bannock?" "How is she feeling?" "Is she warm enough?" As if I wasn't really there. They kept slipping me wee things, a biscuit, an apple, a bit gingerbread, all without a word. It was worrying.

However, when Dad came in for his breakfast just before noon, he spoke to me clear enough. He was mixed in his feelings: annoyed that I had got myself into a dangerous situation, and at the same time pleased that I had done a brave thing and saved the son of his friend. Fortunately for me, he was more pleased than angry. He picked me up out of my seat, turned me up, smacked me hard three times through my good dress, turned me back, and gave me a great bear-hug. "There, now, lassie!" he boomed in my ear. "That's for not taking care o' yourself, nor your kirtle. A pity, that, eh? Well, I've a wee surprise here for you, from Master Spens himself!" He carried me into the main hall and over to his bed corner, set me on my feet, and while I rubbed my bottom, trying to decide whether to laugh or cry, he reached behind the curtain and drew out a package of unbleached linen. It was fine stuff, and I admired it. He laughed again. "Good sakes, Meg, that's but the cover. Open it, lassie, open it!"

Slowly, enjoying the excitement and stretching it as long as possible, I unwrapped the stiff layers. As they fell back, all the women in the house, crowded round to watch, drew in their breaths with delight. For inside the cream-coloured linen lay fold upon fold of velvet. Rich amber velvet. The most glorious cloth I'd ever seen. Silken, shining, rich, lighting up the whole house with a warm glow. I scarcely dared touch it. Why did I smell cloves?

"What's wrong?" Dad demanded, grinning. "It looks fine to me. Is it not good enough for you?"

"Oh, Dad! Oh, Dad!" was all I could say as I at last picked up a corner and held it to my cheek. I'd never dreamed of wearing such stuff, never in all my born days. "Oh, Dad! How can I thank him?"

"It's him that's thanking you, lass," Dad replied. "If it hadn't been for you, he'd have lost his youngest son—and him the apple o' his daddie's eye, the poor wee lad. God knows what's to come o' him, the wee soul, with a face like that and him not able to speak. He'd be best in a monastery, his dad's thinking."

I frowned at him, surprised. He was as bad as Inge. "But he can so speak, Dad," I said. "He spoke to me. He told me his name's Davie, and he's six year old."

Dad, in turn, frowned. "He can make sounds, sure enough," he said. "But you can understand what he's sayin'? You're certain?"

"O' course I am, Dad," I said. What was he going on about? He scratched his head, and Inge caught his eye. She nodded to him.

"Aye, Dad," she said. "Meg can understand the wee lad right enough."

There was something here I didn't grasp, something just between the pair of them that they weren't saying out loud, but my mind was more on the gorgeous stuff lying on Dad's bed. As I started to caress the wonderful cloth, Dad turned and went out without a word, Inge after him.

All my sisters admired the cloth. So they should. It was fit for the queen herself. None of us had ever worn such stuff before, or even seen it more than once or twice. I wondered when I'd ever have an occasion grand enough to wear it.

Birgget was green with envy. That same afternoon, I heard her saying to Domna, "But what can we make of it, that the bairn won't spoil the first day she has it on? You know fine she takes no care for her gowns."

Domna, bless her, snipped her off short as a thin thread. "Maybe you think it'd be better made into a dress for yourself, for your wedding, eh?" Her tone was so sarcastic, Birgget flushed. Clearly, that had been hovering at the root of her tongue, but she could scarcely mention it now.

She consoled herself by telling me for the umpteenth time while we brushed each other's hair how she was going to enjoy being a lady when she was wed. She went on and on about how she'd have many fine dresses, not just the one, how she'd be adding rooms to her husband-to-be's house, how she'd be first lady in the burgh, before even the provost's wife, for the customar was a king's official. I was heartily glad when Inge said I had to lie down for a while, and tucked me in.

"Don't fret, my pettie," murmured Inge, with a secret smile. "All lasses are that way till they're wedded. Nearly all, anyway. Now give me your wrist an' I'll measure you. We'll just decide now how you want your cloth made up, and I'll do it for you when I've time. It'll be ready for the great wedding, anyway. You'll fair put the bride's nose out of joint, you will indeed."

In a way, this was very satisfying, but I wasn't altogether happy as she knotted the twine to the measure of my wrist. It was the only measure needed, of course—twice it was once round my neck, the length of each part of my arm, and from neck to waist; twice that was my waist; three times it was waist to ankle. It was a good idea of God's, that one. "I don't want to spoil Birgget's wedding for her, Inge," I said. "It wouldn't be right."

She tutted her tongue, and shook her head ruefully at me. "Ach, Meg, Meg! You're too soft for your own good. You're that careful o' other folks' feelings, and not caring for your own! But we all love you just the same."

I was stunned. No one ever told me they loved me. While I was still speechless, Inge, laughing, drew the curtain over.

JOININGS AND PARTINGS

———◆———

Three weeks later, Dad told me to go away up the Keithing Burn with a couple of the lads, to see what bulrushes we could find. It was just time for them, and he had a passion that was near sinful for the big reed maces boiled with honey and saffron. Elsbet, giggling strangely, gave us some barley bannocks and the last of the stored apples, and strict instructions that it was to be Hugh and Ian that did the paddling, not me, and we were to be back by noon, or heaven help us! I was quite glad to get out, for there had been an odd atmosphere in the house these last days, with Dad running back and fore to Dunfermline, folk whispering in corners, and sly, half-hidden grins. The three of us had a grand time. Not much after noon, and not very wet, coming home with a full basket and keen appetites in spite of the bread, we saw about a score of horses in the yard, and ran in to find out who was visiting.

The hall was jam-packed with folk in their Sunday clothes. Before I could ask what was going on, or investigate the grand cooking smells, Emma and Inach grabbed me and whisked me into the bower, where to my horror they stripped off my muddy kirtle, stood me in a tub of warm water, and started to wash me. I wriggled and protested I'd been bathed already that year, at the spring-cleaning, but I just got slapped and told to keep still while they scrubbed me all over. They'd give me no explanations. They looked happy, though, so it couldn't be all bad, whatever was going on. They undid my plaits, washed my hair and oiled it until it gleamed, rinsed and rinsed it with camomile in the water, and combed it out smooth, paying no heed to my squeals. They cleaned and trimmed my nails and polished them, and rubbed Inge's special cream in till my hands felt as soft as a baby's. Every time the two looked at each other they squeaked with glee.

At last they were finished. They called some of the lassies who'd been peering round the curtain and adding to the giggles to take out the tub. I stood, wrapped in a good linen towel, pink and shivering, totally bewildered. It must be a feast, but for what? And why hadn't anybody told me?

Then Inge came in, with all my other sisters and many of the womenfolk from the hall and town. They clustered round me, studying me like a dancing bear, and commenting on my hair and looks as if I was deaf. I recognised most of the women—there was Mistress Anna Croft, and Mistress Bessie Fletcher, the provost's wife, and even ancient Lady Aliis de Voylans, the mother of Birgget's betrothed, even older than Asa. What were they all doing here? Most of the comments were pleasant; just one or two about what a big lass I was— I'd never been anything else, even when I was a baby, never slim like Inge—and the scratches and bruises that I always seemed to collect. Inge smiled and nodded and smiled; I blushed. All over.

Emma produced a pair of scarlet stockings like the provost's—for me! They snagged worryingly on my rough heels as they were pulled on. And red garters to hold them up. Then a pair of tan leather slippers, with long fashionable toes. They had a little gold embroidery on them—"Look!" said Emma, and when I looked, it was a tiny whale. I was gasping from sheer excitement. At last, in a final flurry of chatter and clatter, they whisked away the towel, and slipped over my head a new yellow kirtle, of fine, fine wool, far better than my old best dress, tight enough to need lacing down to the hips at the back, then flowing out into a full skirt. It had more embroidery round the neck and the cuffs of the long, tight sleeves. I thought life could hold no more joy; but then while I was admiring it, from behind the curtains on Inge's bed she brought out the amber velvet. It had been made into a surcoat, with a low square neck and long slashed sides to show off the yellow kirtle beneath, just to my shins at the front, but at the back it had a train—short, of course, for I was young yet. There was a beautiful belt of plaited yellow and cream linen cord, with a ball of cord at each end, one yellow, one cream, and a chaplet of the same for my hair. It was like heaven.

Both the dress and the surcoat had huge hems, I noticed. What a relief to find a sign of sanity!

When I was fully dressed, Inge turned me round on display, and the ladies clapped. I smoothed the velvet and looked down, too overcome to smile back. Then old Lady Aliis produced a mirror of polished silver, and I could see what I looked like, inch by inch. I'd not have recognised me if I'd met me.

Inge made me practise walking in the new slippers and the train. Up and down the bower I went, among the comments of the women, all smiling, even Birgget, till I could turn without tripping myself. "Kick the skirts out o' your road, lass! Not like that, up on your toes! Graceful-like! Take wee-er steps! Smooth an' dignified—don't bounce! Head up! You're not a dog after a mole! Look proud o' yourself. Kick the tail round to turn!" And to curtsy; like a cow in a bog, they snorted at first, but finally I managed it fairly successfully. "Aye, you'll do. You look almost like a real lady; act like one, if you can," Inge said, smiling, and all the women laughed again. I was far too excited to be angry; I laughed with them.

And, at last, they led me out into the hall.

Everybody was there, all looking at me in this silly, smiling way. Inge turned me to the head of the hall, and there, at the top table, was the provost, wee Master Fletcher. Sitting by him was my dad, in his good blue tunic. And on his other side sat Master Spens, a fat lady who could only be his wife, and the laddie I'd tried to pull from the water.

Act like a lady. I didn't grin at him.

Inge led me to stand in front of Dad. He turned to Master Spens and his wife. "This is my daughter, Margaret, Master Spens," he said formally. Act like a lady; I curtsied. I didn't wobble, not quite, and the women cooed behind me.

Master Spens rose from his seat by the provost. "Margaret Wright," he said—Wright? Dad was a shipwright, but—think about it later. "My friend Master Rolf here tells me you can understand what my son Davie says."

Whatever I'd expected, it wasn't this. "Er—aye, sir?" I said. The wee lad smiled shyly at me. Elsbet, on Dad's left, shuddered, as did some of the others, and it annoyed me; he wasn't that bad. "Good day, David Spens," I said.

He ducked his head behind a hand and muttered something into his chest. Drat all ladies! I knelt down by him— carefully, not to crease the velvet. He repeated it into my ear; he was glad to see me recovered. "I'm glad to see you're none the worse, neither, Davie," I replied politely.

Then I glanced up at his parents; his father was looking at me as if I was a piece of the True Cross. I got up, rather alarmed, and my heel caught on the train, but he had seized my hands so quickly that I don't think many noticed my stagger. Mistress Spens said, unbelievingly almost, "Aye, you do. You understand him." She held her chest, and sniffed. Was it tears or disbelief?

Anyway, I was annoyed. "Aye, o' course, Mistress Spens, I can make out what he says. Why not?" I said, rather sharply. Why were they all going on as if the laddie was daft? Or—it came to me suddenly—could they themselves not understand him? His own parents? Poor wee soul!

Master Spens smiled, and then sighed deeply, as if in relief. "No reason, Margaret Wright," he said. "I think, lassie, you're the answer to a prayer."

Prayer? Me?

He turned himself and me to face all the people gathered there. He looked at Dad, who nodded, grinning. Then he spoke to us all. "My friends, a few days ago this lass here saved my son—my youngest son—from two dangers." There were a few puzzled looks—one of them from me. "As you can all see, his—his face isn't like normal folk." Again, the wee lad looked down, and a covering hand came up automatically. Hot rage rushed into me, and I wished I had courage enough to kick his father, who was embarrassing him here, in front of everyone. I took Davie's other hand protectively. The women all cooed again, and I nearly dropped it, but thought drat to them all again, and hung on.

Then I found that his father was smiling down at me, his big hand on my shoulder. "She saved him from a gang o' louts who wanted to harm him"—here, I'd forgotten all about them—"and she dived in, to the danger o' her life, to save him from drowning. Whether it was from kind-heartedness or courage, you'll agree she's a rare lass."

I blushed again, as they all nodded and cheered. What could I say? Thank him for the velvet?

But he wasn't finished. "Now, as you've all heard, when they were both recovered, my son asked her to wed him, and she accepted. It was but a bittie bairn's play, maybe, but her father and I are both agreed on it. We are decided to match Margaret Wright, youngest daughter o' Rolf Haraldsson, shipwright o' the Royal Burgh o' Inverkeithing, free tenant o' Duncan o' Macduff, Earl o' Fife, with David James Spens, youngest son o' myself, Patrick Spens, Burgess o' the Royal Burgh o' Dunfermline, her dowry to be one cog o' no less than sixty-five tons burthen, built by her father, to plans to be agreed by us both; to be presented on the day o' her marriage. The groom's part to be two hundred silver shillings." There was a murmur of applause. "Agreement to this betrothal is given by Duncan, Earl o' Fife, and witnessed by Adam Gardner, Provost o' Dunfermline, and by John Fletcher, Provost o' Inverkeithing, here present. And so we declare that these two young folk are promised, the one unto the other, the marriage to take place when the groom reaches the age o' thirteen, that's in seven years' time. And to this we call you all to stand witness before God and man."

There was a roar of cheering and clapping from everybody round about.

As Father Michael moved forward to give us the formal vows, I stood stunned; I'd never dreamed of this. It would suit both our families, I could see that. Master Spens would be linked by his almost unmarriageable son with a fine shipwright, and Dad would be joining his big, seventh daughter to an up-

and-coming merchant—good business for both. But what about us?

The wee lad looked up at me, eyes wide and anxious. Reassuringly, I smiled at him, and he grinned back, gripping my hand hard. Aye, you did get used to his face, after a while. We'd manage fine.

That night was the grandest feast I'd ever had. I had a sore belly next day. Inge said it served me right.

Four weeks later, I left home. Not that I'd not been away before, on trips to try Dad's new ships, out round the Bass Rock, that we couldn't quite see from the house, or up the coast to Crail, or over to Prestonpans for salt. I'd even been to Berwick, the biggest port in Scotland. But never before had I intended to stay more than a day or two.

This time, I was going to live with the parents of my betrothed, to learn from his mother how to run his house as she'd expect. I'd be away maybe for ever. I was thrilled, and scared, and sad to be leaving.

But if I had to keep my husband's house well, I had to show I was worthy of it. Inge and every other woman in the house went into a frenzy of making and mending, so that not a soul in Dunfermline should look down on me, or on my family. They sent to Edinburgh and Berwick for cloths and braids, and sheared into new lengths of linen and wool as if they were canvas rags torn from a sail. I'd never seen such industry. Birgget had claimed that her wedding outfit was grand, and it was. She had sheets, table-runners, wall hangings, and a whole chest of shifts, kirtles, cloaks, and surcoats that she had made and embroidered over the past five years, with all the trimmings a good housekeeper could manage: silk embroidery, beading, even some precious stones—she had a lovely belt with silver thread and river pearls. But for me, my sisters and every wife in the house dropped all other work and stitched like slaves. The cooking, the weaving, the children— all were abandoned to the kitchen wenches, while they cut and sewed for dear pride's sake.

Even Birgget. She made me a pair of gloves, lovely fine work, red kidskin, and she got one of the lads to beat four pennies into tiny silver bells to hang on the cuffs. They were beautiful. I felt ashamed of how I'd resented her sharpness, when she could spend her little silver on me so sisterly.

I couldn't knit or sew well enough, they decreed. I wasn't allowed to do more than hem shifts, but I had to be there all the time. There was a constant cry: "Meg! Where are you? Come here and try this on! Be handy, now! Ach, we'll never get done in time!" And when a needle was lost, so that there weren't enough to go round one day, they nearly came to blows.

In the end, it all filled a big chest. From a lassie with but one kirtle, I ended up after a month with more clothes than I could remember. Well, almost. None so rich as the amber velvet, of course, and there wasn't the time for heavy embroidery, but good cloth and good workmanship. And I'd no need to hang my head, Inge said proudly, over any of my bed or table-linen either. It would prove that young Davie Spens wasn't marrying beneath him.

It took my mind right off the business of the king's death, anyway.

Dad was in fine fettle all this time. He'd never been invited to become a burgess. He was as rich as any of them and richer than most, but some folk felt he wasn't fit, being a foreigner. They used the fact of our house being down near the shore, on the sheltered east side of the inner bay to keep close watch on the slip, and not actually inside the burgh walls of Inverkeithing, as an excuse to keep him out. But now that he'd one daughter betrothed to one of the noble Norman families, and one into a big merchant house, they reconsidered, and his name was put forward.

He was on edge all the day of the meeting; when he was told they'd voted him in, he didn't get drunk, though we'd all expected it; he went to Saint Peter's Church in the High Street, and paid for a huge wax candle. Then he came soberly home, ate his dinner, and still in his Sunday clothes went down to the new logs lying by the slip. He spent the whole May night there, alone, cutting and splitting them for the cog Master Spens had ordered. We couldn't sleep for the constant crash and thud of his mallet, axe, and adze.

He did ten men's work that night, and then met the lads going out yawning bad-temperedly in the morning and gave them their orders for the day. They stood gaping at the piles of freshly hewn timber while he came home to break his fast, joked with us, ate cheerfully, sat down on the edge of his bed to change his boots, fell back on the bed, and slept till nightfall.

From that moment on, he swore, there wasn't a thing could spoil his good temper. He was right—for at least half a day.

Word came of trouble at the other side of the country. Old Robert de Brus and his son raised their men to attack the Balliols in Dumfries and Wigtown, hoping to start a civil war and snatch the crown in the stir, but the land lay quiet. We heard the Guardians were gathering an army to sort out the ambitious family, and some local lads joined up, but it was far away, thank God.

I thought back on that lady, whispering, "King Robert!" as she left. Had she been a de Brus? It seemed likely. And would the fighting spread, with no king now to keep the barons in check? Or would the Guardians do better than Master Spens had feared?

But then word came again that Edward, King of England, had proposed to the Council of Guardians that the little princess, the Maid of Norway, should be wed to his son, Prince Edward, the lassie's cousin. It sounded an ideal solution, in so many ways. If the Pope would allow it, the children being related, it would be the one thing that could keep peace in the realm, for surely no noble would dare to challenge a lass supported by the great Edward, the starkest warrior in Christendom. We all sighed with relief.

The day before I was due to leave, I was sitting out in the orchard with Inge. All the packing was done, the new clothes and linens strapped in the big trunk with lavender and hyssop between the folds. Next day, Master Spens would come for me, and my dress for then was all ready, too. Nobody could think of anything else for the moment. After all the frantic hurry and rush, we had come to an end. Everything seemed to be still, like a leaf the instant before it quietly slips from the tree.

The cherry trees were in bloom. I made a little coronet for Inge's hair.

"Thank you, pet," she said quietly. This last month she'd been quiet, and sad somehow even when she was smiling and busy. I worried about her.

She let me put the ring of flowers on her head and looked at me seriously. "You've been silent these last weeks, Meg," she murmured kindly. And here me thinking I was acting normal! "Now, you've not to mind about the laddie's face. God knows it'll not get better, but as you said yourself, he's a good laddie. And"—she hesitated, and then as I relaxed at her interpretation of my stiffness with her, she nodded at a thought in her own mind—"our own dad had the same trouble." I was surprised, but she took my hand, looking out towards the sea. "Aye. You can't remember Mam. She was a fine woman. But she'd one hand all twisted into a great lump o' bone by falling in a fire when she was wee, and one side o' her face was scarred and twisted. When she and Dad wed, there were folks laughed at them for a good match: the one-handed wife and the one-footed man. But they had the sense to see in behind the scars, and they were happy together all their lives. Just you be sure to look in behind the skin, too, my lass, and you'll find your lad's as good as any in the land."

She smiled down at me, and hugged me close to her side. "Now mind, if you feel strange in the strange house, we're but five mile away, and you can walk down to see us, even if they'll not lend you a garron. But Master Spens is a good man, and his wife's a quiet soul. They'll not be hard on you, and you'll likely be in visiting more often than we fancy! Just you mind what they say, and learn all they teach you—and then you can come back and teach us, eh?"

"But you'll not be here!" I said sadly.

"What makes you say that, lass?" She leaned back to see my face.

My heart pounded as I realised I wasn't supposed to know that she'd be leaving. I'd overheard it that terrible night; had I betrayed myself? She was looking at me curiously. I thought fast. "Ach, you're bound to get wed now, Inge, with both me and Birgget to find grand rich men for you!" I joked. Was I flushing?

It wasn't a good jest, but after a moment, to my relief, she smiled. "No chance o' that, my pet," she said. "I haven't stayed a spinster all these years to be wed so easy now. I'm just too picky, I fear me." She started to hum, as I relaxed again. "Did your teethache ever come back?" she asked quietly.

"No, not after that night, the cloves worked fine," I said. Then I stopped dead, and stared at her in horror. And if my words hadn't betrayed me, my face now surely did.

"Cloves." It wasn't a question. She knew.

We sat in silence for a long minute. I couldn't think what to say—or what to do, except run away in shame, and that was no use. At last she sighed, and took my hand.

"Meg, my pet, don't judge me too harshly. I did—what I had to do. Somehow it's in me, and I must use it or burst. I'm fair stifled here. But I'll not just leave, to walk the streets and turn a living telling fortunes or selling daft wee charms. I've seen my future, and it's not that."

Did she remember, I wondered, saying she'd seen her death too? Then I realised she wasn't scolding me. She wasn't angry. What was wrong?

She paused again, searching for words. I saw that she was trying to defend herself from an accusation I hadn't made, but others could—or maybe one she'd made against herself. "When I see something in the air, is it something that must be, or something that only may be? When I use my power, am I using it truly, or maybe being used by it? Can I do anything that's not written for me? I sometimes think I can't. Meg, Meg, don't you have anything to do with uncanny things, for they can lead you far, far from any straight and easy road." Her hand gripped like a vice, and I winced. At once, looking shocked, she let go. "But my pet, I'll not harm you. Never."

"Aye will you." The harsh voice barked from behind us, and we both jumped. It was Asa, standing as if she'd grown there in the long grass. No whisper of sound from her dress dragging, or her staff tapping, had warned us she was there. Her black eyes were angry as she shook her staff at us. "Aye will you, Inge Rolfsdaughter, I have you told an hundred time."

As I sat, terrified, Inge swept up from the bench, and round to face the old wife. Her own eyes were blazing. "More like a thousand, you old hag. But I'll not do it, whatever you say!"

"Then she will be your death! Have I not seen? The one will death bring on the other. If you no kill her, she kill you!"

No one spoke. That, then, was why Asa hated me, why she had tried to kill me when I was a baby. She had "seen" that one of us would kill the other, and had tried to protect her favourite.

Inge at last drew a deep breath. "Then let her!" she said firmly.

"No, Inge, no! I'd never hurt you! I love you!" My voice was shaking.

She continued to face Asa. "We may hurt worst the thing we love best, my pet," she said slowly. And the old woman snorted and turned away. "Asa!" snapped Inge. "Have you ever tried to harm the lass?"

Asa went on as if she'd turned deaf. She rounded the corner of the bower, and her long skirt trailed out of sight. The day seemed suddenly brighter.

"Has she ever hurt you, lass?" asked Inge worriedly. I shook my head, but I remembered a dozen times the old woman had tempted me to do something dangerous—never openly, but daring me, scorning me as too weak or too scared to risk myself. It was she who had said I hadn't the nerve to join in the climb to smash the corbies' nest away up the North Queensferry cliff. She'd told me I was too wee to go out late in a blizzard to fetch in firewood from the stack fifty feet from the house. She'd told me only brave folk, fit to be a Viking's child, could run across the sty where our biggest, most vicious sow was suckling her litter. And all in a sneer that made it a challenge. Each time I'd survived; when I fell on the cliff, I landed on a ledge only five feet down; when I was lost in the blinding snow, I turned into the wall of a bothy, and the owner found me sound asleep in his bed when he and his wife left the hall; as the sow leapt up screaming in rage, she tripped over a piglet, and I just had time to scramble out again as her foul green teeth slashed at my heels. But I couldn't say Asa had ever told me to do anything I shouldn't.

"She aye said I was a coward," I muttered.

Inge understood at once. "Old bitch! But you know now, pettie, don't you? You're not feared o' nothing. You're the bravest lass I know."

This was too much. I knew how my insides crawled with fear sometimes. But it was so good to hear her—especially her—say it! I couldn't blame Asa for trying. I loved Inge, too. "I swear to you, Inge, as God's my judge, I'll never, ever cause you harm," I said solemnly.

Inge took my rough brown hands in her fine white ones. "And I swear you the same, my lass. I'll not harm you, ever." Then her gravity broke down, and she grinned, more like herself than she'd been in ages. "Not first, anyway! But if you scratch me, I'll scratch you right back!" We both laughed in relief from the tension, and went in.

I woke first next morning. More accurately, I couldn't sleep. I roused up when there was a glint of grey in the dark and was out having a last look round before anyone else was about. That was how I was the first to see the troop of soldiers riding down the track.

I raced down to the hall, screaming a warning. The dogs barked, and all the men tumbled out of bed cursing. But they were too late. By the time they were up, the soldiers were at the door.

Dad put the best face on it he could. He stumped out, innocently tying the laces of his tunic, made his best bow, and politely asked what he could do for them. Behind him, all the men seized axes and hammers from under the benches and crept up to listen, while the women dressed in haste and seized or hid their most valuable jewellery.

The captain in charge of the men was polite, too, which was a relief, but his message was surprising—except to me. He had been sent, he said, to escort Mistress Inge, daughter of Rolf Haraldsson, to be one of the handmaids of the lady his mistress.

Dad's jaw dropped. Of all the things he might have expected, this wasn't one. Was the captain sure? Yes, the captain was. Where was the lass?

In the baffled silence, Inge stepped forward. "Here I am, sir," she said quietly. The captain's eyes took in her beauty, and he bowed to her as if she was a lady. "When do you wish to leave?"

"As soon as we may, mistress," he answered firmly.

Dad spluttered. "But who is your mistress, man? I can't just allow my eldest daughter—any o' my daughters, that is, to be carried away by any soldiers that happens by. She's not setting foot out o' here without I know where she's going. And that's—"

He stopped, for the captain had gestured and half a dozen of his men had swung down from their horses and drawn their swords with a scrape of steel. There was a kind of gathering of strength inside the hall, as the men raised their axes to rush out to Inge's defence, but she calmed them. "Dad, I'm sorry it's come so sudden-like, but I know where I'm away to, and who I'll serve. You'll see me again, don't fret. I'll be safe, and well cared for."

He looked at her bitterly, without his usual smile. "One o' the lords at court taken your fancy, eh?"

"No, Dad," she said, patting his arm kindly. "It's"—the captain coughed, and she smiled up to him—"it must come out sometime, sir. It's the Lady Marjory de Brus, Countess o' Carrick, Dad, that I made tryst with a while ago."

"And you couldn't tell me?" he asked.

She shook her head. "No, Dad. I couldn't. For it all depended on—something happening as I'd said. If it hadn't, I'd never have left you. But it did. I must go."

"Inge!" he cried. "Are you sure? Certain sure?"

She smiled waveringly at him. She was near as upset as he was, but quite determined. "Aye, Dad. I'm sure." Turning to the captain, she said, "Give me three minutes, sir. I'll not keep you longer," and came back through the throng in the house.

All my sisters were at her to say what was happening, but she answered none of their questions, none of their comments. She ran to her bed and hauled out her box from under it. Into it, on top of her neatly stowed clothes and linens, went her combs and brushes, her bead-loom, the elderflower cream for her hands—all the little things that had cluttered up her bedside for the past years. As she dragged it out in the gathering silence, rucking up the rushes, no one came to help her. Even I stood back silent at this sudden leave-taking. Only kindly Emma at last stepped out, to call the captain to send a man in to take it for her.

As Inge went out, old Asa started to wail. In a moment, half the women were at it. Inge went over to the old wife, took her in her arms, and whispered to her a moment, but Asa still wept, heart-broken at her loss. The tears came to my eyes, too, but I blinked them back. This was what she wanted, after all.

At the door, she paused. A soldier was strapping her box onto a horse, and another offered to help her mount behind him, but she shook her head. She reached over to a servant at the door, who was holding a torch, and took it from his hand. I suddenly knew what she was going to do.

She went over to her own store, and unlocked it. After a minute inside, she came out with a large satchel on her shoulder, and something small in her hand. "Here, Meg," she called me with a lopsided smile, and handed me the whole bag of cloves. She bent to kiss me, but I ducked away, and her smile faded. I felt I'd betrayed her, but too late. Then the first streamers of smoke uncoiled from the door of the store-house, and after only a few seconds it was blazing fiercely. More than anything, that told us she was really not coming back.

She gave Asa one last hug, and then kissed Dad and all the sisters. Suddenly I could stand it no longer, but ran away, up the field behind the house into the woods. I didn't kiss her farewell. I didn't see her ride away.

PEEM

———◆———

In all, I spent nearly six years with the Spens family, just across the hill from Saint Margaret's huge kirk. Theirs was a grand house, on two floors and a cellar, its beams and doorposts carved like twisted vines and painted bright red. The finest house in the street, though there were many merchants in the burgh, all trying to outdo one another in displaying their wealth.

My sadness didn't last long. I wept sore the first night, Mistress Spens's plump arms round me. She thought that it was homesickness; how could I tell her it was for a sister gone, not a home? But the next morning I was up bright and early, exploring. It was so different from Dad's house! It spread up, not out. Master Spens's counting-house was by the big kitchen on the ground floor, with a grand wide stair twisting down to the cellar and up to the hall and chambers on the upper floor, that jutted out on huge beams above the street. There was a tiny garden and herbery, and a high-walled yard to ward Master Spens's wine casks and hang the washing.

I shared a bed with the two unwed Spens daughters and

the servant lass. It was a fine room with a cloth ceiling to hide the thatch above, and plastered walls. Its shuttered window looked south over the town to the Firth of Forth. I told myself sometimes that I could see home, but that was just daftness. Our bed had a fine feather mattress that we beat up every day, a feather quilt with a woollen coverlet, and a green rush mat on the red-stained boards beside it. In front of the window stood my box.

Inge had been right. I did need it. Before the week was out, every stitch had been examined and approved. "Aye, good stuff. Good stuff. I'm glad to see it, lass, it makes up for a many other things." What other things, I'd like to know? Or, "Ah, Meg, what fine gloves! See the wee bells!" Thank you, Birgget! "I must admit you'll not disgrace us, my dear." In other words, I was fit to be seen out of doors. I thought thanks to my sisters for all their labour.

The mistress of the house had a bad leg, and walked limping with a stick, grown fat with more sweeties than sweat. Her long-suffering smiles and sighs of disappointment rather than scolding and slaps near drove me daft till I realised that "If it's not too much bother, Meg, would you care to . . ." meant the same as Dad's "Get up off your backside, lass, and do . . ." and that "What a pity Meg didn't think to do it this way . . . ," said with a sad, smiling shake of the head to one of the others in my hearing, was her version of Domna's slap on the ear and cry of "You daft skyte, Meg, get that mess cleared away and do it right this time!" If she was crossed or upset at all, she'd clutch at her heart and moan that she was faint, her breast was fair bursting, and we all ran to calm her. I must call her Mother Alison, she told me, sweet as honey.

Her daughters, Mary and Anna, were ages with me. Mary, about eleven, had her eye on the only son of one of the bailies, and took the greatest care of her looks to make sure he kept his eye on her. Even Inge had fewer creams and lotions. And ten-year-old Anna took after her mother in figure and energy, without her mother's excuse. She was just a wee butter-ball that had to be pushed into motion—except towards the table. I soon found I had more to do in the house than both put together, but since I learned from it, I didn't mind.

Within two weeks, much to my amazement, I also had a manservant.

The second Friday after I'd come to Dunfermline, Master Spens walked me up the town to see the market and be introduced to his friends. I'd met most of their wives already, calling casually in, oh-so-surprised and, I hoped, pleased to meet the future daughter-in-law. I put on a good new gown and surcoat, to do him credit, as they said—often; asked Mistress Spens what I could get for her, and went out with my hand light on Master Spens's wrist like a lady. Inge would have been proud of me. No, I mustn't think on Inge, I told myself firmly when my nose started to prickle, and I turned my mind to keeping my head proudly up and my eyes modestly down, and walking smoothly.

With Davie's hand tight held in mine—which didn't help the smoothness—and Andra, Master Spens's man, grumbling behind, we walked up by the Great Kirk to the marketplace. My, I thought, there's as many here as at the Lammas Fair in Inverkeithing—or even at the whale! Then I was being introduced to this one and that, merchants, shopkeepers, shoppers, passers-by. Everyone seemed to have heard about the whale, and they were all very flattering about my courage. I fear my head started to swell a bit from all the praise.

"What all have you left to get now, eh, Meg?" asked Master Spens at last.

"Some rose sugar, sir, beeswax for candles for when you've company, and a good root o' rhubarb for the herb garden. All the main things is in already."

"Aye, she's aye up and about early, is Alison," he said fondly. "It's a good habit for a wife."

"Oh, I know, sir," I said eagerly, anxious for him not to think of me as a slugabed. "I'm aye up before daybreak myself."

He smiled down at me. "Don't fret, lassie, I know that," he reassured me. "Alison says you're set fair to be a grand housekeeper."

Again, my nose prickled. He was so kind to me—far kinder than my own family, who more often scolded me than praised. I determined never to give him trouble, or cause to think ill of me in any way.

"My greetings to you, Patrick Spens!" A loud, arrogant voice behind us made Master Spens turn quickly.

"Sir James! A good day to you, my lord!" Although his words were friendly, Master Spens's voice showed him not best pleased to meet this man, and wee Davie's hand that had been tugging to get away gripped fast in mine. "Is your good lady wife well? My service to her." His voice altered subtly. I knew him just well enough to hear the touch of malice. "What was it I was hearing—another bairn to carry on the family name? My congratulations, sir!"

"Thank you, thank you, aye, but it was a damned lassie, sir!" said the other man. "Another useless baggage needing a dowry."

"Ach, a pity that, sir," said Master Spens smoothly, his eye forbidding me to giggle. "But better luck next time! How many's that you have now?"

"Just the two lads, sir, and four bairns." Well, that was one way to look at it. Heavens, I thought, what would he have said if he'd had seven, like Dad, and not a boy among them?

He was clearly rich; a grand surcoat of fine blue broadcloth, trimmed with squirrel that almost matched his wiry hair, was stretched over his vast belly. Fat, aye, but strong with it. He'd a gold chain round his neck, like Provost Fletcher at home. Was he the provost here? He looked at me, sandy eyebrows raised over keen dark eyes, a bulbous, pock-marked nose, and a thick red mouth. Master Spens could not but name me to him, though I felt somehow he didn't want to. Why not?

"Sir James, this is Mistress Margaret Wright, daughter o' Rolf Shipwright, Burgess o' Inverkeithing." Dad's acceptance as a burgess was standing well for me here, I knew. I curtsied, politely deep. "Meg, this is Sir James Macduff o' Donibristle." The lord nodded to me. Me, Meg Rolfsdaughter, introduced to a real live lord! If only Birgget could see me now!

Sir James gave me a cold stare. "Oh, aye, Patrick? The quoy all the talk's been about? Dived in to fish out your open-steek bairn?"

Suddenly I was thrilled no longer. Never mind calling me a heifer; to call wee Davie "open-stitch," to his very face! Fat hog! He was as bad as the cottar lads; worse, for he should know better manners! I was furious, and felt my face turning scarlet. Davie hid himself behind my skirt, as far as he could. The lord grinned jeeringly down at me. "Quite the heroine, my kitty? You'll be fair puffed-up, eh?" If anything was needed to save me from pride, it was his tone; it would have curdled new milk.

Not waiting for an answer, he turned back to Master Spens, who was near as red as I was. "I'm not in for the market, Patrick. I've lost a cottar's lad. Run. I nabbed him with a hare two days by, and whipped him. Can you credit it—a cottar, taking a hare! They'll be in my warren at the rabbits next."

"Imagine!" said Master Spens drily. His tone wasn't as shocked as Sir James expected, and the lord frowned slightly, but he didn't stop.

"He'll be heading for one o' the burghs. Here, or Crail, most like. The whipping I gave him, he'll not run far, anyway. I've told them at the ferry there's a reward, and I'm here to warn the provost to keep an eye lifted for him. When I catch him, I'll see he'll run no more—I'll have the foot off the scoundrel! Run! From me! The rapscallion! The Lord have mercy on him!"

"For you'll have none, eh?" muttered Master Spens, as Sir James nodded and turned abruptly away. We glared after him as he bulled up the street expecting every soul to step out of his path, and exchanged grins as not everyone did.

"Why should the lad run to a burgh, sir?" I asked as we walked on.

"If he can stay a year and a day in a burgh, lass, his lord can't claim him back. Did you not know?"

"But is he a slave, then?" I asked.

"Not exactly. But he's eaten and drunk from the produce o' his lord's estate while he was growing, and he's bound to stay there and work on it, and pay his dues on it. And if the estate's sold, or whatever, his duty goes with it. He can't leave, or wed, or even turn priest, without his lord's permission, to leave the land wanting his labour. That's the law, anyway, but there's not that many will take it as far as Sir James there."

"If the lord whipped me for taking a hare, I'd run," I said.

He smiled at me, while Andra, behind me, sniffed, and Davie jerked at my hand, growing impatient. "Do you mind, lass, when you were betrothed—"

My mind went back. "You said, 'With the permission o' the Earl o' Fife'! I thought it was just—just words!"

"No, lass," he said. "Your father holds his bit ground o' the earl himself. We had to go to him and pay a fee for you to wed off his land."

This was news to me—that Dad had to ask anyone's permission to marry me to the man—or boy—of his choice. But it had worked out all right for me. Just one thing bothered me. "Sir—how much was it?"

Master Spens roared with laughter. "You want to know how much you're worth, eh? Well, lass, want must be your master! For it's not me that'll tell you!" I was quite huffed.

We went down past the mercers' booths, selling rolls of cloth and trimmings—I was introduced to the man who had provided the amber velvet, who looked pleased when I praised it—down to the apothecaries' row, to find the sugar, wax, and rhubarb for Mistress—Mother Alison. I'd get used to it yet. Davie kept bouncing and tugging to get away ahead; he clearly knew where we were going, and liked it. The scents reminded me of Inge's store. No, I wouldn't think on that.

Master Spens turned in to a shop like the rest, in the front room of a house, its heavy shutters open to the street. It had a big table, and shelves full like Inge's of bags and packages, small and large. "Good day, Manfred!" he called, stepping up into the house, and an untidy pile of black woollens on a stool in a corner at the back rose to its feet and greeted him warmly.

"Mine greetings to you, Master Spens! And to your son! And who is dis so charming young lady you haf brought to visit old Manfred?" His breath smelt deliciously of liquorice, and his hair and moustache looked like strings of it.

I looked round, wondering who had come in with us, and then as I realised it was me, I blushed. The two men laughed delightedly.

"Innocent youth! You vill not do so in ten years, or five, liebchen!" said the old man. "Sit, sit! I vill anoder stool bring for such a valued customer." I'd never heard anyone talk like that. It was very odd, and hard to catch unless you thought hard on it. A bit like Asa, but different. He turned and called into the depths behind the shop, and a younger version of himself, without a moustache, carried out a second stool, bowing to me as he set it down and vanished again. I wasn't used to this, but thanked him and sat, pretending to be at ease. The two men laughed again, as if they shared a joke. Davie grinned obligingly, and the old man cackled.

"Vould your fine son care for a sweetmeat, Master Spens? And de lady? Or is she too old for bairns' things?" Immediately, my mouth watered. I was, as usual, hungry. But I couldn't say it, and admit to being a child, could I?

While I wrestled with this problem, Patrick Spens laughed heartily and heartlessly. But then he reached over to the bowl the old man had produced from a shelf, took out two lumps of something sticky, and handed one to each of us. "Eat up, Meg! Don't be feared, it's but marchpane!" He laughed again, as I tasted the stuff cautiously. It was lovely, sweet and nutty, shaped and coloured like wee apples. I nibbled to make it last. Davie stuffed his in, and chewed messily. I'd really have to teach him to eat more tidily.

Master Spens introduced the old man as Herr Manfred Grossmeyer, from Lübeck, the finest apothecary in Scotland. The man snorted, pleased at the flattery, and when I asked for a root of rhubarb, he was most helpful.

"Ach, rhubarb! A goot herb, ruled by Mars, to clear der blood and dispel evil humours from der stomach. Wise you are to haf it by you. I haf it, I haf it, mistress." He offered me another piece of marchpane while his assistant—or his son?—dug up a root for me.

While we waited, I bought six pounds of wax, and rose essence to scent it. Then he and Master Spens talked about the troubles of shipping. Every captain, it seemed, given the chance, would turn pirate and attack any ship smaller than his own. Even Master Spens! He traded with many countries, and they discussed the problems of money-changing across seas and frontiers. You had to watch French silver, they agreed; it wasn't as pure as it should be. The wee bowl of marchpane was on the table at my elbow. Davie and I ate quietly—well, I ate quietly—and I slipped a piece to Andra, squatting by the door.

A far-off shouting gradually made itself clearer. Somebody was being chased up by the Great Kirk and was dodging down towards us. Davie and I stood up and peered out, to watch the hue and cry, and Andra reached an arm out to hold the wee one back, and lift him to see better.

A lad, a good bit bigger than me, was ducking and dodging half a dozen of the sheriff's mounted soldiers in and out the cloth booths at the top of the street. The men were trying to drive him with their spear butts out into the open where they could grab him. As a stave thudded on his leather tunic, he yelped. The two men behind me stood and watched with us, Master Spens applauding the lad's cleverness, Master Gross-meyer tut-tutting.

"See him dive below the booth, eh? Not easy caught, that one! My lord, Meg, did you see that?" A soldier had been belted right off his horse by a wife whose stall he'd knocked over. She lambasted him with a roll of trampled linen, and his friends stopped to rescue him, their horses rearing as the cloth flapped. She and her neighbours were shouting, and the soldiers swearing.

They lost the lad, and cast round like hounds to find trace

of him again. "If they'd get down off their horses, they'd find life easier," said Master Spens. True enough, the horses turning in the cramped, crowded lanes were causing enough stir and commotion to hide a dozen boys, as stallkeepers leapt to the defence of their wares, all yelling and shoving and making the horses rear and kick worse than ever.

"Look there, it's Sir James, isn't it?" I asked. Master Spens nodded. We could clearly make out his bulk of blue cloth, as he directed the soldiers from the back of a horse not that much larger than himself. "It must be his cottar they're after, not a thief." I felt a sympathy with the lad.

Suddenly wee Davie tugged at my sleeve. He was pointing over at the other side of the street. The lad was slinking up the far side of the booths there.

As bad luck happens, one of the soldiers saw Davie's gesture and caught sight of the lad. He shouted, and charged his horse through the scattering shopkeepers down towards us, the rest racing after.

And it was at that very moment that I caught what wee Davie was trying to shout to me through the din. This was the lad who'd brought word of the whale, who'd gone into the water with Master Spens and helped find us and pull us out. The lad who had helped save our lives.

As soon as Davie said it, I knew him. And I knew we couldn't let Sir James cripple him. I turned to tell Master Spens, but there was no time—if I was going to help, it had to be at once. As I shouted, and waved the lad over, I hoped Master Spens would back me, for Davie's sake if not for mine.

They looked at me as if I'd gone daft, and Master Spens even reached out just too late to stop me as I ran out, grabbed the exhausted lad, and hauled him up the step into the shop. The soldiers and Sir James clattered down the street, hauled their horses to a halt outside, and leapt down. But as they reached for the lad, fallen to his knees behind me, I screeched at them as I'd done at the louts on the whale.

"What the devil d'you mean, attacking my man?" I screamed.

They stopped dead.

There was a pause of almost silence. The crowd following the chase, to cheer the soldiers or trip them—for the sheriff's men were not entirely popular—stopped shouting to listen and find out what was happening.

Sir James's jaw dropped. He swung down with agility—I'd known it wasn't all fat—and strode towards me. But I faced up to him, not stepping aside as he'd expected, and he had to stop or knock me down. He lifted his hand to hit me aside, and my prayers were answered. Master Spens gripped his fist.

He made it look almost like a greeting, for to strike one of noble birth was a serious offence. "A pleasure to meet you again, Sir James," he boomed, holding that gentleman's hand in a grip that could control a ship's rudder in a gale. "But why so hot? Come in and have a bittie marchpane."

He'll be lucky, I thought. How daft, at such a time!

Sir James was no weakling. He tried, and failed, to free his hand from that painful grip, and glared at me, spluttering, too angry to speak clear.

I took a deep breath, and carried on yelling. "What's my lad done that you should be so sore on him? Tell me, an' it's me that'll sort him for you, sir. But you attack him like that, and I'll have the law on you for assault."

Little did I know that I couldn't have. But the words served their purpose, which was to make him pause. And I used the pause to call on Master Spens for help, though Sir James, I hoped, wouldn't realise it.

I changed my tone—I was afraid I'd gone too far, seeing

Master Spens's frown growing. "Pray forgive me, sir, if I've been too forward, but I'm deep in the lad's debt. You were speaking about me saving wee Davie there when he fell off the whale?" I could see puzzlement in both their eyes, and I went on as fast as I could, to say it before I could be interrupted. "Well, sir, it was him helped Master Spens pull me and the wee laddie from the sea. We both owe him our lives."

There. I'd got it out. I knew Master Spens was quick on the uptake. I'd done what I could. If he backed me, there was a chance; if not, I'd be whipped till I bled. But for Davie's sake, I thought he had to. I was sure in any case he'd never forgive me if I just stood by and let his son's other saviour go back to torture and maybe death. But could he—would he— thwart Sir James?

The lord was spluttering again. "Your lad? He's my lad! Bred and whelped on my land! You damned wee bitch, mind your screeching tongue, or we'll have it out by the roots! Sergeant—"

He was turning to the soldiers when Master Spens interrupted. He still held Sir James's hand, and he simply put a few more pounds' pressure into his grip. The lord stopped dead, with a gasp, and Master Spens said mildly, "Now, sir! Now, Sir James! It seems to me there's a bittie confusion here, would you not agree? Here's you claiming the lad, and there's Meg claiming him, and the both o' you can't be right, is that not true, eh, Sergeant?"

The sergeant, no servant of either man, agreed. He'd been sent out with Sir James to bring in a runagate, not to get into disputes with one of the merchants who ran the burgh where he lived. He was in a difficult situation, all over one worthless laddie, and he cast a grim look past me at the lad crouched by the table. But Master Spens offered a solution.

"Why do we not sit down a wee minute to talk it over,

eh? He can't get away from you, in there. And there's no sense bothering the earl with a daft wee matter the like o' this, if it can all be settled friendly-like." It seemed like sense, even to Sir James, whose hand must have been feeling as if it had been hit by a hammer. They all nodded. The sergeant dismounted his men and sent a laddie off with a silver penny from Master Spens for a jug of ale. Another pair of stools and some tankards appeared from the back shop—Master Grossmeyer had vanished, keeping out of trouble, I wished I could join him, but he must have been watching—and Sir James and the sergeant sat down.

One basic fact of life is that it is much more difficult to shout if you are sitting on a low stool. Everybody calmed down. The crowd gathered round, nosy and noisy, until pushed back by the soldiers. The ale arrived, and the sergeant mellowed a little more.

Sir James supped his ale, angry and frustrated. I was glad he'd none of his own men here. "I know the rascal fine!" He'd moderated his voice to a bellow. "It's nonsense to say he's not mine. Just take a look at his back; I whipped him not ten days past." He tore back the rotten leather of the lad's tunic, showing the half-healed weals bleeding, newly burst open by the soldiers' spear shafts. He lost a lot of sympathy as the women tut-tutted.

Master Spens looked at me questioningly, and I realised I had to carry it on. He wasn't about to do everything for me. I gathered my wits.

"I'm that sorry," I said, "to have to argue with a nobleman as noble as yourself, Sir James." It was a clumsy way to put it, but I'd no time to think of a more elegant style. "But sure as death, this lad's mine. He's worked for my dad at Inverkeithing over a year now. Even if he was your bondsman, sir, he's been in a Royal Burgh for long enough to have won his freedom." My politeness gained me back some of the crowd's support that my bad manners—screaming at her elders and betters, the bizzom!—had lost. And if I was scarlet from lying, well, it could easily be taken for embarrassment. I hoped.

"But what about his back, then, mistress?" asked the sergeant. He was still civil; he hadn't made up his mind yet. Or maybe he just hadn't finished his ale.

"When I left home, sir, it wasn't like that," I said. I couldn't think of a reason for me to have done that to anyone. "But maybe my dad did it? He's got a fierce temper when he's roused."

"Have you any witness, mistress?" asked the sergeant. "If you haven't, I must accept Sir James's word. It's not sense that he'd lie . . ." Sir James smiled.

I turned to Master Spens. "Sir," I begged, "don't you remember the lad? At my home? And after, at the shore?" As I waited for his answer, my heart sank, for he was long about it. It came to me that if he supported me, he'd make an enemy—maybe a powerful one, I didn't know. He might well think the lad's life not worth that.

At the last, he nodded. My heart started to beat again, and the lad behind me sighed deeply, as if released from pain. "I do that. I mind on him in your dad's house, Meg. Aye, I've seen him there. As God's my witness, I'll take my oath on it." Well he might, the clever man; it wasn't a word of a lie.

Sir James's eyes narrowed, and his face turned a mottled red. "Would you cross me, man?" He looked vicious, and dangerous.

"Cross ye, Sir James? Never, sir, never! But you'll grant I must tell the truth! You wouldn't have me lie, now?" Master Spens was the picture of honesty.

Something still worried the sergeant. He was a common

man, and to be acting as a judge on a lord, even if unofficially, worried him. "What about the whipping?"

"How should I know?" said Master Spens. "Why not ask him?"

Once again my heart near stopped, but I'd underestimated the lad. He'd been listening. He crouched by me, looking up at the men. "I wis stealin', sir," he whispered. "I wanted tae come up tae Mistress Meg, an' I lifted a penny for tae buy her a wee gift. An' the maister caught me, an' said it wisnae the first time. He beat me sair, an' cast me oot. An' I came here, tae see if Mistress Meg would tak' me in." He looked up at me like a dog begging its master.

"Will ye, mistress?" asked the sergeant curiously. "Will," not "would." He believed us, not Sir James! Tears came to my eyes as I nodded. Davie, held safe in Andra's arms, grinned at me. He knew, too.

Sir James was furious. He knew this was his man. And I realised if it was left like this, he'd go up to the sheriff and bring up witnesses from his estate. Something more was needed. What? What?

Suddenly something Inge had told me hovered in my mind. What was it? How could I use it? Maybe . . .

"Sergeant." I smiled at him. Across his empty ale-cup, he smiled back, a young man for his rank. An older one would have had us all up before the sheriff long ago, with none of this carry-on. "It's plain, sir, you're not that happy, an' it's not to be wondered at." I could see everyone looking at me, asking themselves what tricks I was up to now, and knew I'd have to be very careful not to seem too clever, and put all their backs up against me. Had I gone too far already? Apparently not; the sergeant was nodding.

"There's maybe a way we can prove it?" There was a doubtful pause.

"Well?" said Sir James. Master Spens eyed me thought-fully.

"If the lad's mine, I'll know his name; if he's Sir James's, he'll know it, won't he?" The crowd nodded and muttered approvingly. As soon as I saw Sir James frowning, trying to remember, I knew I had him, and the struggle not to smile was dreadful. I had to bite my tongue really hard, so that it hurt.

Master Spens's eyebrows rose, but he supported me. "That's sense, now. But how to test it?" We left it to the sergeant to find the answer.

"Mistress, you tell the name you know to one o' my men, and you, Sir James, will you say yours to another? Then the lad will tell me his own name, and we'll compare. That's fair, eh?" He looked triumphant; here was real proof.

I stepped over to one of the soldiers, and prayed my memory was right. "His name's Peem Jackson, sir," I whispered, making sure neither the lad nor the lord could possibly hear me.

Sir James argued. "How in the Devil's name am I supposed to know the name o' every damned cottar and his whelp?" The crowd jeered him.

Master Spens asked him, perfectly politely, "Did you not think to find out the name o' the lad you were chasin', Sir James?"

"What for? Would it not be the first thing he'd change? I knew his looks, damn you, and that was enough!" he snarled. But all round us, heads were shaking.

His stiffness showing how much he was displeased at being sworn at, the sergeant asked the lad his name. "Peem, sir," he said, with an anxious look to me. "Peem Jackson." When I couldn't help smiling in relief, and the soldier confirmed what I'd said, he started to cry and the crowd cheered.

Within five minutes, the street was near empty. Sir James had mounted and spurred off so that I pitied his poor horse, and folk cursed him as they had to leap for safety. The sergeant and his men had told Peem how lucky he was, and clattered off with another silver penny to the nearest ale-stall. And the crowd had gradually trickled away, laughing and swearing at Sir James.

I sat silent on my stool, my fingers tight clenched together. Now that it was over, I felt scared. I'd taken Master Spens's name in vain; called on him to aid me in a lie, in stealing a bondsman from his legal lord. I didn't know what he would do.

He studied me thoughtfully for a long minute, pulling at his lower lip. Then, as I quaked, he picked up the sweetie bowl and swore. "Hell mend you, Meg Rolfsdaughter! You've eaten all my marchpane! Manfred! Manfred, you hound! Would you look at this! Beelzebub's bum, a right wee piggie, this one!"

Davie started to giggle. Even Andra's grimness cracked. Peem grinned shakily, the tear tracks smeared white on his broad, dirty face. I started to relax and smile, and sniff, with relief. Master Grossmeyer, coming back in and shaking his head at me, handed Master Spens another bowl, and he stuffed his mouth gleefully before picking me up, whirling me round in one arm and Davie in the other, roaring with glee and kissing us both equally.

THE *PETREL*

———◆———

$\mathcal{T}$he next six years, Davie, Peem, and I were aye together. I couldn't get away from them. I was the only one who could understand Davie well enough for conversation, so he clung to me, and if I tried to get away, maybe with his sisters to a fair, he'd mope and droop. Not sulk: his temper was clear as spring water; but he was so unhappy when I wasn't there that unless I had to, I never left him behind.

Peem was aye with me, too, but not for the same reason. He turned into my watchdog. Nothing, but nothing, was allowed to come between us. He served me at table; he slept on a pallet at my door. Anything I wanted, he'd do for me; if I'd told him I wanted his right arm, he'd have cut it off instantly. As he ate, he grew; enormously. First up, tall and gangly, like a daddy-long-legs, and then out, to control of his limbs, agility, and strength. Talkative he never was, nor ever seemed clever, though his wide, happy grin spread goodwill round him like a warm sun. But he'd remember a word spoken for ever and a day, and for faithfulness he'd no equal. It was embarrassing.

Master Spens laughed at me about it. He'd not blamed me at all for helping Peem, although it could have got him into trouble. Indeed, he said how grateful he was to me, for giving him the chance to repay the lad who'd helped save his son. But if he gave Peem an order, the lad checked for my nod first. As I said, it was embarrassing.

Every summer, we three went to my dad's house, leaving the stink and disease of the town for the fresh air by the sea. Mother Alison fretted about her baby boy, to Davie's vast annoyance. She was aye on at him to mind change his hose, and wear a scarf, and take care. We only got away by promising faithfully to avoid every possible risk. He'd not be near harm, we promised. Not a splinter, not a drop of water would get within yards of the bairn, we swore all three.

In a shipyard? She was daft to believe it.

The next summer, when we went there in June, the weather was clear. Lucky for us. We spent the first afternoon touring the house and steading. We watched the men re-thatching the byre, introduced the lads to Wolf, admired Domna's weaving and the size of the young pigs, and helped feed the lambs, which Davie loved doing, and the geese, which he didn't. There was something new, called carrots, in the garden. We were told they grew like long yellow teeth, which didn't sound very pleasant. Davie lifted a few of the biggest of them, and got a smack on his bottom, but was let keep them. He was everybody's favourite, in spite of his looks. Or maybe because of them. The carrot things were quite sweet, but stringy.

Next morning we asked Dad if we could come down to the slip, and he told one of the apprentices to show us round. He never let me run round the yard alone, for there were too many ways I could hurt myself, he said. In fact, it was in case

I damaged something. When I was six, I'd tried to climb a rope, and brought down a mast the men were just wedging in position. I aye said they shouldn't have left it alone if it was so delicately balanced, but ever after, Dad was wary of me, and naturally he included the others in the ban.

Anyway, that fateful morning, Jackie was told off to see we didn't get into any mischief. We put on old clothes, for tar has a way of jumping out onto you as you pass by it, begged Elsbet for some bannocks that Peem tucked away in the huge wallet aye hanging from his belt, and ran down to see the latest ship. She was a small cog, half-way ready for launching. Some of the men were cutting planks to deck her out, and lads were hauling up the big bags of linen and wool scraps to the tar boiler. The noise echoed in your skull as they hammered the tarry rags in between the hull planks to make her watertight.

We four toured her carefully. "Wha's 'a'?" was Davie's constant question, and Jackie was kept busy explaining. Peem trailed along behind, but not dully. His eyes were bright, happily taking everything in.

The boys stopped to watch the men smoothing the planking, and Dad shouted, "Hey, Peem, would you like to try your hand?"

Peem doubtfully eyed the great razor-sharp adze offered to him, its heavy cross-set blade near five inches across at the end of its three-foot handle. He looked at me, and I nodded permission, so he grinned, shrugged, and agreed. All the men stopped work and gathered round happily, which should have warned me.

"See, I'll show you," said Dad heartily. On his mettle before his men, he demonstrated on a long, thin triangular beam split from a whole log. "We'll start you easy. Here's a good bit beech, no knots to throw off your blade. See, you stand astride, swing your adze up to about your shoulder height, and bring it down in a long draw between your feet." Dad took off a shaving from near three feet in front of him to a foot behind his heels, not the sixth of an inch thick at the deepest part, all even and curling smoothly like a lady's hair, and nodded in satisfaction. "See, it's easy. And you just do that till it's smooth. See?" He repeated it exactly. "Now, son, you have a wee shot."

Peem stepped up, and a mutter of anticipation rose. He hesitated.

"Never mind them," Dad urged him. "On you go, just do your best."

"Mind you don't cut your leg off, Peem," I called. "One peg-leg in the family's enough." Everybody laughed excitedly. Peem glanced round and nodded as if in decision.

At the first swing, the blade stuck straight in, and as Peem grunted, the men roared with laughter.

"Not so hard, son. Reach for it," Dad said. "You're doing fine."

The second stroke missed altogether, the heavy blade swinging between Peem's legs within a fraction of his ankle and twisting up behind him. "Careful!" I shouted, and was shushed. "Let the laddie try—he's got to learn—leave him alone, lass!" Davie was biting his lip anxiously, and I suddenly realised what I should have seen earlier: they were hoping—not exactly for Peem to be hurt, but certainly to make a fool of himself. A rough joke, that could end in harm to Peem. And I couldn't stop it now. Ach, men!

For the third stroke, Peem took a fresh grip. He spat on his hands, eased his shoulders, grinned innocently round, raised the blade—and drew off a perfect shaving, near as long as my dad's and not much thicker. There was a shout of disbelief as he swung over and over, each time lifting off a long, smooth curl of wood. Then all the men, seeing that he'd turned the joke on them, started to laugh and cheer like dafties.

At last Dad shouted, "Stop, lad, stop, before you shave it to a splinter!" Peem stopped, grinning even wider. Dad seized him by the shoulders. "Where did you learn, you rascal? Having us on like that! Playing that you couldn't do it! You rogue tink! Who taught you?" He thumped Peem's back, roaring with laughter.

Peem actually blushed. "My dad worked tae a carpenter ower tae Inchcolm, when they wis buildin' the monks' house there," he muttered, "an' he teached me." He grinned again, fidgeting shyly as they all roared and cheered him, Davie laughing in the middle. I was so proud, not just of his skill but of the way he'd played them all at their own game—I stood at the back of the crowd and grinned till my jaw ached.

When the men were called in for their morning meal, an hour before noon, we were surprised. We'd been so busy and interested, we'd not even stopped to eat our piece. I told Jackie to go on up and break his fast, and we'd just sit in the sun by the blocks supporting the keel, and take our ease. He was a bit doubtful, for he'd been told to stay with us, but I promised we'd get into no trouble, and he went running up to the house for his porridge.

We sat on bags of wool for comfort, and ate our bread. Fine thick beremeal bannocks, heavy with butter, satisfying. We'd no need of more, even with the sea air to set us sharp. Then I fell asleep for no more than five minutes, I swear, and when I woke with a jump the lads had gone from my side.

I nearly fell off the sack in my hurry to rise. Where had

those daft fools gone to? I called them, and ran round to the far side of the ship; and there they were. Fifty yards from shore, in a wee shallop, its sail half up and trailing in the water beside the boat, which was tilting and tumbling under them, shipping water to a chorus of yelps, laughs, and giggles. They'd clearly no idea what they were doing.

I shouted and waved. They saw me, and cheerily shouted and waved back. The wind and tide were pulling them farther out all the time towards the black Ness point; past that and they'd be among the fierce currents of the Forth, and its mercilessly rocky islets. What could I do? Get Dad? It was much too far to shout—I'd have to run up, if there was no one about—there wasn't. A glance along the shore showed me that there wasn't another boat ready for the water this side of the quay. It would be near half an hour before Dad could get after them, and by then they'd be half-way to the Bass Rock.

Or overset. And I didn't know about Peem, but Davie couldn't swim a stroke.

No, there was only one thing for it. And even before I started, I knew I was as daft as them.

Grimly I pulled off my kirtle. I tucked it carefully under some wood—at least I wouldn't lose this one. I tied up my shift in a knot at my hip as I ran down to the water and waded in. Then, as I'd done the year before, I launched myself into the water to rescue Davie. As I went, I knew Dad would have my hide for this, betrothed or no betrothed.

Dod, it was cold! Don't think about it. I struck out as hard and fast as I could. I just hoped I could catch them before they struck either a rock or a current that would whip them out of my reach.

It was my lucky day. They dropped the spar as they were

trying to haul it up, and the whole sail landed over the side. For several minutes they lay still—well, sploshing about— carried only by the tide, which carried me as well. And in those minutes, I got close enough to shout to them.

If I'd been in any mood for laughing, I'd have split myself at their faces as they turned from fighting the sail and saw me churning towards them. In surprise, Peem dropped the rope again, and again the boom clattered down, burying Davie under the folds of wet grey canvas. They screeched with laughter like a pair of popinjays.

As Peem helped me haul myself over the stern—he wanted to take me in over the side, and couldn't understand why I'd not—some inkling of how I felt hit him. His grin faded, and he started to look anxious. Well he might.

First things first. I'd deal with them after. I helped heave the sail off Davie. "Sit down in the stern there out o' the way, hold the tiller straight, and if you dare twitch you'll get a sore ear!" He gaped at me, bit his lip, and did it. Peem and I pulled the sail up out of the water into a big soggy bundle at the foot of the mast. At least now we were fairly level, but we had inches of water in the boat. I set Peem to bailing it out, using his beloved wallet—if it was ruined, serve him right.

While he was busy, I wrung my shift damp. He took off his tunic without a word, and handed it to me. My teeth were chattering, and I was shivering violently as I slipped it on. It was nearly dry, and warm, but I was still so angry I couldn't bring myself to thank him. He kept his head down and got on with the bailing in just his breeks.

By then we'd been swept right out of the Inner Bay, and the tide race was sweeping us down the Firth. And of course, there were no oars. They'd been taken out to stop thieves. Huh!

It took me nearly two hours to fetch that shallop back to the shore. Fortunately, the tide turned, and the wind swung round eastwards, so that we could sail back, and was light enough that I, never more than a passenger before, could cope, yet strong enough to push us against the currents. We could scarce have been luckier. No one had to row out to fetch us in, and we'd no need to seek shelter—and me without my kirtle!—on the far side of the Firth.

But it was bad enough. I scarce said a single word to the lads, save to tell them when to move and which ropes to pull. They hurried to do as I said, at last realising, as we struggled and lurched past rocks and sand-bars and whirlpools, some of the danger they'd been in.

By the time we entered the bay, I was calmer.

"That was the daftest thing you've ever done!" I said to Davie. "You near killed yourself. And me!" He didn't answer. "I could have drowned myself, swimming after you." Still no reply. "And you needn't think I'm taking a whipping for you, for I'll not!" Silence, head down. "Well?" I asked. "What's the matter? Cat got your tongue?"

He looked straight at me, and I saw he was grinning. "Fun, eh?" he asked.

Peem was grinning, too.

I couldn't help it. I joined them. As we sailed in past the East Ness, and turned up towards my dad and all the household, the owner of the boat, and a fair few of the townsfolk, too, standing waiting for us on the beach, staring, puzzled, anxious, relieved, angry, all three of us started to laugh. Cold, wet, hungry, heading for a sure beating, we hooted and honked and brayed like jackasses. It was indeed fun.

It didn't last, mind you. Dad saw to that. But he didn't tell Mother Alison, which was my greatest worry, for she'd have forbidden us ever to come back. What he did do, two days later when his temper and our backsides had all cooled down, was pay one of the fishers to teach us how to sail properly.

We learned how to steer, handle the sail and tiller to go downwind and across, judge wind and tide and wave; how to see where shoal water, rocks, or currents lay in wait; and how to row, if the wind dropped. Our hands turned first red-raw and then tough and leathery with hauling and tugging rope and wood; mine, too, for Dad said if I was a member of the crew, I had to work at it, and not just be a passenger—and that suited me, for I was never one to sit back and watch if I could help. We took that wee boat out all the summer, at first in gentle breezes, just round the Inner Bay, and then out into the Firth, and in stronger winds. And we ended up sailing to the isle of Inchcolm, in one direction, and to Culross in the other, and thinking little of my sisters because they worried about us. The lads thought it was marvellous.

I enjoyed it, too, I must say. I cut an old kirtle into a tunic just below my knee, almost like a lad's, to my sisters' shrieks of horrified mirth, plaited back my hair—I had just enough sense not to cut that—got one of the lassies to make me a straw hat to keep off some of the sun, and had the best— the freest—summer of my life.

When Master Spens returned from his latest voyage and found out about it, he frowned, and laughed, and agreed not to mention it at home. He also checked that I'd taught Davie to swim, which he did well, like a trout, once he caught the trick of it. Peem was slower in the water, but tireless. I ended up sort of in the middle: a better stayer than Davie, though slower in a short sprint, and faster than Peem, though not for so long.

The next summer, when we came down to visit, there was a strange air in the house. All the first evening, everyone was looking sideways at us, talking too loud and innocent, and hiding grins. Davie was a bit worried, but I reassured him. "Don't fret, pettie"—at his frown, I apologised. He was too old now for that kind of talk—"I know what it is. I've had this before now. That day we were betrothed. Everybody knew but me, and they giggled like dafties. They've a secret for us, but we'll not let on we suspect, to irk them. But, Peem," I said as they nodded, "see can you find out what it is." We were itching with suspense. But not a soul let it slip—even Peem couldn't find out. The sly looks and grins near drove us daft.

Next morning, I could stand it no longer. I rose early and roused Peem silently from his pallet at the door of the bower, and we lifted Dad's clothes from beside his bed and hid them.

When the roars erupted, and all the household were holding their sides laughing at Dad rampaging about with not a stitch on, I refused to return the clothes until we found out what was happening.

Dad glowered at me. "I might have guessed there'd be a carry-on the minute you set your foot in the house!" he bellowed. "Aye, well. You'd have found out the day anyway. Give me my tunic back and I'll show you." He grumbled to himself, pretending to be angry, as he dressed, and then the whole house swept us out and away down to the slip, to show us this surprise.

It was hidden down behind the rope shed. A new skiff, all of our own.

We walked round her in silence. Dad and the rest stood back and watched, delighted by our delight. We touched the fine new ropes, fingered the blue paint on the clinker-built sides, hefted the oaken block, smoothed the lovely red-dyed canvas of the sail. "Oh, Dad!" was all I could say, just as on the day I'd first seen the velvet. "Oh, Dad!"

Peem couldn't take his hands off the boat. "Would ye look at this!" he kept muttering. "Look here!" Everything was of the finest—beech planking, pine spars, a fine new anchor of ash stuck with so many nails the wood was totally covered. She was beautiful.

Suddenly Davie, who'd been gasping with joy, sat down on the sand and burst into tears, overcome with happiness. Everyone understood. It somehow said all that I couldn't.

The boat was a gift to Davie and me from both our fathers. They'd planned it the summer before, and Dad's men had been working on her off and on all winter. We named her the *Petrel*, after the little bird that skims the foam, and spent every summer after that on—or in—the water.

My sisters weren't best pleased. Domna scolded me; I was a young lady of eleven now, I shouldn't be carrying on like this. I'd get brown! I agreed with her, and went on swimming and sailing.

Three summers later, when I was fourteen, Davie eleven, and Peem about seventeen, we made a great expedition. We planned it carefully, storing bannocks and cheese and a cask of water without telling anyone, for we'd be away all day, and if the wind was wrong, maybe more; and they'd not let us go so far, if they knew. Not alone, at least—and we didn't want anybody else with us, as if we were babies.

When the boat was in good order and all prepared, we hid our eagerness as we best could, and waited for a day of fair weather; but none came. More than a week we hung about, sailing just round the bay, or up to the monastery at Inchcolm. We prayed there, too. Maybe we were answered, for at last, at the end of August, only four days before we'd have to go back home to Dunfermline, the weather turned right. There was a good breeze from the north-west, that would carry us out and back, and all the old men that we asked—cautiously, not to arouse suspicions—said it seemed settled to stay a week.

We'd wondered how to slip away, but that was solved too—the sprats came into the Firth, and every boat in Fife was out before first light to harvest them. We just joined them. We carried down our bundles, Peem lugged the water cask aboard, and we shoved away off the muddy shore, raised our new brown sail, and set off.

Even though I was a grown woman now, I risked a beating, but had decided it was worth it. For today we planned to sail near forty miles right up the coast to the big port of Crail, buy a fairing there, and come home again the same day if we could. Though we'd been as far as Berwick over two days with Dad's fisher friend, we'd never been as far before on our own.

That day was perfect. The wind was just right, a fine stiff breeze. The skiff flew over the glittering, glimmering waves like the petrel she was named for, slicing through their white-capped swirl with a fine spray of foam as she leapt and dipped, dancing among the racing swells. We were near flying through the green gleam of the sea. We sang and riddled, and made jokes, and laughed with sheer joy as we sailed sweeter than ever before through a world jewelled and enamelled like a reliquary: gold sun, silver water set thick with emerald, sapphire, and beryl, and the wide lapis arch of the sky above.

We steered just near enough the shore to see the little fisher villages, Pettycur, where the king had died, Dysart, the black cave mouths at Wemyss, Buckhaven, Largo, Elie, Pittenweem, the two Ansters, the huts clinging on the ledges of their cliffs like fulmars nesting. Every boat on the coast was out for the sprats, rowing and shouting like a seagoing market-day, happy and excited with the sea's bounty, a full belly for weeks and plenty to salt and sell, and we exchanged jokes and good wishes with them as we soared past.

Davie took the tiller as we entered the harbour at Crail. He had perfect judgement when steering, and he brought the skiff in to the great timber baulks of the quay as light as a floating sea-gull, between two great ships.

One was loading hides. Raw hides. The master, seeing Peem, leaned over his bulwarks and tried to tempt Peem to give him a hand to load, offering a whole silver sterling for the afternoon, but Peem shook his head, pointing to the glowering onlookers. "Naw, sir," he called back, clearly enough to be heard. "That's work for the shore porters here. Would ye hae me tak' work frae honest folk?" A sterling was above the normal rate for longshoremen, and I guessed the guild was asking extra to handle the stinking hides. The captain cursed, the folk standing by beamed, and I knew our boatie was safe while we went round the town. Peem had sense, so he had.

They helped us climb the side of the quay, and when they noticed I was a girl, they whistled. I blushed, to my annoyance. The shipmaster, resigning himself, agreed to pay the extra they'd asked for, and they called on Peem to join them, out of sheer high spirits, but I had to refuse. We couldn't stay that long, I said. We'd but come to see the town. They were relieved, I think; he wasn't a member of their guild, and they shouldn't have asked him. One woman, a strong wife that hefted her great bundles of hides as easy as any man, called to a runny-nosed child on the quay-head to take us round and show us the best stalls and shops, and warn the stallkeepers if they tried to cheat us, she'd sort them personally.

We spent a grand two hours in Crail. It was a good bit bigger than Inverkeithing, near as big as Dunfermline itself, and one of the great ports of Scotland. Nothing like Berwick, of course, or even Leith, but busy. Even on ordinary days it was aye crowded, rising up its hillside above the harbours. Ships from all over the world traded there, and Davie and I spent a good few sterlings.

I got blue glass beads for Domna that would have cost me near double in Dunfermline, and a strange-coloured fruit that the man said was an orange. It was from far away over the seas to the south, he said, where it was so hot the folk all had been burned black by the sun. He thought I'd not believe him, and was surprised when I told him I'd spoken to two black men, slaves to Sir Alexander Dalrymple, who'd brought them back from a pilgrimage to the Holy Land years ago. They were wed on lasses in Falkirk now. When I bit into the fruit, rather doubtfully, the juice squirted into my eyes and stung, and I near threw it at the man laughing at me. But he showed me how to take off the bitter skin, and the inside was tangy and delicious. I thought so, anyway—Davie didn't like it. At a silver penny each I could just afford two more to take back, and some sugared apricots from Burgundy.

Davie bought figs from Spain. He loved figs. I told him to keep them, but he nibbled and nibbled and nibbled at them as we went along. A sailor had an ape on his shoulder that jumped at Davie and grabbed a fig he was eating, and chattered at him as he yelled with fright; he was a bit ashamed of himself when everybody laughed at him. We wandered on, looking at walrus ivory and magical amber, peacock feathers, currants, and fine leather from Italy. Suddenly Davie turned to me, and said he thought was it not time we were getting away home? He was right. We were going to be late back as it was. And looking at him, if he wasn't to disgrace himself, the sooner we were away the better.

Our skiff was quite safe. I gave our young guide a farthing, which delighted her. And Davie lost the greenness round his mouth once he'd lost his precious figs into the sea. "A pure waste of silver!" I told him.

"Ach away, Meg!" he replied. "You're getting near as bad as Birgget!"

Peem had had little to spend, but had a bulge in the breast of his tunic. I asked what it was, for I'd not seen him slip off to buy anything, but he'd not tell me until we were well on the way back, and wishing we had brought more to eat. Then he produced three fat, juicy pies, stuffed with mutton and prunes. As I said, he had real sense. And a kind heart.

I'd worried what Dad would say if we were too late, but I needn't have. We arrived just about sunset, after a wonderful, fast run back under a high heaven, the few clouds like pink petals floating in the yellow lift. We spoke little, content to sail and enjoy the sea. The boats were ashore, the sprats gone by till next time. As we turned the tiller and sail to head into the bay, the sun was just sliding down the back of the Ferry Hills, so that we glided home into a quiet, grey evening. All was peace. They'd scarce missed us, they said when we arrived, except for salting the sprats down in their wee barrels, and they'd guessed we'd be hiding far away from that back-aching, messy task; so when we told them all where we'd been, and handed out our gifts, they couldn't really scold us.

Indeed, Dad was quite proud. He sat at the dinner table, Davie by his knee, a piece of orange dripping in his huge hand, and boasted about the fine wee skiff he'd built. "She just all fell together, lass, as if she was enchanted," he said, grinning at us. "I never had a boatie build with as few snags. She's just grand. Grand. You could sail to Norroway in her."

In the warmth of the fire, among all my family smiling approvingly at me for a change, Peem steady as any rock behind me, why did I suddenly feel cold?

NEWS

◆

*M*other Alison, though she was half crippled, was a notable housewife. I learned in the six years I stayed with her more than I'd have done in twenty at Dad's.

I learned medicines and cordials, that Inge would never teach me, and the charms to ward off evil. Mother Alison wept, telling me of the hare she'd seen only a month before Davie was born, and how she'd not then known the proper charm, so that he was born with the hare's split lip. I learned that one first.

I learned prices and measures. Like a stone weighed fifteen pounds, if it was wheat, but a stone of wax only eight; unless you used the tron stone, of course, for butter or cheese, which was nineteen pounds and a half. The dry measures, for salt, maybe, were the forpit, peck, firlot, boll, and chalder.

I learned how to produce both a diet for an invalid in September's heat and a banquet for a visiting bishop and his train of eighty in Lent, when no meat was allowed—and a right panic that was, too, since we got only three days' warning, and the weather so stormy the fishers couldn't get out!

But we found four swans and a porpoise, and with a fine subtlety, a marchpane ship, laden with sugared almonds, they kept the Merchants' Guild from disgrace. Roasting a porpoise isn't easy. Nor is seating a mixed company of merchants, priests of varied ranks, guildsmen, and nobility, in proper order of precedence.

I learned how to store food and drink, bake and brew, make sweet candles and scented soap and ale and mead; how to judge and care for cloth and fur, make stylish clothing for myself, the men in the house, and the servants—the hardest to please—and how to design a pattern for weaving or embroidery.

I learned how to play chess and draughts, sing in harmony, and even make fair music on a gittern, joining the rest in their music-making of an evening, though I came to it too late to be expert. I was best in the house at inventing riddles. I even tried to learn my letters from one of the priests at the Great Kirk, but found it so hard I gave it up. I had enough to do without bothering about clerks' matters.

Davie came to that easier than I, and did fine. Master Spens had thought to make him a priest, but his third son was already settled in the seminary near Rouen. Davie would never have been happy in the Church, and probably the Church wouldn't have been happy to have him, either. Once he sneaked up into the bell-chamber in the Great Kirk and rubbed the dollies on the bell-ropes with rotten mackerel, so that the monks had the choice of stinking for days or not ringing the bells for the Divine Service. He was caught, of course, by the smell of the fish on him. Oiling his back after his whipping, I told him he should have used a brush.

Another time he climbed right up onto the high tower of the kirk and hung a pair of breeks like a flag on one of the gargoyles. He was near whipped for it, for sending his mother into one of her "turns," but I told Master Spens how he felt he had to prove himself to the street lads who made fun of him, and the master turned from anger to pride in his youngest child.

Davie was small and looked delicate, but if he couldn't do a thing straight-ways because he was too wee, he'd find a way round it that ended up just as good. He was clever, and quite dauntless. Though he was wee, he was wiry and tough, and the summer sailing brought him a new confidence, so that year by year he paid less heed to the lads about, and they left off teasing him. He joined them at the butts, and with practice became one of the best archers in the town—not for long shots, for his bow was short, like himself, but in the gold near every time at fifty paces. He wasn't as self-conscious about his face as he had been; it was no fault of his that other folks had to look at it, and if they jeered or sneered at it, that was their ill manners.

His father decided, after a lot of thought, that the laddie couldn't make himself understood well enough in speech to go out as a captain or supercargo. Though he was better than he'd been, it was still hard to understand him, and he hated to speak in front of folk. Besides, his mouth did put people off him; we had to face facts. But he was such an expert clerk, in spite of not being in holy orders, that he'd be a grand secretary to his father, writing letters to the merchants all over the world with whom Master Spens had dealings.

So, as well as the international Latin that the priest taught him, he started to spend most of his time learning languages. He said the tongue of England was the worst, being in some ways like the good Scots English we spoke, and yet queerly twisted. I could help him with the Norse I'd learned at home.

French and Spanish, he said, were like the Latin, and then there were Flemish and German, Danish and Erse—enough for a dozen lads, I thought, but he loved the challenge, and soon could read, write, and understand them all well enough.

Peem just grew. He'd the biggest hands and feet of anyone I'd ever seen, and filled out to the strength to go with them. His beard began to sprout, fair and curly like his hair, and the girls started to glance sideways at him in the street—and though he grinned and reddened, he started to glance back.

We chose the cloth for his yearly suit together. We both liked blue; so he usually had a dark blue tunic with tight sleeves, a grey-and-blue-checked cote-hardie over the top, a bright red capuchon hood with a fine long tail to it, grey breeks and hose, and big black boots. I gave him another pair of hose, blue ones, and suggested he wear one leg of each, as the fashion was, but he said that particolours were for the gentry, not for him. Anyway, I thought he was the finest-looking lad in the town, and no hardship to have as an escort; better than sour-faced Andra any day. And his speech improved: not as broad, more civilised. And best of all, he was still my man.

Myself, I was a sturdy big lass of fifteen, well-dressed and—well, not exactly pretty, but not bad-looking neither, and I no longer blushed at a second look or a whistle when I passed by. My hair was growing darker brown, and the white streak showed clearer, right down my plait. I'd be wed next year, and have to cover it.

All this time, there was a constant unrest. The various claimants to the throne would not settle, even when at last Edward of England got his permission from the Pope for his son to wed the little Maid of Norway. There were clashes all over, on the roads, round the castles, in the towns, between supporters of the various rivals, and the common folk suffered sore from their lords' disputes. Our own young Earl of Fife was even murdered, in an ambush near Brechin, but all the murderers were hunted down and brought to justice.

The Guardians did their best, for they knew that when eventually there was a king, they'd be called to account for all their doings, and in some ways the land was even better ruled than it had been. Master Spens said it was hard for a man to turn an honest penny now, with so many rules and regulations. But the roads were full of broken men and soldiers, and trouble waited round any corner. Even in Dunfermline.

That January, we were out at the market, Peem at my back, Davie away ahead of me, and fat Anna dragging behind at the food stalls. I'd got near everything. The braid, the twine, the holly-wood tweezers for Mary's eyebrows—she kept losing them, there must be a dozen pairs down the floorboards somewhere, or maybe her mother was lifting them to pull the black hairs starting on her chin—aye, there they were. Peem had the dried apples. "Now, what's left?" I muttered, slipping off a mitten to poke in my flat tray basket.

Peem, behind me with the deep, heavy basket, said nothing. He knew there was just the spice to get, and then the fish that I aye left till last because of the smell, but he'd not speak unless he had something to say. I sometimes wished he'd talk more—and other times I wished some folk were more like him.

"Aye, just the saffron. And the fish. Hake, maybe? We'll get it on the way back." Anna came up, as she aye did when food was mentioned—it was instinct with her—and we turned into the Saltmarket towards Master Grossmeyer's. "Cry on Davie, Peem, will you?" I said, craning my neck to find the lad.

As we moved on, and Anna started to suggest crayfish for the dinner, or perhaps a few dabs, for she didn't like hake, I slipped on the cobbles where the snow hid the holes, but Peem's hand was under my elbow same as always to steady me. The huge leather boots he was so proud of were solider than our pattens, but Mother Alison insisted. We had to wear them, strapped over our low-cut shoes. I thought it was daft, but "We have appearances to keep up, lass! What would folk think—the idea! You'd disgrace us all, wearing boots!" So we had to slip about, frozen-toed and wobbly on the high wooden platforms. This business of family pride was a right nuisance at times.

There was a shouting and the clash of steel from the street above. We stopped, and Davie came wriggling back through the surging crowd. "Comyns!" he called to me. They were fighting the sheriff's men. Anna started to whimper.

I took only half a second to realise we had to get into shelter, but even as I turned to Peem the group of horsemen at the top of the hill, swords clattering, broke apart, and came galloping down towards us. Davie and Peem were already dodging, and I jammed Anna and myself safe in a shop door.

Then there was a wail from the far side of the street, and a scream from just by me. A wee bairn, maybe three years old, had been parted from its mother when the crowd split, and carried to the other side. When folk stopped, it had found itself lost, and was wandering out into the street to find her. And the horses nearing, their hard hooves battering on the stones.

The child's mother screamed again. She was a beggar wife, not yet twenty, thin and ragged, her face white below her tatty shawl. With a desperate glance up the street at the charging horsemen, she raced out, snatched up her babe, and turned to come back. She should have gone on. As she turned, her bare feet slipped in the snow and she fell and lay twitching. The child wailed again.

I didn't stop to think. The crack as her head hit the cobbles sent me out there, sliddering to a halt, grabbing up the child, and dragging at the woman's arm. She slid a yard and then stuck. The first horse was only yards away, and someone nearby was screaming. Anna. My feet slipped again, and I lost a patten.

Drat, I thought, boots next time, whatever she says. But then, there'll not be a next time . . . The broad chests and iron-hard hooves were upon us.

Then Davie grabbed the bairn from me, and Peem's great fists on our arms hauled me and the woman wrenching and slithering back off the street, as a dozen horses galloped by my toes, the blue and gold Comyn livery sped on its way by curses and a shower of snowballs and fish from the folk around me. I sprawled among bumping knees, gasping, "Where's my basket? And my mitten?" and trying not to remember the man who'd been dragged by me, his foot caught in the stirrup and his head and hands bouncing and flapping red on the ice.

The woman, when she recovered her senses, kissed Peem's hand. He was horrified. All the folk about cheered him, and collected money for him as a reward, which I insisted he had to take, but I know he gave most to the poor wife. She went away with probably more silver than she'd ever had in her life, vowing gratitude, her son's teeth happily glued together by a lump of chewy liquorice that Anna had given him.

I made them all promise not to tell Mother Alison, but Anna told Mary, and Mary told her mother. She had another "turn," the worst yet, and Davie and I got a right telling-off, for risking our lives for a beggar woman, but I remembered her face as she hugged her child, and didn't care. On the quiet, Master Spens gave Peem a new knife, with a carved walrus-tooth haft and fine red leather sheath, for saving me. His eye had been green on it in the cutler's for weeks. He took it tender as a baby, his grin reaching his ears.

It wasn't long after that that Master Spens came in early one night looking fretted. He didn't even wait for Andra to pull off his boots before he called Mother Alison up the stair to speak privately. There was something about the way he didn't look at me . . . When they called me, she was white as her barbette, huddled on her padded seat by the brazier. He bade me sit on a stool beside his big chair. "Meg, my dear," he said, "I've ill news for you."

Aye, I'd known. "What, sir?" My heart was jumping in me.

He rubbed his hand over his mouth near half a minute before he could bring himself to speak. "It's your sister. Inge, aye. I'm sorry to bring you the word, my dear, but she's accused o' witchcraft."

Aye. The maids were all peeking. "Is she for trial, sir?" I asked calmly.

He seemed relieved by my matter-of-factness. "Aye, that she is, lass, before the Abbot o' Cambuskenneth." Mother Alison, opposite him, muttered consolingly. Davie stood by the brazier and stared. "She'll be tried as soon as may be. They say she's brought about the deaths o' two o' the Guardians, to aid old Robert de Brus in his claim to the crown. You mind the Earl o' Fife was murdered last year? And now Comyn o' Buchan, he's dead as well, and they're claiming that your sister put a death-spell on him."

"How?" asked Davie.

His father frowned at him. "Mammetry. They say she made

a wax image o' the Comyn, with a strand o' his hair stuck to it, and melted it gradual-like so he'd die slow. It's a hard case. Her mistress, the Lady o' Carrick, she's standing by her. She says it's all lies, put about by a Balliol man Inge wouldn't wed. With such a great lady to protect her there'd be no danger to her in the normal way, but you see—"

"When it's a Comyn she's accused o' killing, it makes all the difference."

"Aye, lass. It's a terrible crime, murdering one o' the greatest men in the land. They're saying the Bishops o' Glasgow and Saint Andrews will be judges as well. Wishart o' Glasgow's fair, but Fraser o' Saint Andrews is a Comyn man, and hard with it. Lucky for her it's a church court that'll try her, for she'd be dead already o' the torture if it was left to the Comyns."

Torture? Oh, God! "Can I go to her, sir?" I asked. Mary and Anna were whispering. I had to go. Even if I could do nothing. But surely there must be something? "I could speak for her." I rose, as if I could go at once.

He gripped my wrist and turned me to look straight at him. "Could you? Could you swear, on your Bible oath, that your sister wasn't a witch? That she never showed any strange powers? If they asked you, lass, what would you say?"

I hadn't thought of that. My mind went back to the night of the king's death. But aye, I'd swear she had no power. To save her life, I could. But I was flushing already. He shook his head, before I could speak. "No, lass, you couldn't," he said firmly, and Mother Alison murmured in agreement. "You're not that good a liar. Your face gives you away every time. No, Meg, you're one o' them that's born to be honest. I'll not take you to Stirlin'. Your dad'll be there to speak for her, and your other sisters, and likely the priest from Saint

Peter's as well. But not you! Mind me, now! You're not to testify! You hear me?"

"Aye, sir." I nodded.

He wasn't quite satisfied. "Am I not right?"

I nodded again. He was, of course. Then what could I do? I should pray for her. I should . . . I should . . . I couldn't think straight at all. "I'll see to your dinner, sir," I said blankly, and went down to stir the pots.

The days after that passed slow and long, for I could neither sleep nor find any activity to take my mind off Inge, jailed in Stirling, questioned, maybe tortured. Everyone was very kind, but their eyes turned sideways to me, and their muttering about the dreadful torments put on witches to make them confess weren't aye quite out of earshot. I heard Peem argue that folk would confess to anything if they were tortured, just to stop the pain. How could that be taken as proof? They just asked how else he'd get a witch to confess.

A week before the trial, the feeling in my heart finally took words to itself. I turned to Peem, as we walked down to the oil merchant for some sweet oil of olives, and said, "I must go, Peem."

I don't know what I expected. What I got was astonishing. He just nodded. "Aye," he agreed. "It'll not be easy, for they're watchin' ye. They know ye better than ye know yoursel', mistress. Andra or one o' the other men's aye near ye. It's Tam the day—he's at the corner o' Pie Lane there." As I glanced round, he tut-tutted at me. "Don't let on ye know, mistress!"

I'd never heard him say as much at the one time. But he wasn't done yet. "Davie and me's got a plan. A good head on him, the wee one. We was just waitin' on ye makin' up your mind. Just you be sure ye wear a warm gown, wi' a wide skirt, an' a cloak, whenever ye get out tae the market. I don't know just when we'll manage it. It depends."

He'd tell me no more. In a way, I was relieved; I couldn't have kept up a lie. An honest face was a great handicap.

I was on tenterhooks, but for days I couldn't get out at all. Mother Alison kept me by her all day, and the younger lasses were sent for the messages. "Never fear, we'll try the morn, mistress," said Peem each night. I felt sick.

Even the day of the trial itself, again Mother Alison kept me busy about the house till half the morning was away. But at last, about three hours before noon, trying to hide my fretting and worrying—though truly I'd reason for them—I found a second free to take up my cloak.

"Where are you off to, Meg?" demanded Mary behind me. Drat the girl! She'd been like my shadow all week. On her mother's orders, of course, but she could surely relax now?

"Ach, just down the souter's. I've a hole in my slipper. See?" I had, too. I'd made it myself the day before. I had to get an excuse somehow.

"Hold on a wee minute!" she called, and nipped up the stair. After some muttering, Mother Alison's voice came from the hall, ". . . too late now, anyway—aye, let her go, but you stay right by her, and straight back, mind," and after a moment Mary ran down.

"I'll come with you, Meg," she said, pulling on her red cloak and blethering nervously about the camlet wool she wanted for a new lining for it. I was desperate, but Peem nodded behind her and gave me his wide, innocent grin as he fell in at our back. Tam came out as if to shut the heavy door, but as I went up the street I glanced back. He was watching us, his head poking out past the jamb, just waiting to come after when we'd not see.

We turned into Souter's Lane, and instantly Peem grabbed my hand and raced me off downhill towards the river. Mary, taken by surprise, wasted a minute gaping before she started to shout, and we had a fair start on Tam when at last he rounded the corner. We doubled back, scurrying through lanes and closes, gradually gaining on him, though passers-by staring after us would give us away every time we dodged. "No far now, mistress!" Peem grinned as I gasped for breath. "The wee one's had mounts held ready for us at the livery in Spital Street this week past, in his dad's name!" We ran on down to the road by the leper hospital, and there stood horses waiting, a lad holding the reins, all three looking round startled at us as we panted across to them.

The horses were both saddled for men. "Up wi' ye, mistress!" cried Peem, and punted me up into one saddle. As I tried to arrange my skirt so that I could sit astride—it had never struck me before just how thick a horse was—he stuck my feet in the stirrups, grabbed my reins, and heaved himself into his own saddle, and we cantered off round the back of the town, towards the road for Stirling. Tam, too late, shouted angrily after us. Peem waved. I didn't.

We were off!

I was near off in more ways than one. I'd never ridden astride before. I'd aye been seated comfortably on a pad saddle behind Peem or one of the other men, hand tight in his belt and feet secure on the footboard, on a quiet, sensible, easy-paced beast, warranted suitable for a lady's use. It was a bit boring, but quite safe, even if the front rider managed to stir the horse into a trot for a bit. This—this racing along, bouncing and bumping, clutching desperately at the saddle to hold myself on—this was no riding I'd ever done before. But after a bit I started to get the hang of it. Fortunately, the back and front of the saddle were very high, to help beginners like me stay aboard, and I found if I pressed my feet into the stirrups, they helped me stay on, too: a good idea. I even started to think of taking the reins myself. And where had Peem learned to ride like this? There was aye more to him than you'd think.

When we stopped a mile or two outside the town for me to pick myself up the second time, or maybe the third, I asked about the reins. Peem shook his head. "No if you want tae reach Stirlin' the day, mistress," he said, but finally consented to use his belt as a leading-rein, attached to the bit ring of my mount. We got on better that way, and I didn't fall off more than twice more, in spite of the speed. It was a good road through the forest and farmlands, for pack-horse trains used it fairly often, and that no doubt helped me. But oh, I was sore when that afternoon we reached Stirling!

I was in such a state I scarce noticed how full the town was. Braid Street, the market, was crowded with folk. Townsfolk out for the holiday, for the trial of a witch was a rare thing, and this was no daft old crone but a great sorceress, it was said. Shopkeepers and stallkeepers out to make money. Apprentices, journeymen, housewives, cottars in from all round—they made the town fair buzz. But in and around them all, spoiling the holiday atmosphere and making sober men look to their goods and families, were the soldiers.

Each lord had brought his best men, to make a good showing before the others. Everywhere blue, red, and gold liveries swarmed in the street, clustered round their chosen ale-stalls, watched each other jealously across invisible borderlines. They clotted in groups like bees from different hives, ready to attack any intruder, any disturbance. The mailcoats gleamed under the bright cloth, and they kept their steel hats on ready, not slipped back comfortably onto their shoulders. When we arrived, they were still under control of their sergeants, but as more ale was being drunk, they were growing more and more offensive—and more ready to take offence. And the townsfolk noticed, drew off from the street, bolted their doors and shutters, and hoped.

We were told the trial, being a religious charge and not a civil one, was being held not in the Castle but in the Kirk of the Holy Rude, in the South Gait just off to one side of the long hill that led up to the Castle. Soldiers of the two bishops were all round the church to keep order. It was as well I'd my purse to bribe a sergeant, or we'd not have got in. With Peem's breadth of shoulder and of grin to clear a way for me through the packed spectators, we worked our way up the side of the building. At last we squeezed between two gaily dressed backs, he slipped me forward under his arm and I could see.

There was Inge.

Voices were echoing in the high stone arches and in the hollows in my skull, but they made no sense. All I could think for a minute was that she'd not been tortured. She was standing alone before the row of three judges, in a clear blue surcoat and white kirtle, pure and lovely, just like a statue of the Mother of God. And I was sure—knowing her as I did—it was deliberate.

Her silvery hair curled smooth from a maid's chaplet of twisted white and blue. She wore no jewels, and the belt of her plain linen surcoat was merely a thick white cord. Nothing could have seemed simpler, but I knew that it was all planned carefully to give the effect of purity, innocence, a simple maid caught mistakenly in a coil not of her making. Though she was now twenty-seven, she looked less than eighteen. The commons, staring brown and grey from the body of the hall, were mostly for her. The nobles, packed fidgeting in bright, intent rows round the nave, were mixed in their feelings, depending whose side they were on. But her judges, the vital men, the experienced faces eyeing her steadily above their vivid robes and rich vestments, were among the cleverest in the country; would they be impressed? I feared not. The very effectiveness of her appearance must surely have warned them she was more than she seemed.

Dad, in his best tunic and hose, his hat twisted in his hands, was red-faced, angry, and confused here. By him stooped old Father Michael. On the other side were the accusers, two men in Balliol and Comyn blue and gold. And some of our neighbours, too—Mistress Barnes, whose man we all knew had only asked her to wed him when Inge refused him, and four of the meanest-minded wives in the town, all in their finest, looking smug and sweaty.

No witness was being questioned. All the evidence must have been given. Now the judges were arguing among themselves. I heard one say, ". . . Put to the question," but the old man on the left, one of the bishops from his mitre and white robes, shook his head determinedly, and after some protest the others nodded and sat back. What had been decided?

The bishop beckoned to a clerk, who approached respectfully, head bowed, listened to a brief instruction, and stepped forward. His tonsure gleamed freshly shaved in the light from the long windows.

"Lords, gentles, and commons!" His voice echoed like a psalm. "My Lord Bishop of Glasgow commands, if there be any here who knows this woman but has not yet spoken, let him stand forth and truly and rightly speak, that the truth of this matter may be resolved." His Lordship must be unhappy about the evidence. Should I . . . ? No. Mind what Master Spens said. And he was right.

A pinch-faced woman seated in front of me eased her back. I recognised her as she moved: Marjory, Countess of Carrick, who had called on Inge all those years ago, and started all this. Now at least she did not desert her. Then the old man beside her, richly dressed in crimson, bounced up.

"My lords, why waste more time? There's not a soul here, see you, that can claim this is more than a ploy to bring me an' mine into disrepute, aye, an' cause us harm! This is no more than a plain lass, a bit strong-willed maybe, but none the worse for that, that had the sense to refuse an offer from that mumpit mowdiewarp—"

He was interrupted by another man, in blue. "Hold your tongue, de Brus! Your turn to speak's past! Disrepute, he says! A de Brus worried about being thought disreputable! My God! This 'plain lass' "—his tone was cutting—"has untimely done to death my uncle, to clear your way to the crown! She's—"

"Untimely! God, Comyn, the old fool was seventy-five if he was a day! Did you expect him to reach the hundred? You've no proof o' any crime!" shouted de Brus, in a voice that was used to carry across a battlefield, his bald head matching his cote-hardie. "Not as much as would hang a flea! Hearsay an' old wives' clashmaclavers—"

"Honest women from her own town, you old scarecrow, here at their own costs—"

"You'll pay them later, you mean!"

There was uproar throughout the kirk. A younger man beside de Brus pulled at his sleeve. "Will you sit down, Father!" he snarled. "You're making a—"

"Sit!" yelled the older man. "Wi' that ill-favoured hound miscallin' me!"

"My lords! My lords!" The centre judge, the Abbot of Cambuskenneth, had risen to his feet, the clear belling of his voice cutting into the bellowing of the two lords, and the shouts of their supporters. "Is this the way to conduct yourselves, in God's own house? Or is it any way to arrive at the truth, by shouting and bickering like fishwives?" The angry stir faded as the tall, spare figure stood firm before them, his naturally kindly face set today in severe lines. He gathered the eyes of the two other judges, and they also rose.

Dad was white now. Inge looked over at him, with a strange pity in her face. She was the one in danger of her life, yet she thought of him. Then she looked up again to her mistress, the Lady of Carrick, and her eyes travelled a fraction farther. She saw me in the crowd. Her face changed, to surprise, a smile, a frown. Her hand half rose, and fell again.

There was a pause. The bishops looked in some puzzlement at the abbot between them, but he was looking at Inge. Then he, in turn, lifted his eyes up towards me. I tried to hide behind Peem, but I felt those deep eyes pick me out of the crush. He murmured to the other judges, and they sat again, the Bishop of Saint Andrews tugging bad-temperedly at his robes, while the abbot called the clerk and pointed. Everyone was turning to seek what had drawn his attention.

The clerk straightened, turned, walked over the aisle. He paused by my side, looked back for a nod of confirmation, and said clearly to me, "Lass, it seems to the holy abbot that you may know something about this woman, accused here of witchcraft, that might well help us to a just and true decision. Will you step forward, and tell us what you know?"

THE TRIAL

———◆———

My breathing stopped. The clerk, the judges, the officers of the court, the witnesses, the spectators noble and common, all stared at me. Inge's eyes, blue-grey and wide, were gazing at me with mingled hope and apprehension.

"Come, lass," the clerk said, still kindly, "you're called by the abbot. Step forward and give your testimony, if you have anything to say."

At last I found my breath. "No, sir!" I whispered. "I've nothing! I don't know anything!" I leaned back on Peem's steadiness behind me, shaking my head desperately. I couldn't go out there! I couldn't lie, on my sworn Bible oath, to all these people! I'd betray Inge—I knew she had power—I wouldn't be able to deny it. Peem put his arm round my waist, as my knees threatened to give way under me.

The clerk frowned, and then returned to speak to the judges. I gasped in relief, but then I saw Inge. She was staring at me as if she was drowning and I offered her a rope to pull her out. Hope, joy, love—they were all in her face. But I couldn't!

The clerk spoke. "My lords, the lass says she doesn't know the prisoner."

Inge, oh, Inge, I'm sorry! I thought. I couldn't look at her. I buried my face in Peem's tunic. Oh, why didn't I listen to Master Spens? Why did I aye think I must meddle? I'd but hurt her more.

But worse still came on me. An old voice chirped up. "Doesn't know her? That's a queer thing, then, when she's her own sister!"

One of the wives from Inverkeithing was standing among the murmur that grew to a roar, pointing a knotted finger at me and screeching, "Aye, her sister! Meg, that's her! Her that's promised on the half-faced laddie! The Spens youngest! Too fine now to know her own blood, eh? But I know her! See her hair! Ask her about that!" She was delighted by the stir she caused.

There was a quick nod from the judges, and the clerk returned. I couldn't go! He beckoned a soldier. I couldn't refuse. I had to step out from among the crowd, conscious of the greedy eyes on my stained dress and ruined shoes, my wild hair, my dirty, mud-splattered hands and face, knowing I'd done nothing but bring harm and notoriety to my future family, without helping my own one. Trying not to cry with shame and fury, I wished I could scream at them all, as I'd done when I was little at the louts attacking Davie. I couldn't. Well, maybe I could do better than Master Spens feared. Peem held my arm as I limped forward, and I took a little comfort and courage from his firm hand.

As the noise died away, I smoothed my hair and kirtle, drew a steadying breath, and raised my head to face the judges.

They were all old men. The abbot, in the centre, in a grey habit with a white hood, was the simplest-dressed, and seemed the simplest man. His face showed the kindness and sympathy that old Father Michael at Saint Peter's had. But now he was regarding me sternly.

"I'm sorry, sir, that I didn't come forward before," I said. "It's not that I don't know Inge—just I've nothing to say that will help."

He nodded. The man on his right, the Bishop of Glasgow, a broad man in gold-embroidered white, sat forward in his high chair. "What's your name, lass? Are you indeed the sister o' this woman? And betrothed to young—what's his name—David Spens? I know his father. A fine man."

I tried to smile, not very successfully. "Aye, sir."

"*Your lordship!* Not *sir!*" hissed the clerk at my back.

"Your lordship—your lordships," I stammered, "my name is Meg Wright—Margaret Wright. An' I know nothing against my sister's good name. She's aye helped whoever came for help, with good advice, and never—never harmed none." Except a king—except a king. Don't think of that. Don't speak of it. Never. I bit my lip. The blood, in spite of myself, rose to my face.

The third judge leaned forward. "Margaret Wright. Daughter o' Rolf Shipwright o' Inverkeithing? Eh? Aye. Take the oath, Margaret Wright."

As I laid my hand on the Bible and swore before God that I would tell only the truth, I could feel the church tremble. No. It was me that was trembling. There was a clerk speaking to Mistress Barnes. Dad was wringing his hat to rags.

"Now, Margaret Wright. On your oath before God." The third judge, the Bishop of Saint Andrews, was thin and pointed of face and build, with eyes and voice cold enough to freeze my heart. He was the one who questioned me, the clerk who'd spoken to the old wife whispering in his ear.

At first I managed fairly well. I said aye, I loved Inge, everybody did, except mean old wives, which raised a laugh. Aye, she'd raised me when my mother died. Aye, I knew Asa. She was my dad's old nurse, and—I had to be careful, I didn't know what else had been said—I thought she was a bit wandered in her wits. No, I didn't think she saw the future. No, I didn't think she was a witch. No, I didn't know she'd been questioned, and boasted about Inge's powers. I wasn't surprised, though, I said; she aye thought the sun shone out of Inge's backside. That got another laugh; was I doing the right thing? If anybody suggested Inge could do anything, Asa would agree to it, even if it was unlawful. She'd lost her sense, like I said.

God forgive me my lies. But I could do nothing else.

The Bishop of Glasgow nodded. He seemed ready to accept that, and to take my red face for shyness. The other bishop frowned, eased his mitre a touch, and started about my hair. Aye, I said, it was Inge hitting me had caused the white streak. There was a gasp, and the bishop looked pleased, but when I explained about the weight from the spindle in her hand, he sat back in disgust. One of the ladies watching supported me that a blow could cause hair to turn white; she even kindly offered, with a simper, to remove her barbette and show them a streak in her own hair, but they politely refused.

But then the Bishop of Saint Andrews, the Comyn one, with the face of a hoodie crow above his purple and gold robes, turned cruelly on me. What did Inge keep in her storehouse? Spices, eh? Nothing else? Then why was no one allowed in? Only the value of the goods? Why not keep them in the main store, then? Had I ever seen people come by night to ask her aid? Did I know what any of them wanted? Why did they come under cover of darkness, if it was all legal? Who had I seen? Anyone here present? Was I sure? Was I quite sure?

The blood was rushing to my face all this time, and though I denied everything, it must have been plain to them all that I was lying. And then, somehow—I still don't know how—he winkled out of me that Inge had not told Dad that she would be leaving to go to the Lady of Carrick; that she had burned down her store before she left; that none of us knew of any connection with Countess Marjory that could have made her take Inge as a waiting-woman.

In triumph he turned to his fellow judges. "Nothing o' any help, indeed! Nothing that would help the woman there, she meant! If all was innocent, why did she not tell her father she was leaving? If there was nothing harmful in that store-house, why should she burn it when she left? Why, indeed—maybe the Lady o' Carrick will tell us—why should a common lass be given such a high post? A laundry-wife, a sewing-maid, that we could understand—but a waiting-woman? A companion? And why did neither the lass herself, nor the great lady concerned, think to tell us any o' this? Could there be clearer proof o' conspiracy? An' if there's one thing hidden, you can be sure there's another! She must be put to the question!"

"No! No! You can't! You mustn't!" I heard myself screaming at him. Inge's face was linen-white before me. Then Dad came behind me before the soldiers did, gripped my shoulders to turn me, and slapped my face. I stopped screaming in shock. He took me in his arms and held me tight.

I missed the next few minutes. Peem and Dad drew me back to sit on the chancel steps, stopped me crying, and at last I could listen again.

I bit hard on my lip as the abbot and his fellow judges

again rose to their feet. The Bishop of Saint Andrews didn't look as pleased as he might, Peem whispered. Maybe there was hope yet. Dad just shook his head, grey-faced.

"Let it be known by all the folk o' this Realm o' Scotland, both noble and common, that here, in the case o' the accusation o' witchcraft made against Inge, eldest daughter o' Rolf Shipwright o' Inverkeithing, this is our decision, and we call on all Christian men to accept and support it!" There was a hush. Somebody cleared his throat, feet shifted, a spear butt scraped. Then absolute quiet. Inge took a deep breath, and stood proudly tall.

The abbot's voice, trained in singing the kirk services, echoed musically in the crowded silence. "We judge that there is not good and sufficient evidence to prove to us, beyond any doubt, that this woman is a witch." Tears sprang to my eyes. Inge let out her breath in a gasp. There was an answering gasp, and then cheering and catcalling mixed down the church. The abbot raised his hand, as the Balliol and Comyn men started up from their seats in a rage, and in a louder voice went on. After a moment the sense of what he was saying reached them, and they settled back. "But we're not satisfied either that we can just dismiss the case against her. There seems to be a good deal that cannot just be cast aside as malice or envy. In especial the evidence given, and given against her will, by the sister o' the accused, raises questions that require an answer."

Oh, why did I come? I'd just made things worse for Inge! Why did I aye stick my nose in? I aye thought things couldn't be done without me there, and now see what I'd done! Sh— the abbot wasn't finished.

"We have considered the use o' torture, but on the strong recommendation o' His Grace o' Glasgow we have decided against it at this time." God bless him! "However, we feel that a test is needed, to find out for certain if this woman is indeed in league with Satan or not." He turned to Inge, alone before them all. "Woman, will you abide the trial by water at our hands?"

Dad's face turned from grey to white.

For a full half-minute, Inge didn't stir. Then slowly she nodded. "Aye, my lord, that I will. For as my God is my judge, I pray for proof that will satisfy ye all that I am not now, nor ever have been, a servant o' Satan."

Was I the only one that noticed she'd not said she was innocent?

Though I'd not expected to, I slept well that night. Dad had a place hired at an inn, a fairly clean one he'd known for years, where they'd let us stay, witch in the family or not. I couldn't eat, for my throat choked me. Dad kept on and on at me, why had I come, did I not see I'd hinder instead of help, on and on and on till I was cried out. At last I fell asleep on the bench, and Peem just picked me up and carried me up the ladder to the sleeping-room, rolled me in my cloak and his, and laid me down on the bed. Dad tried to get in to see Inge, but the guards wouldn't admit him, and at last he returned to the inn. He slept on one side of me—when he wasn't praying—Peem on the other, and the four other folk that shared the big bed came in after I slept and left before I woke. But when I did, I found new trouble.

Master Spens had arrived seeking me. He was not pleased, with me or Peem.

"I have dealt already with David James," he said. He never used the lad's full name except in a rage. "He's but a lad, easy to lead astray by his elders. Peem even, he's your servant, and he can claim he was but obeying orders from his mistress. Not that it'll save him a whipping, mind, but at least he'll not be cast out for it. But who, then, shall we say is totally responsible for this catastrophe? I can understand, you'll be aware, that you wished to help your poor sister, to be present to aid her; but when I'd already forbidden it, and you'd admitted that I was not only legally entitled to do so, but correct in my judgement . . ."

Long before this I was in tears again. It didn't stop him. "Is it pride, would you say, that you can't believe the wind can blow without you there to see it's done right? You'll maybe keep in mind in future that you're not God, Meg Wright. The position is already filled, to the general satisfaction o' most folk—excepting yourself, it would seem. You think you're responsible for every action on the face o' this earth. Well, you're wrong! Cultivate humility, and we'll maybe have a bit less capers from you, and less trouble for the rest o' us to suffer!"

I was in such a state that Dad, who agreed with every word, was moved to intervene. "Master Spens, I'm far from defending her actions, but I think she knows what she's done by now, and if we don't move, we'll not be there for the trial. You'll mind I have—I have another daughter I must see to."

I didn't want to go, but Master Spens insisted I had to see the final result of my meddling. A very subdued Peem brought a damp cloth and a borrowed brush and tried to make me look respectable. I was past helping him, or even caring, but he got me a mug of ale and some bread and cheese, coaxed me to take them, and talked quietly to me till I was at least fit to walk out on my own feet.

Master Spens, looking through him, bade him wait in and mind the horses, but Peem firmly but politely refused. "I can't do that, sir. I can't see my way tae leave my mistress when she's in this state," he said, while Master Spens turned puce. "I'm Mistress Meg's man, sir, while she needs me."

I was near collapsing again, but Peem knew his man better than I did. After a moment when I was certain he was going to knock Peem flying into the fireplace, and the landlord was reaching for a broom handle to defend his house, suddenly Master Spens relaxed with a resigned, disgusted, even amused snort. His colour faded to its normal walnut, and he turned to take Dad's arm without another word. They went out together, Dad stiffly, like a scarecrow, and Peem and I trailed behind down to the bridge.

When we got there we found a huge crowd already gathered. It took all the efforts of Master Spens and Peem, for Dad seemed to have little strength in him, to force a way through for us to the front. When folk realised who we were, though, they usually let us through without too much trouble, sometimes with a sneer or a curse, sometimes with a rough sympathy. "Poor lassie! An' her tryin' to help her sister!" I heard once behind me. My eyes would have watered again, but I felt drained of tears.

At last we stopped, right at the corner of the bridge. It was a low wooden structure, the first bridge over the Forth, just above the old ford. This was why Stirling was such a stronghold; it guarded the roads to the north, to Perth and Aberdeen, and round into the rich lands of Fife. No enemy could pass there while the fortress on the rock was firmly held. The river under the middle arch of the bridge was about five feet deep, running clear and cold, and crowded along the banks and even out into the shallows with all the good folk of Stirling and the surrounding countryside, come to see the witch swim. The far end was full of the blue and gold wheatsheaf badge of the Comyns, well separated from the yellow with red saltire crosses of de Brus on our side by the bridge itself, kept clear by the bishops' men.

We waited and waited. It was near noon when at last there was a stir up towards the Castle, and the sound of chanting. A troop of horsemen clattered down the rocky road past the hospital, and those who had inched forward had to shove back hard to save their heads from the swinging spear butts. Then the procession flowed slowly into sight.

A dozen guards marched down to join the others already on the bridge. After them trod a long line of monks from Cambuskenneth by two and two, their grey robes flapping in the cold breeze, singing the Te Deum. Many of the older folk in the crowd sang with them, knowing the sounds, if not the meaning, and the chanting rolled solemnly out over the river. The monks stopped at the far end of the bridge, jostling slightly to get a clear view.

Behind them, between two files of soldiers, walked Inge. My heart jumped. The folk cheered. She was in the same clothes as yesterday in the church, all blue and white, pure innocence. But it wasn't people she had to impress today.

And behind her came her three judges, surrounded by a flock of lesser priests. First the abbot, tall and somehow ungainly, lurching along as if striding on stilts; then Bishop Wishart of Glasgow, shorter and square-built, marching steadily, frowning slightly; and last, in the place of honour, stalked Bishop Fraser of Saint Andrews, more like a hoodie crow than ever, his triumphant eyes flicking from Inge to the crowd, judging their growing sympathy for her and despising it.

The whisper went they had held a Mass in the Kirk of the Holy Rude, and prayed for God's blessing and judgement to be made clearly known. Inge had taken Communion without crying out or fainting, which many thought showed she was innocent.

"How could a servant o' the Devil swallow the body an' blood o' Christ, an' not choke, eh? Answer me that!" a man behind me demanded of his friend.

I was cheered a little, till the other replied, "Maybe she's stronger than ye think, John. Maybe she's that armoured in evil she can face even the bishop himsel'. But the water'll show us. See, they're blessin' the river now. Once they get going, they're quick, eh? An' then they'll put her in. If she's guilty, the blessed water'll no accept her, an' she'll float. But if she's innocent, she'll sink."

"Aye," said John, "an' they'd best be ready for to pull her out, before she drowns. She's in a sore pickle, the lass; if she's guilty, she'll hang, an' if she's innocent, she's like to drown. Aye. It's no me would like to be in her shoes this minute!"

I remembered what Inge had said, six years before. She'd neither drown nor hang, she claimed, and I'd believed her then. But how reliable was her vision? Maybe she was wrong. I felt Dad sway beside me, as he shifted his weight. When I looked up, he was grey in the face again, and one hand clutching the cross he aye wore at his neck. The other was rubbing his chest, across and across. I gripped his elbow, and Peem's hand moved from mine to Dad's other arm. I felt Dad lean gratefully on him, and was looking up at him when the sounds changed.

Inge was kneeling down before the bishops at the centre of the bridge, and I could see their lips move, praying, though I couldn't hear the words over the chanting of the monks and the crowd shouting.

Then a silence fell, slowly, as Inge unfastened the laces of her blue mantle. She slipped it off. Then her shoes and her white kirtle. Underneath she wore a short shift, only down to her knees. She was barefoot now, and shivering, but whether from fear or from cold no one could tell.

Soldiers moved forward with a rope. When they stepped back, she was sitting in a strange crouched-up position on the rail of the bridge, supported by two monks, and with a fresh twist at my heart I saw that her right hand was tied to her left foot, and her left hand to her right ankle. The prayers and incense rose again. As they fastened a rope round her waist, she looked up with a wild toss of her head, and somehow out of all the crowd I felt she saw me. She drew a fast, deep breath and screamed, "God! O my God! Help me now!" Then suddenly she wasn't on the bridge any more. A shout, half scream, half cheer, tore from a thousand throats, and we all surged forward to see what was happening.

My hand was pulled from Dad's sleeve, and I was carried forward onto the bridge and jammed up against the parapet. It wasn't till next day I found the bruises. At the time I'd no mind for anything but Inge. Where was she?

She was downstream of the bridge. Her white shift bobbed just on the surface, and there was a roar of "Guilty!" But one of the bishops spoke sharply to the soldiers holding the rope, and they slackened it. She sank. It seemed clear that it was the rope that had held her up. Now another cry rose: "Innocent! Innocent! Have her up! Pull up!" There was more argument among the bishops. Could she could stay under so long and not drown? "Up! Up!" the shout rose. And at last the rope tightened and my sister was dragged from the river.

She lay, still tied, not moving on the planks, her hair tangled round her neck. Nobody seemed to know what to do. She wasn't breathing.

She was dead. She was dead. I'd killed her. Maybe this was what Asa had meant when she said one of us would kill the other.

There was a shout from the heart of the crowd, and a man

shoved through with no ceremony. "Will you just stand there and let the lassie die?" he bawled at them all. "You handless fools! You've seen her sink—what more proof d'you need? Let me by, there!" He pushed through the fluttering monks to Inge's side. One of the soldiers won a nod for having cut the ropes at her wrists, and then the man, swearing blackly, swung her up onto the rail of the bridge, face down, long legs trailing to the bridge, her hair dripping into the river. He rubbed up and down her spine, as so long before he'd rubbed me—for, of course, it was Master Spens—hunching her back and fore over the wood. I knew his words before he said them. "Wake up, you bitch, don't dare die on me or I'll kill you! You've caused enough trouble already. Wake up!" And at last she coughed through the trickling water, and her hands twitched, and Master Spens stood back and eased his shoulders.

The cheer that went up startled crows off the fields for a full mile round.

I found I wasn't cried out after all.

When I started to be aware of my surroundings again, the churchmen were gone. Most of the crowd was still there, singing and merrymaking happily as if they'd not come in hope to see the witch found guilty and hanged. Dad, Master Spens, and even Peem were nowhere about, and I was crouched almost under a horse's belly at the corner of the bridge. I got up hastily and backed off.

Then I saw Inge. She was sitting against the parapet wrapped in a cloak, with half a dozen women about her, just going to lift her into a litter slung between two horses.

I had to speak to her before she went out of my life again, maybe for ever this time. As I edged forward, she drank something from a green glass, handed it back with a smile, wiped her mouth, sighed—and caught sight of me.

Instantly the smile vanished, and something I'd never seen before peered at me from her eyes and hid again. She gazed at me levelly, and all the women stared, too. One started to shoo me away, but with a gesture Inge stopped her.

I ran to her and dropped to my knees beside her. "Oh, Inge!" I stopped. I couldn't think what to say, how to apologise. "I'm that sorry!" Such feeble words.

A queer twist came to Inge's lovely mouth. "Well, if it's not my wee sister!" she murmured huskily. "Come to see whether I'm drowned? Last time, if I mind right, it was me looking after you. But I was trying to help."

It was a second before I understood. "Oh, Inge, so was I! I just came to see if there was anything I could do for you!"

The twist showed again. "Do for me? Aye, you near did that, all right. Right clever you were."

"No, I wasn't, Inge. If I was clever, I'd never have come."

"True," she smiled, and coughed again.

"I never mentioned the—that night."

"No. They could have asked you why you never spoke before. That was clever, too."

"No, Inge. Master Spens told me I'd just make things worse for you—"

"Did he so? Well, he wasn't wrong, eh?"

"Aye, but—I couldn't leave you alone. I had to see could I not help."

"Help who?" The cold inquiry stopped me dead. She couldn't really believe I'd tried to harm her.

"No, Inge, I wanted to help you!"

"I hear you." She motioned to the women, who started to assist her to her feet. I was elbowed aside.

"It's true, Inge! Say you believe me! I still love you, Inge!"

She stopped, leaning on a tall woman's shoulder, elegant in spite of everything in a gorgeous fur-lined cloak that made me think little of that velvet I'd thought so fine, so long ago. I felt small and crumpled, though I was only two or three inches shorter than she was. She looked down at me thoughtfully. "Do you so, then? Aye, well, I love you just the same."

I sighed with relief, and as she was helped to climb up into the litter, I grinned, happy at last. "I'll tell Dad you're well, then. I don't know what's become o' him—he was here while you were—eh, and it was Master Spens saved you when they pulled you out the water an' didn't know what to do." She seemed to be paying me no heed, settling into the blankets in the litter, coughing again, the horses sidling at the weight. "Will we see you again soon, Inge? We're all wearying for word. Will you not come by and see us?"

Comfortable at last among her cushions and furs, she lifted an eyebrow at me. "Aye, you'll see me again. Maybe before you expect it." The terrible thing glinted in her eyes again— or was it not just tears? "My—my thanks to Master Spens. He came here with you? Aye. I'll see if I can return him the favour one o' these days."

She rubbed gently at her wrists and throat, and swallowed painfully. I knew how she felt. "Away in now before you catch your death in those wet things, Inge." The women, who had been eyeing me resentfully, laughed. "We'll see you when you can come. Take care, now!"

"You too, Meg. Take good care." She relaxed back with a sigh, and was carried off up the road, a troop of de Brus horsemen protective round her. Clearly a lady of importance, our Inge! I waved, but she didn't wave back.

I came to myself with a jump. What had happened to Dad and the rest? I felt distinctly unsettled without Peem close at hand. Maybe they'd lost me in the crowd and gone back to the inn.

When at last I'd worked my way back, I found Peem on the point of setting out to seek me. He near jumped on me and hauled me up the stairs so fast I'd no time to trip. "Your dad's sick, mistress!" he told me on the way. "Come on! I got him back here from the bridge—I'd lost ye, and I'd no time tae search, for your dad just collapsed at my feet. Master Spens found a physician, an' he's away down tae the apothecary's for a draught. But ye've to be quiet now, an' no disturb him. Wheesht, now!"

Warned, I crept into the room. Dad lay there on one side of the huge bed, snoring. His eyes were half open, but blind, and his face still had the grey, pinched look I'd seen on the bridge. Father Michael was praying at the bedside, and scarce nodded to me.

I bathed Dad's face and hands with warm water. How on earth had Peem got him back? He could only have carried him—and Dad was a big, heavy man, to drag through the crowds all the way up here. Maybe he'd got help—but who would leave the river just at the exciting moment? No, he must have done it all himself. "Thank God for you, Peem!" I whispered. "What would we do without you?" He grinned widely.

While I knelt praying by Father Michael, Master Spens came back with the medicine. "Foxglove, it is, to slow the heart," he told me quietly. "He just got too worked up. He'll do, if he's right quiet for a week or so, and then he can travel home."

"In a litter?" I asked. "Like Inge?" Then, of course, I had to tell Master Spens everything that had happened after he'd been thanked by the bishops and left the bridge. As I talked quietly, I somehow felt that Dad was listening, and when I looked down at him, his eyes were fully open. "Wheesht now," I told him, tucking the blanket round him. "I'm here, Meg. I'll look after you."

"Aye," said Master Spens. "It's the one good thing that you've done this day." And glowered at me.

THE START OF THE QUEST

◆

*D*ad recovered well, and in about six weeks was up and about the shipyard, leaning at first on a stick. But the illness had left its mark. He'd never been sick before, except after accidents, of course, and to find he was mortal came as a shock to him. He shouted less, and though he was still cheery, it seemed forced. And he found fault less often, as if somehow he'd lost interest.

I spent as much time there as I could. I liked to get out of the way of Master Spens, who forgave me slower than my own family for going to Stirling. Well, it was him I'd disobeyed, not Dad. He showed his annoyance. Davie was kept hard at his work, and so was I, with few smiles and more complaints than normal. Little wonder I often asked leave to visit home. There, at least, they gave me credit for what I'd tried to do, not what I'd actually done.

Inge didn't come home. Asa, back from Stirling, sat by the fire growing more and more evil-tempered, spitting at us as we worked round her. Domna would have cleared her out, if she'd dared.

Birgget's old husband, Master de Voylans, died that spring, and she was left a rich widow. Not for long; a young merchant from Berwick had her promised within a scandalously short time. Good luck to her, I thought. She'd had little joy with the old man; let her choose this time for love—and she did. It made her look quite different, younger and softer, somehow. I even liked her.

That spring, too, the Council of Guardians, with the clergy, nobles, and community of Scotland, sent a message to King Eric of Norway asking him to send his daughter to be married to Prince Edward of England. The princess was seven or eight now, old enough to leave home, and King Edward sent out a great ship to Bergen to fetch her. It was fine, and stocked with walnuts, gingerbread, figs, and raisins for the little lass—the word said that it had cost near two hundred and seventy pounds! One of Dad's ships, fully found, cost about eighty. But King Eric refused to let his daughter go aboard.

When the news reached us, in June, Master Spens was just back from the biggest fair in Europe, at Troyes, with all the latest fashions. He'd a new kind of mantle, called a pelicon, for Mother Alison: a huge oval, near fourteen feet long, with a hole near the middle for a hood, and two slits for the arms. It used a terrible amount of cloth, and only the richest folk could afford it. Mary, of course, was desperate for one. He teased her for a while, and then fetched out his gifts: fine camlet wool and brocades, to make the new fashion for each of us. Even for me. Had he forgiven me? "Well, I'd not have my family looked down on by the rest o' the guild," he explained. Oh, well.

But then the talk turned serious. "I hear the de Brus isn't that happy about this wedding," he said at dinner that night.

"And if there's any trouble, we'll see more fighting in the streets." I felt slightly sick. Mary, Anna, and Davie looked excited, and the servants at the far end of the table muttered briefly. "It's not likely, here in Fife, but you'll need to be on your guard, Alison. The new door's strong, and the shutters, but when I'm away, take good heed not to open them if there's any hint o' trouble—and see the door-ward's aye ready to bolt them fast if need be. You hear that, Rab?"

"Is there no word why King Eric wouldn't let the lassie leave, Patrick?" his wife asked, shaking her head and tut-tutting.

"No, wife, not a thing," he replied heartily. "Maybe he wants her to go to her new home in a Norwayan ship. They have fine ships, you know."

"That'll be it," she said, smiling, and nodded to Davie to pour him more wine. After a moment's thought, she asked, "Why not a Scotch ship, then? She's our queen, isn't she? They call her the Damsel o' Scotland."

"Or the Maid o' Norroway. But she's not the Queen o' Scotland, and never will be, even when she's crowned at Scone." As we looked up from our meat, puzzled, he nodded round at us. "Aye, the land o' Scotland belongs to the folks that owns the land. When she's crowned, she'll be accepted by the lords and commons as Queen o' Scots, o' the folk, that is, not o' the ground. And she's not our queen yet, not till she's crowned. That's our earl here's task. By tradition, you see, the Macduff has the right and duty to set the crown on every king's head. If he doesn't, it's not a right crowning."

"Then what'll they do now that the earl's a bit laddie, with his daddy dead?" Mother Alison asked. "What is he—three year old? Poor wee soul—he can't put a crown on the lass!"

"I don't know, wife," he said cheerfully. "But they'll think on something! Anyway, about the ship, I wouldn't be surprised if you're right. They'll be looking for a grand ship, and a braw captain, to fetch her back to her own country. And whoever it is, I feel heart sorry for him!"

"Aye? Why that?"

"He'll have a ship filled with seasick lasses and ladies and lords that would rather drown than step aside for you, getting in the way o' the sailors and tripping on all the ropes. Can you not just imagine them?" We all laughed at the affected voices he put on. "Can you not stop the ship rolling just for a wee whilie, Captain? Turn back a minute, Captain, I've forgot my hankie! There's water coming in the door o' my room, Captain, can you send a sailor with a wee cloth to wipe it up? Beelzebub's bum, I'd not have that job for all the wine in Scotland! When I get some!" At the pointed reminder, Davie jumped to refill the cup. "No, lass, I'm but new back; I'm not for leaving home awhile yet."

"Patrick, Patrick! Don't say that!" his wife begged him. "It's the surest way to bring it to pass!" We laughed again, and he drank off his wine.

Somehow, I knew what the knocking was at the great door below, before ever the messenger entered the room. The Council wished to see Master Spens in Stirling at once, on a matter of the gravest importance. Mother Alison sighed in resigned exasperation.

"That'll maybe teach you, Patrick Spens! Asking for trouble, you were! But the Council should think shame on theirselves, calling you to ride all that way, at this time o' night! Thank God it's June, and not dark till late! Aye, well, Mary, would you favour me? Go through and set out his good tan fustian tunic, and that blue garde-corps with the vair trimming, you know it? Aye, and fresh hose and the new boots, while he finishes his dinner. Rab, I'll trouble you to run down to the livery. Will they saddle up for the master and Andra and—two others, Patrick? Will that be enough to keep you safe on the road these wild times? Aye, John and Tam, then. They'll all be ready to leave in a half hour, won't you? Good lads. Eat up, my dear," she said to him as Mary and Rab left, and the other men gulped down their stew and apple pie and hurried to find their cloaks. "It'll be near midnight before you reach Stirling!"

When he'd left and we'd cleared away the boards of the table, she turned to me. "I pray you light the brazier, will you, Meg? And turn down the bed, for I'm wearied." As I put the bedcover away in the cupboard at the side of the hall and helped her loosen her laces, I said I feared a fire would be uncomfortably hot for her, that warm evening, but she shivered, and complained softly, "I'm cold. Put some coals on the fire, Meg, pet. It's cold."

Next afternoon, Master Spens returned. Silent for once, he dismounted at the door and trod heavily up the steps to the hall before he said a word. Rab knelt to help him off with his boots, as he sank wearily into the big chair, and Davie ran up from his books to bring him wine.

"Is it Norroway, Patrick?" Mother Alison asked from the pillows, for she'd stayed abed. He nodded. "Aye," she sighed, shivering. "I thought so. Aye, well, we must just do what's the Lord's will for us."

"Which lord?" he asked bitterly. As she frowned at him, he drank, wiped his beard, and said, "I'll tell you! Sir James Macduff! O' Donibristle! Peem's old master! That's the lord that's willed this on me! He's a second cousin to the Earl o' Fife, you'll mind. So when the Council o' Guardians was looking for a captain to go fetch home the Maid, and he happens to be in Stirling, does he not whisper in their ear that my new *Andrew and Margaret* is the biggest and brawest ship in all Scotland, and I'm the finest skipper o' them all!"

"Is that not a compliment, sir?" I asked, rather surprised. It didn't seem to me to be as bad as he believed. If anything, I was puzzled that Sir James had done Master Spens a good turn, after all this time. The servants, clustered round the door, thought the same, for they muttered approvingly.

"Compliment?" he snorted. "Aye is it! And it's got me into just the hole I wanted to stay out o'! See you, Meg, I've a business to run. I'm contracted to carry wool out to Dieppe, and wine back. I've six ships on the sea, lass, and no time for wandering all over!"

"Away, Patrick," Mother Alison protested. "You've a son as supercargo aboard four o' them, and good masters on them all, and clerks that know their business. Or you can bring Jamie or Alan back while you're away, can't you?"

Davie looked annoyed she'd not mentioned him. "Me too, Dad," he mumbled. "Can I not help?"

"Aye," he snapped, "but—ach, I don't like it! See you, wife, it'll be July before I can leave, and with all the delays at the court in Norroway, likely another two month before I'll get away back. That's us into the September gales, and we'll maybe be delayed more yet. Who's to say when we'll get home? And my trade going to rack and ruin all the while." He saw Davie's frown, and with a rueful grin pulled the lad to him, an arm clasping the wiry shoulders. "Ach, I know you've sense for ten, lad, but you haven't the experience! Aye, I'll be paid for this trip, but—you can't hurry a queen, nor tell a gaggle o' lordlings that the tide or the wind'll not suit. There's aye trouble when ye mix ships and land folk, specially the gentry. Ach, I just don't want to do't, an' that's a fact."

"But if they've chosen you . . ." said Mother Alison.

"Oh, aye, I'll have to go. I can't refuse the honour!" he snarled. "Well, if they want me to be civil to their lords, they've picked the wrong ones. David Macduff o' Wemyss, the stiff-necked ass, he's one—and his ill-tempered bitch o' a wife to be a lady to the poor wee lassie. And the other's Sir Michael Scott o' Blawearie. A dafter popinjay never carried sword, and his wife's as bad. And the old bizzom Gray o' Cairnglas—with a mouth like a sewer, fair running with dirt about folk. It'll be a grand trip, this—a real pleasure."

He sighed, shrugged vastly, tossed off his wine, and rose stiffly. "Meg," he said, "I've the *Andrew and Margaret* in Leith the now, unloading. But she'll need seen to before I sail again. There was a Flemish cog ran into her in Dieppe harbour, and I'm not that happy with the new strakes we set in. I'll put her in to your father when she's empty. Will you go down and tell him what's afoot, and say it's by order o' the Council, and he's to put by all other work till this is done. I might as well get some good out o' it, eh? And then we'll leave Davie in charge"—Davie's face lit up like a sunrise as his father grinned down at him—"load the lairds, and away bring the lassie back to her husband-to-be. Like you, Meg, lass." He took the tip of my nose in his big fingers and waggled it gently. "And if she can keep from sticking her wee neb into what doesn't concern her, she'll do well to do as well as you." He hugged me. "There, now. Off you go and pack your boxie for the morn, before I change my mind."

I was so pleased to be forgiven, I'd have gone with nothing. But I packed the cloth for my new pelican as well as my other clothes. I might find time to sew it, after all.

Davie got leave to desert his books and come with me for a week, but Dad was too busy, he said, to spare a man to put the skiff in the water for us. Two ships were in for repairs; one had been attacked by pirates, and had one side half stove in where she'd been rammed. The other was just old, and needed her bottom scraped and the worm-holes filled with wooden pegs. All the men looked busy, but there seemed to be more noise and running about and less purpose and order than there had been before, as I remembered the yard. Peem had the strength of two men, though, and among the three of us we got the *Petrel* afloat and the rigging set up within a day, and spent three happy days revisiting all our old haunts.

Then the *Andrew and Margaret* sailed in. At once Dad, almost like his old self, stopped all the work on the others and concentrated his men on making this the finest ship afloat. She was a nef, not a cog, with the rudder at the stern and a great square sail. She got new planking—Dad was scathing about the repair done in Dieppe—new ropes, two new sails, new flags and pennants, new paint—all of the best. They built platforms with battlements like castles at the prow and at the stern, to hold the royal guard of archers if the ship was attacked, and all carved and decorated like no ship I'd ever dreamed of.

When Davie went back to his desk, sailing without him wasn't the same, so we beached the *Petrel* and I let Peem earn himself some money working in the yard. All hands were needed; the carpenters of the other ships even came round, and instead of grumbling because their own ships were put back they joined in. All the women helped, too, stitching at the fine new sails. The flags had been embroidered, Dad said, by the ladies of the court. I'd never known such a joyous atmosphere in the yard before, all because our own little princess was returning to us, in a ship of her own land, of our making, and the times of uncertainty and strife were ending.

The first week of July, the main work was all done. Master Spens brought a tun of ale for the men and a cask of wine for Dad. Davie, who rode along with him, was full of snippets of news about the voyage. He was as proud as the Devil that he was to be left in charge—with the experienced clerks to help him, of course, and whose word was final I'd not like to wager—but as well as his instructions for running the business he could reel off the sailing directions and marks to Bergen, and, talking more than I'd ever heard him before, he told us all about the plans for the ship. She wasn't coming right back to Scotland; she was going to take the Maid to Orkney first, for it seemed the lass wasn't in strong health, and the journey was to be done in stages. First to her father's lands of Orkney, to meet the ambassadors of England; then across the Pentland Firth to Caithness, and on down by land in easy steps to meet King Edward and the wee prince in the North of England.

The stores started to arrive. The *Andrew and Margaret* was a big ship—fully seventy feet long—but Master Spens packed her. Twelve salted beefs, hogsheads of wine, barrels of beer, hams, dried and salt fish, live lampreys in a barrel of water, sacks of onions, cabbages, mustard by the gallon, salt, pepper, spices—a pound of cloves!—ship's bread, oatmeal, sugar, raisins, dates, figs, gingerbread for the Maid; enough to feed a crew of forty, twenty archers, three priests, and a fair number of nobles and their servants for three weeks, to allow for bad weather and a long time at sea. Then the gifts for the Maid and her father, under guard: parcels of clothes, cloth, fur; Scots pearls, cairngorm, amethyst, set in Scots gold and silver; carved horn, embroidery, French perfumes, scented Spanish leather, glass from Venice, toys from England.

And last, the people. The lords and ladies came with their friends to visit the ship, and exclaim and argue over their sleeping space, and how many chests and servants they could bring with them. There was no cargo except the stores and gifts, and plenty space left below the deck, near the stern. It was fully twenty feet long and about fifteen wide at the broader end, but the three ladies were horrified. It would be bad enough on the outward trip, but on the way back, when the Maid herself and her attendants were with them—how would they manage then? They made more fuss than geese watching a fox.

I began to see what Master Spens had meant at the table.

Lady Grizel, wife of Sir David of Wemyss, was severe and harsh, rigidly upright in carriage and behaviour. She was a fearsome woman; but she understood that if this was all the space there was, then there was no more, and her very pride forbade her to argue. Her maids looked at their sleeping corner and sighed, but dared say nothing. Her husband smiled serenely.

Little Dame Mathilda Scott fluttered helplessly while her very competent maid arranged her boxes and bedding. She talked without a pause, aye fiddling nervously with her bar-bette, and never paused for an answer; as well, for Sir Michael never heeded her, too intent on stowing his own multitude of boxes.

But old Lady Gray was the worst: never a word that wasn't a moan or a complaint. And I'd thought Mother Alison was bad! The sailors called her Old Groaner. Or worse.

At last, early in the damp and windy morning, July the fifteenth, the quay crane lifted the water barrels down the hatch to the hold. The passengers had sworn faithfully to arrive by an hour after dawn, and by noon the most of them were there, with their friends to see them off on their historic journey, the Earl of Mar, the Bishop of Glasgow to bless the ship—sensibly, he'd brought his own chair—half the nobility of Scotland, and every soul from Culross to Dysart, from Leith to Bo'ness, all dressed in their finest to honour the occasion. Dad, Davie, and our family were right at the front of the crowd, with Peem helping hold back the press off the wee lad.

The nobles were packed like barrelled herring on the quay, velvets and silks marking with the rain and the crush, their piled hats and veils nodding agitatedly, Master Fletcher's new striped hose fluttering round in an ecstasy. He'd holed one on a nail, and the sawdust he'd padded his calves with left a trickle after him until it ran out, and he was left with one fat leg and one skinny. John Jamieson was earning good silver just rowing about in his coble, fishing out the hats and scarves that landed in the harbour, and hoping for a lord. The rain slowed to a light drizzle and then stopped, but the air was still damp and the ladies found all the barrels and bollards wet. Dannie Dunn was hiring out stools he'd begged and borrowed from all over the town, with a cushion for another penny. Tam Bakester and his mother had been making pies for days, to sell hot. There would be a grand party in Inverkeithing tonight. The alehouses were fair bouncing already, but most folk stayed jammed in the steep streets and slopes round the harbour, up on every wall and creaking roof to watch the ship sail. But she didn't.

Master Spens was keeping his temper admirably. The earl wasn't.

Where the devil was Old Groaner?

At two hours past noon, even Master Spens was growing irked. He'd allowed for time, and yet more time, for latecomers, and hadn't expected his passengers till noon, ready to leave on the high tide four hours after; but even he hadn't thought they'd be this late. If he missed this tide, he'd not get away till next day, and have it all to do again, maybe, even if the wind held steady, which wasn't likely. Where was that woman?

At last, a boat came in past the East Ness, with a woman in it. But it wasn't Lady Gray. It was Inge.

She stepped gracefully from the coble, smiling to the lords who rushed down to hand her out, and curtsied to the earl and the bishop. Then, clearly, so we could all hear, she said, "I'm sorry to bring you bad news, my lords. The Lady Gray can't come. She's broken her leg, falling down the stair."

There was an uproar of consternation.

Inge seemed unaware of the effect of her words. She glided over to where Master Spens stood by the gangplank, cursing very near under his breath. As he glowered at her, she smiled, and his frown faded. "Meg told me, sir, I've you to thank for my life at Stirling," she said to him sweetly. "It's been a sorrow to me to have no leisure before now to come thank you as I should."

He took off his great hat, folded and pleated with yards of cloth, and held it almost like a bashful callant as she drew his head down and kissed his cheek. He reddened slightly in the glory of her smile and the burning glares of all the young lords. His new garde-corps, of red Flemish serge, the hanging sleeves trimmed with expensive rabbit fur, looked like a rag beside the elegance of Inge's cream and gold pelican. Of course she was in the fashion, I thought; I'd not had time yet to make mine up.

As if she heard my thought, she turned her eyes straight to me, standing with the family. "Ah, Meg, my dear!" she murmured. Her eyes glinted in the thin sunlight struggling through the clouds, and her smile was warm. "I'm that glad you're here!" Her voice was changing, I thought; almost a court accent. I ran to her, and she bent for me to kiss her scented cheek, but put aside my hands and turned to Dad. "Are you well, Dad? They told me you'd been sick." There was real feeling in her voice. As he reassured her, his voice choked. All the others surged forward and she was near hidden in a cloud of sisters, but after a wee minute she slipped away to where the nobles were discussing what to do.

"What now, eh?" Mar was demanding. "You can't sail with no proper attendants for the princess, eh? There was to be three. Would the two do, eh?"

"No, two wouldn't do!" snapped the bishop. "We must just away back to the Council and find ourselves another!"

A groan went up from all the watchers, and especially from the two ladies on board the ship already. "Ach, not again!" snarled the Lady of Wemyss.

"Is there nobody here could just go?" asked the earl, gazing about vaguely at the congregation of nobility. No one volunteered.

The bishop eyed him with a most unsaintly exasperation. "With her gear all packed ready? Or would you have her go naked?" The sailors and the crowd cheered this idea and suggested some names. Some of the ladies mentioned looked pleased, some embarrassed, and all the lords amused and interested.

Inge entered the group round the earl as if by right. "Maybe it's as well, my lords," she said. "I was aye worried for the wee lass, with none but old fogies about her. Maybe the Council could take thought and find her an attendant more her own age this time, to cheer her and play with her. Maybe a lass who could speak Norse, even." Her dark eyes gazed serenely on them all.

Master Spens's head, that had been lowered in defeat and disgust, came up and round like a dog hearing a whistle. "What was that?"

Inge's fine-plucked eyebrows rose inquiringly. "I said someone who could speak Norse, sir," she said with a puzzled smile. Her eyes gleamed.

"And more the same age, you said—and all packed—Meg!" I jumped a foot. "Meg! Beelzebub's bum, where's the bizzom at now?" he bellowed. "When you don't want her she's aye underfoot, and when you do—Meg!" Dad, frowning, pushed me forward, and Inge nodded encouragingly. Something felt wrong—but—

"Come over here, lass, quick!" I stepped forward reluctantly. He couldn't mean . . . "Meg, your chest's packed to go home this night, isn't it?" I nodded. Oh, dear God, he did mean! "And you speak Norse?" I nodded again. "Well, is that not God's providence, just!" Peem started to grin. I wished I felt like it.

The nobles looked first blank, and then angry. "Don't be daft, man! Look at her—she's not fit to attend on the princess!" snapped the earl, the bishop nodding in agreement. And me in my best kirtle—well, the best I had with me!

"Not fit? She's to be my good-daughter, my lord, and she's been trained in my house this six year by. What house would you say she's not fit for? She's sister to Mistress Wright here, who attends on the Lady o' Carrick! She can sing, play chess, make music—she's a better maid for a wee lass than that whining old crone! And she's here ready! Would you rather wait another month till the Council can gather to pick a new lady, she makes and packs her things, and then wait again on the wind? We'd be six weeks more! At the least!"

There was no doubt about it, even Lady Wemyss, who had been horrified and insulted, started to look thoughtful. The two great lords eyed each other doubtfully, not wanting to take the responsibility.

"She's not o' noble blood," protested the earl.

Master Spens looked triumphant. "Aye, isn't she?" he barked. "When old King Hakon, the Maid's great-grandfather, came here, near thirty year ago, my lords, who was the heart's friend that stood in the place o' honour at his right hand? Was it not the father o' that man there, Meg's own father? Is that not true, Rolf?"

It was convincing, as he put it, and there was a cheer. Suddenly I saw why Master Spens was such a good merchant. He left them no time to think. While Dad was still spluttering, he turned back to the lords. "Sirs, would you rather wait another two month maybe, when it'll be too late in the year for safety? We might have to wait till the spring, even! And how would the Comyns and the de Brus enjoy that? Or King Edward?"

They looked appalled. Well they might. "Aye, well," said the earl, considering, half convinced. "But—what would the rest o' the Council say, eh?"

"What should they say, but thank you for saving the peace o' the realm? It's as well it's you here, sirs. There's not many men with the decisiveness that's needed this hour!" Master Spens eyed them rather carefully, to see if he wasn't maybe laying it on too thick. The bishop's eyebrow was raised, but he glanced at the earl, and said nothing. Reassured, Master Spens went on. "What would you have folk say o' you, that you couldn't put a lassie on a boatie? Come, sirs, there's no time to be lost. It's seize this tide, or likely wait till next year.

What say you?" Davie was hopping and cheering on the quay.

Well, what could they say? With the cheers from my friends and family on the quay, and Lady Wemyss's baleful eye on them? And nobody asked me at all.

Peem was sent running for my chest, while the bishop hoped that I understood the great honour being done me, and that I'd prove worthy of it. Master Spens glared, and I promised them all, and him in especial, that I'd behave perfectly, I'd be respectful, I'd not cause any trouble. At last they seemed to accept it, and turned to their own talk again. Master Spens, grinning, started readying the ship to cast off.

Dad held my hand tight. "Ach, Meg! To think o' you, lady to a queen!" He was quite overcome. My sisters, and Davie, and all our neighbours were grinning and giggling with glee. I wished Birgget was there.

Inge put an arm round my shoulders and drew me gently away from Dad. She put a tiny bottle in my hand; a pretty thing, green glass with a silver top. "Here, Meg," she said, smiling. "Take this. They say the wee lass isn't a good sailor, poor wee soul. I made this up for her, if she gets seasick. It'll settle her stomach. I meant to give it to Lady Gray. Is it not as well I forgot?" She laughed gently, her teeth very white.

My own stomach tightened. "What is it?" I asked doubtfully.

She was surprised. "Poppy and camomile, in a drop wine. Naught to harm her. Did you think—you did! Meg, Meg, would I harm a bairn? How could you think it of me? Even to help my mistress and her son? They don't need it, my dear; I know what's to come, and it doesn't need my help. Don't you know me better? No, no, Meg; as God's my witness, I swear when the lassie reaches Scotland, she'll have no more loyal and obedient subject than myself."

In a great rush of love for her, and shame for my doubts,

I hugged her, and stowed the bottle carefully in my pouch, while she quietly smiled down at me. All at once I started to feel all the excitement, and giggled like the rest.

Peem came racing up, grinning even wider than usual, my box on his shoulder, his own bag in his hand, and Inge handed me across the gangplank. I jumped down to the deck, and turned to help Peem aboard. But just as he came by Inge, the plank somehow wobbled. Down he crashed, his right foot twisted under him. When he tried to rise, he fell back with a gasp.

In ten seconds it was clear he'd not be fit to go with us; his ankle was already swelling, and he could put no weight on it at all. He couldn't go; then how could I? My heart hurt me, as I tried not to show my disappointment. But Master Spens cut through the panic; I'd just have to make do with a loan of a servant from one of the others. I looked at the row of unhelpful faces and sighed. But there was nothing else to do. I shrugged to Peem, and he, reluctantly, shrugged and nodded back, grinning reassuringly. I felt as if I'd lost an arm, somehow.

The earl made a speech, the bishop prayed, the monks of Inchcolm, over for the day, sang; Master Spens, watching the wind and the tide, called his orders; and a bittie before the bishop was ready for it, the ship hoisted her sail and the long poles turned her from the quay. The bishop's hasty sprinkling of holy water mostly missed the ship and fell in the harbour.

To the cheers and prayers of near two thousand people, the *Andrew and Margaret* sailed off, to bring back the hope of Scotland's peace for the years ahead. As we left the bay I strained my eyes to pick out Davie, waving wildly, and Peem, disappointed and worried, on one leg by Dad. But what stood clearest among all the rich reds, blues, browns, and greens was the pale gold and silver glimmer of Inge, smiling as she watched us sail away.

THE MAID

◆

$\mathcal{W}$e had a good journey out to Norway. The great square sail drew the *Andrew and Margaret* along steadily, east and north before a fine smooth wind, bellying evenly out over our heads in a huge swell of new red canvas.

Our own quarters were fairly crowded. What had looked to be a big space, empty, was filled full with two lords and their wives, three maids, three priests, five menservants, four dogs, a talking popinjay for the little queen, and me, with all our—or rather, their—chests, boxes, and bundles. We were lucky that the weather was so good, for in bad weather the hatch would be shut down. As it was, it was quite airy and light, and nobody was badly seasick, so that it still smelled fresh. Even so, when we all settled down to sleep, it was a squeeze. On the way back, we'd have the Maid and her companions, and the menservants would have to sleep out on deck, or with the archers or the crew; they weren't looking forward to it.

I had a wee corner to myself, for no one quite knew whether I was a maid or a lady, and I snuggled in quite cosy on old Lady Gray's feather bed that Master Spens thoughtfully hadn't cleared out with the rest of her gear. He hung me up a spare blanket for a curtain such as the others had, and I had as much privacy as I was used to, or more. I was fine and comfortable.

On deck, there was much more space, even with the archers as well, but the lords complained that the sailors and their ropes kept getting underfoot. Master Spens was most apologetic, and winked at me behind their backs.

The new castles built up on the bows and stern gave even more room. The archers and sailors used the forecastle, which was on wooden posts about six feet above the deck. The aftercastle was near seven feet high, all beautifully carved with saltire crosses and painted blue and white, with little carved and gilded thistles and lions on the pillars and arches. With a curtain hung to windward, it made a fine pleasant bower for the ladies and lords to sit, and in the best of the weather— not that it was at all wild, just a touch fresh at times—they even climbed up the ladder to the deck of the castle, and stood by the big gold flag with its red lion, holding the battlements and getting Master Spens to tell them stories of sea battles, pirates, and monsters, and of the new lands far to the west, where men of Iceland had found the finest timbers ever seen. "Some day," said Master Spens with a deep draw of breath, "I'll go there myself, and see . . ." He paused.

"See what?" asked the lords scornfully; going on pilgrimage to pay for your sins was well enough, even Dame Mathilda had been to Compostela in Spain, but they saw no good in unnecessary, uncomfortable, dangerous travel. This voyage was bad enough. But I could feel the lure of the venture, and smiled with him.

We spoke a good deal about the land we were to visit. I

could offer tales and songs I'd learned from Dad or Asa, about the old heathen gods. Dame Mathilda wept at the tale of Baldur the Bright, killed by the wickedness of Loki, Master of Mischief. Sir David told us how King Olaf the Fat had made Norway a Christian land, by giving all men a choice: convert or die; and was made a saint for it. He had a quirky mind, Sir David, for all he never said a thing straight in five words if he could talk round it in a hundred; there was a wee sly twinkle hidden in his smooth, round face that his wife never saw. Or never admitted to seeing, anyway.

We talked of King Harald Hard-Counsel, who invaded England, and his defeat by another Harald, King Harald Godwinsson, before my grandfather's grandfather's day; and how that battle so weakened the English king that Duke William of Normandy had been able to defeat him and his army, and become King of England in his place. This interested the lords and ladies, whose forefathers had been Normans. They had tales of battles and skirmishes, and how their families had gained lands in Scotland as well as England. Sir Michael held estates of King Edward, like most of the Scots nobles. The de Brus had lands at Huntingdon.

I wondered that Master Spens had so much time for talk with the lords, but at least, he whispered to me, it kept them from under the sailors' feet.

Feeling shy and awkward, I sometimes slipped away from the elegant noble company to speak to the archers and sailors, who were below the dignity of the lords, and even of their servants. The sailors reminded me of home. I helped them with their mending when I should have been doing my own sewing, and they told me about mermaids, whirlpools, and serpents, and the great Kraken itself, that we might see on this journey, for it lived near Norway. Luckily, we didn't.

What did happen was that the second afternoon, as I took along a pair of hose I'd mended for one of the men, I heard, "An' a right botch he's made o't. Dod, I could dae better mysel' wi' twa spoons an' an Arbroath smokie!" Naturally, I thought this was something to do with the cook, and quite agreed—Lady Grizel had had words with him already. But then I discovered they were talking about Dad, and the way he'd patched the hole in the ship's side.

I was furious; even more because I'd felt in myself somehow that his work wasn't what it should have been. I flared up at them: how dare they, Dad was the best shipwright in Scotland. They tried to quiet me, but I'd not be calmed, and at last Master Spens came forward to see what the noise was.

He hauled me off, and scolded me. "What are you at, Meg, sticking your neb into other folk's business as usual? I know all about the mend, and your dad and I checked it together. If it did him it'll do me. Now, get away aft and stay there or I'll melt you!" I went, subdued but still upset.

I didn't go near the bows again. Instead, with the help of Martha, Lady Grizel's older maid, I finally finished my pelican. I was very pleased with it: green camlet with a red lining, and a strip of red and gold braid to trim the hood and the arm slits. I thought I was the cat's whiskers; even Inge would have been pleased to wear it, I judged.

Three days only, the journey out took. Master Spens was delighted. If all went well, we could be back home long before the middle of September.

We were to pick up the Maid in Bergen. It was a dangerous sail among the islands and up the fiord, but Master Spens knew the waters from his younger days. All the passengers hung about, getting in the way, gazing at the cliffs and mountains with snow on them still, even in July, towering all round us. There was a fair amount of shipping about, nearly all low, oared ships, I noticed, mostly small, but some longer than our own. A great cog of the Hansa League veered close to inspect and maybe attack us, but our archers stood ready, and the captain decided to exchange only shouted greetings, not arrows.

Half-way up the fiord we stopped, anchored in a small bay, and spent a couple of hours making ourselves and the ship as fine as we could. The red sail was changed for a brand-new blue and white one, the saltire cross of Scotland, with a picture of Saint Andrew painted in the centre. A new flag, with real gold threads in it, was raised on the stern flagstaff. Embroidered and painted pennants and pencels were brought out of their chests to hang all over the ship's stays and spars. The sailors even had new clothes handed out, blue tunics and grey hose, a present from the Council members.

Meanwhile, we passengers were busy. We washed our faces and hair, and the men shaved carefully. We were to wear our second-best clothes, saving the best for the meeting with the Princess Margaret herself, but even so the nobles' brocades and velvets were glorious. The ladies' fillets, the stiff bands round the top of their barbettes, were starched rigid. Dame Mathilda had embroidered hers; Lady Grizel sniffed that they should be pure white. They both worried that they'd droop in the drizzle. I was annoyed to find that Lady Grizel didn't yet have a pelican, so, not to seem impertinent, I had to wear my old mantle.

Master Spens, having seen to his ship's appearance to his satisfaction, put on his own holiday wear—russet and blue, rich and substantial, but not competing with the nobles' glitter. He nodded when he saw my mantle. I could read his thoughts: "Getting some sense at last, and not before time!"

It took another three hours to reach the quay at Nordness. The houses were wooden, not even as much stone as Dunfermline, but narrow and high near the quay. Most had a cross at the ridge end, but some still had the old dragon's head soaring above the steep shingled roof. It gave the place a queer foreign feel. Then I realised: it was a foreign place! My heart leapt in me.

Master Spens stayed with his ship. As the rest of us walked up to our lodgings after the speeches of welcome—which were mercifully short, because of the worsening rain—I listened to the shouts of the crowd. I could understand only a few words at first, but then my ear tuned itself to the speech around me, with its queerly tightened vowels, and I found I could grasp what folk said, and even answer them, though their accent wasn't just like Dad's. Maybe his had changed, with being in Scotland so many years?

Our house had plenty of room for us all. It was a merchant's house, much like Master Spens's but bigger, and all wood. I even had a tiny room all to myself, the first time ever. I didn't like it much.

The lords and ladies were received by King Eric after two days, to give us time to recover from the journey. I wasn't there, I wasn't enough of a lady, but Dame Mathilda told us all about it. "The king was that braw and handsome, and that kind—he told me if I wasn't quite comfortable, just to tell his groom o' the bedchamber, and he'd see to it personal—if I wasn't married already I'd have fairly lost my heart, so I would!"—with a flirtatious glance at her husband, wasted, for as usual he wasn't listening. "The Bergenhof Palace wasn't grand, though—not a patch on Kincardine or Edinburgh."

The Maid, it seemed, was not very well. We would maybe meet her next day.

We didn't, though. She was still unwell; maybe tomorrow. What was wrong with her? Nothing serious, just a child's upset. Then could we not visit? Better not to disturb her. We sent her a few toys and the popinjay.

We didn't see the Maid the day after, either. She was better, and thanked us for our gifts. The popinjay was very amusing. Maybe tomorrow . . .

We went shopping, and Lady Grizel picked a fine blue-and-purple-checked wool for a pelican. I helped her maid cut and pin it, using mine for a pattern.

Next day the Maid was still indisposed.

This went on for a week. We started to wonder just what was going on.

One afternoon, Lady Grizel's maid Martha and I slipped out for a breath of air to a tiny garden we'd seen nearby, very pleasant, just two willows on a grassy slope by a wee pond. The street noises dwindled away. I sat under one tree and started some mending. Martha sat below the other seaming the blue wool, and we stitched peaceably together, scarcely speaking. I was near asleep.

Two girls came round the corner. One was eight or so, well dressed, with embroidery on her sleeves; the other, being towed by one of her long plaits, was rather smaller, in clean but ill-fitting clothes like the other girl's cast-offs. Something indrawn about her face made her look old, like a wee ancient wife in a child's kirtle. As they saw us, the wee lass hesitated, but the older one jerked her forward by the hair. My hackles started to rise.

They greeted Martha in Norse, and she, not understanding, smiled widely and gave them, "Good day, bairnies!" The taller smiled, and they turned to me.

"Snakker De norsk?" she said, curtsying politely, with a

sweet smile. I was about to say yes, I did speak Norse, but she didn't wait. "But of course not. You must be one of the maids, you fat cow." The little girl bit her lip. "You are too ugly for a lady. You don't even understand, do you, you stupid—"

"Do I not, you unpleasant brat?" I said sharply in the same language, and noted with pleasure her lying smile vanishing and her jaw dropping. "In my house we don't insult our guests. My father would warm your backside with a strap for such rudeness. Stamp away, you'll not scare me. What you need is a good whipping to mend your manners."

Scarlet with humiliation—or rage—the child whirled and raced out of the garden, her fair plaits flying. The wee girl put a finger in her mouth and turned her blue stare on me. Among the shock, was there a hint of a smile?

"Do you think I'm ugly, too?" I asked. Slowly she shook her head. Martha, frowning after the lass who'd run, shrugged to me and returned to her sewing. "Well, I'm glad of that," I said, smiling. "What's your name, my pet?" The wee girl just gazed. I laughed. "Is it—Martha?" Martha glanced over and smiled; the girl never looked at her, clearly not understanding, and after a moment shook her head. She seemed a bit slow-witted, or maybe just shy.

"Is it—Elizabeth?" Another shake of the head, finger still well in. Her nails were all chewed; her mother didn't look after her well. Maybe she was a poor relation—or a maid herself? "Is it—Inge?" She started to back away. Why should my sister's name make her frightened? Quick, try another— "Is it—is it Margaret?" To my delight she stopped and nodded, and a wee smile started round her finger. "Why, that's my name, too! Two Margarets, isn't that funny?"

Like Anna Spens, Martha aye had a sweetie handy, and in a minute or two the wee lass was sitting beside me, playing cat's-cradle with a bit of thread, chewing away and smiling, but still silent. She wasn't used to being cuddled, for when I touched her arm she jumped and stiffened.

Suddenly the other girl ran back through the gate and pointed me out to three women following her, one small and thin, the others big and heavy-set, not so well dressed, clearly her maids. Martha glanced at me, rose warily, and slipped quietly away behind them. The wee girl dropped the cat's-cradle guiltily and sat frozen. Her smile vanished, and she began to breathe heavily. I looked at her in alarm, but then the thin woman in the fine green mantle spoke.

"Who are you, slut? Do you not know it is forbidden to come here?" She spoke Norse, and more sharply and rudely than I'd have spoken to any servant. I was taken aback by her rudeness, when I'd been half expecting an apology. "Stand when I speak to you, you bitch! On your feet! Don't you know who I am?"

I looked up, but didn't rise. "No," I was saying, when she gestured to the two maids. Before I knew what they were at, they grabbed my arms, pulled me to my feet, and held me while she slapped my face twice, across and across with the flat and back of her hand.

"There!" she snapped in satisfaction. "Let that teach you to show respect for your betters!" I put a hand up to my smarting face in dismay, and found a trickle of blood. Her rings had cut me! I couldn't believe this was happening. "Now," she snarled, "Audfinglas, my daughter, tells me you were rude to her and threatened to beat her. You must learn your place! Now you will be beaten instead!" The big girl smirked, gloating. The maids were still holding my arms.

The lass beside me, wheezing, pulled herself to her feet by holding my skirt. As I glanced down, the woman reached out and casually pulled her away from me by the shoulder. "Stop that nonsense, Maritte! How dare you talk to strangers! How often have you been told you must not disgrace your family by—are you eating something? Spit it out! At once! If I tell your father, what will he do? Tell me? What will he tell me to do to you?" With a ghastly eagerness she twisted the girl's face up to her own. The wee lass's breath was whistling in her throat, and her cheeks were grey.

I finally found my wits and my voice. Who did I know that could deal with this? Ah! "Madam," I said icily, as Lady Grizel had spoken to the cook, hoping my grammar was correct, "I neither know nor care who you are. I am a stranger in your land. But I shall lodge a strong protest with my host His Majesty King Eric himself about your behaviour!"

It was my turn to be satisfied. She stopped smiling, and released the child's face. There were more ways of making folk heed you than screaming insults at them, I was learning. "Who are you?" she demanded.

"My name, madam, is Margaret Wright. I have the honour to be sent by the Council of Scotland to attend on Her Grace the Princess of Scots on her journey back to her own land. For your daughter's discourtesy to me, and for your attack, you must answer not to me, mistress, nor even to my companions here, but to the Princess of Scots!"

Martha was leading Lady Grizel, Sir Michael and his wife, all the maids, and half the men charging round the corner to my rescue, but at that moment I felt I didn't need any of them. I knew I could manage this, all on my own, as I threatened this vile woman with the wrath of Scotland. Knowing how highly the Scots were regarded by the king, I felt gloriously confident she'd be taken aback, dismayed, maybe even terrified. I certainly didn't expect her to burst into screeching laughter, and her maids with her.

My triumph vanished, and I looked helplessly over at Lady Grizel. She and Dame Mathilda were shocked at the blood on my cheek, and added their anger to my own. They called on the woman to stop that crazy carry-on; this was no way to behave to the representatives of Scotland.

The woman turned her face, convulsed with laughter, on us, tried to control herself, and laughed again. We were starting to wonder if we had to do with a madwoman. The child sat like a dropped glove at the woman's feet, her chest heaving as she struggled for breath. She was really ill. This was more important than my dignity, or anything else. Worried, I knelt beside her, and the woman and her maids laughed harder still.

With their hooting above me, and Sir Michael and the others exclaiming and demanding explanations, I tried to help the lass. I rubbed her chest and back, talked to her quietly, and finally, realising there would be no cure for her in this crowd, I picked her up to take her away to a quiet place.

At that the woman's laughter died, and she seized my arm. Over the lass's strained, wheezing breaths, she said to me in Scots, "Set her down, fruken. For you have not her yet got."

We all gazed at her in a mixture of frowns, gapes, stares. She reached out, lifted the lassie from me, and set her back on her feet. Holding her firmly by the shoulders, she turned her to face us. The grey wee mouth gaped like a stranded fish's; the eyes rolled white in the child's rolling head.

"Look well at her, my lords and ladies!" crowed that hateful, sneering voice. "For Fru Ingibiorg Erlingsdatter, wife to Thore Hakonsson, cousin of the king, I am. I am governess to this child, who in my care is till she be wed. Wed to Edward, Prince of Wales. And after, maybe. Where are your manners, my lord? My ladies? Kneel to the Princess Margaret, your Queen of Scots!"

And as Sir Michael and the rest of us, white-faced, began

to sink to our knees, Fru Ingibiorg roughly spun the child across to a maid, who picked her up in massive arms, heedless of her gasping. She stared at us, laughed again, and, followed by her daughter and her maids, stalked out of the garden, carrying the Maid, our little princess, with her.

There was nothing we could do.

Next day the message came: we were finally to be presented to the Maid. Somehow, though we brushed and combed, prinked and pressed, put on our finest gowns kept for this occasion—yes, I was to go this time—there was more of grim determination than glad excitement about us. Sir Michael even, the least imaginative of men, decided not to wear his expensive black garde-corps. It was just too like a funeral.

I was worried; what had the king been told about our meeting with the Maid? How would I be received? But Lady Grizel had insisted I must come.

"For we'll not let a soul think that we're not pleased with you. No, lass," she said as I drew breath again to protest my innocence, "I know you did nothing save speak sharp to an ill-mannered bairn, but you seem to have a habit o' being where trouble is." True enough! "Mind yourself the day, anyway, and don't give that—that corbie a chance to complain o' you. We'll see can we not get you in to speak with the wee lass. If a chance comes, be ready—but don't push yourself forward, now!" Easy said; not so easy to do.

I was afraid to meet the king. A few years back, I'd been thrilled to speak to a lord; now, though I couldn't say I thought nothing of it, it came fairly easy to me. But a king was different; he was God's anointed ruler of all his land. And this one could be angry with me. Did he not know what that woman was doing? Maybe not. I was afraid. But I thought of Dad; if his father could fight for this king's grandfather, and die for him, his daughter could fight for the king's daughter. Though not, I hoped, with the same result.

We were ushered down long stone corridors in the Bergenhof Palace into a fair-sized hall, with bright embroidered hangings. They showed ships in sail, and Master Spens's eyes kept straying to them as we waited. He was very fine, too, standing by me. I was grateful for his solid bulk at my back. I missed Peem.

It was a good sign, I thought, that we were kept waiting, but not too long. Only half an hour after we'd arrived, King Eric and half a dozen of his court marched in with no ceremony. He'd been hunting, and was pink and full of fresh energy from his bath. He was as handsome as Dame Mathilda had said. Tall, dark, with bright blue eyes, in magnificent crimson and gold, he outshone everyone in the large room.

He greeted us all warmly, with a word of welcome for each. When I was introduced, my knees nearly melted. To be so near a king! He nodded to me to rise from my deep curtsy, and smiled. He wasn't angry, at least.

"Margaret Wright? Ah, you the same name are as my daughter! That is goot. You will be goot friends, ya? How many—how old are you, Margaret? Fifteen? But not yet wed?"

"I'm betrothed, sir—Your Majesty. To the son o' Master Spens here." Should I have said that? Did the king want to meet Master Spens?

To my surprise, the king apparently knew Master Spens well. "Ach, ya, Patrick!" He clapped him on the shoulder. I kept forgetting how widely Master Spens travelled. "An' when this wedding will take place?"

Master Spens bowed. "Next spring, Your Majesty, when my son's thirteen."

"Ach, so! He has one good luck!" I'd thought I'd grown

out of blushing. Under the king's openly admiring gaze, I hadn't. "So, Patrick, you to us bring a fine cargo this time, ya? But you one take away even more precious!"

He turned to the side, where a group of women were entering. There was the little Maid, in pink with blue trimmings, not very much too big for her, and the child Audfinglas, holding her hand as I'd once held Davie's. Almost. And behind them, smiling honey-sweet, walked the one Lady Grizel had called the carrion crow: Fru Ingibiorg, with her hard eye tight as a rein on the Maid.

"Come, my little Maritte. Sit here." The high chair the king indicated at one end of the hall was too high for the lass, who paused uncertainly. Fru Ingibiorg, smiling still, nodded to her daughter, whose lips pursed for a moment before, with a great show of attention, she ran to fetch a footstool for the smaller girl, placed it at her feet, and charmingly helped her mount to the chair, where she sat absolutely, uncannily still. Audfinglas smiled as sweetly as her mother at us all, tossed back her long plaits confidently, and stood by the Maid. Her eyes met mine; the smile wavered, but returned fully. Strange that she should be that inch taller, when she was actually a year younger than the Maid, but then she was stronger all ways.

The king, standing jovially beside his daughter's chair, smiled as he said how sorry he was that she was not in such good health as he had hoped before he presented us to her. "But now I hear she has some met of you, ya?" Just how much of the truth had he been told? He didn't look at the red line on my cheek. "So my good cousin Ingibiorg agreed my Maritte might well you meet all. She very glad is see you, an' know she goes to meet her husban' an' her people. Not so, my heart?" Though he liked her, maybe loved her, he didn't look at her—not to see her clearly. Like many strong men, he'd have little sympathy with weakness in others. And as a man, he'd not see with a woman's eyes.

The fair head nodded obediently. "Yes, Father. Glad." She neither smiled nor looked at us. Her eyes remained on the floor in front of her, her thin hands clasped meekly, her tiny blue slippers just tiptoeing the stool, more like an old wife than ever. Her gown's bright pink made her face look yellow. The dye had faded a bit on the shoulders. A man wouldn't notice it.

In turn, we were called forward to kneel to our tiny princess. She nodded as we kissed her hand, but did not meet anyone's eyes, and said nothing.

"The poor child shy is," said Fru Ingibiorg, smiling. "So many strangers—an' you understan' she not is strong." Her teeth glittered as she smiled. Dad had once warned me about people who smiled with their teeth, not their eyes. Somebody else had done that recently. Who? Never mind now.

"May we ask what is wrong with the lass?" Lady Grizel's spine was at its straightest. "Mistress Wright here has much skill with herbs." Me? The back of her neck dared me to deny it. It would certainly let us near the child . . .

Fru Ingibiorg threw me a smile that would have frozen a furnace. "It not is serious. But when she upset, the princess sometime trouble has to catch her breath." That was one way to put it—but it didn't describe that dreadful wheezing. "Our doctors say it go in the warmer air of England. I scarce think that a young woman improve can on advice of our wisest men." Without insulting their doctors, we could hardly insist, especially when the child seemed in fair health at the moment, though wilting under her heavy gown.

A priest stood forward from beside the king. "My lady, your doctors have done their best, but a fresh mind—"

"No, Father Haflidi!" she interrupted, smiling balefully.

"Let us not the child disturb so soon before her voyage." She turned to us again. "My own daughter, Audfinglas, support her tenderly. They are inseparable." The King nodded approvingly at the strong, healthy girl standing demurely by the little princess's side. "An' His Majesty wish that she travel to England with her cousin an' myself, so our little Maritte her best friend has by her side always." Fru Ingibiorg smiled again, daring us to object. The Maid's shoulders seemed to droop even more, as Audfinglas took her hand lovingly. King Eric didn't see the nip that made the lassie jump, and then look scared up at her governess, but we did, and I could feel the outrage all round me, all the stronger for being held back.

We returned to our lodgings seething with rage, muttering like sulky children, but Lady Grizel cheered us up. There was no way that we could remove the Maid from that woman now. But soon, soon, they'd be on board the *Andrew and Margaret*, and then we'd see, my lady!

THE WARNING

◆

*M*aster Spens's earlier fears came to pass. There was so much fussing and delay, petty argument and niggling nonsense, that we didn't get away until the end of September. The storms of the equinox were due; overdue, even. But he was so irritated that once he'd got the Maid and her train all on board, and the wind and the tide right, he'd have sailed in the teeth of a tempest.

If the ceremony of leaving Scotland was grand, the leaving of Norway was grander far. Fru Ingibiorg and her husband, Thore Hakonsson, with their daughter, were not the only attendants on the Maid; there were also Bishop Narwe of Bergen, three canon priests, and twenty-eight servants. Including, we were glad to learn, a new cook. And, of course, the popinjay back again. We all—except the popinjay—with all the court and clergy of Norway, and four hundred soldiers, made a glittering procession down to the quayside, the monks singing the Te Deum, and last the king and his daughter in a gilded litter borne by two horses. The streets were full of folk, weeping and cheering as their little princess left them, for whoever might not love her and want her to be Queen of Scots, and later of England, the folk of Norway did.

At the quay, the king at last showed sadness at losing his daughter. Kissing and hugging her, he wept. She didn't. Like a tiny, pale statue of ivory and lapis she stood by Fru Ingibiorg's side without response, not even lack of breath. When I saw her eyes, the vacant pupils hugely black, I knew why. She'd been drugged with poppy, and could scarce keep awake. Lady Grizel saw it, too, and her eyes met mine with a determination Fru Ingibiorg should beware.

As the Maid was lifted aboard, the priest Father Haflidi started the great hymn Veni Creator, and to its rolling chant from all those hundreds we cast off and set sail.

The ship was packed, and the menservants did have to sleep on the deck among the sailors and archers. Fru Ingibiorg had demanded that Master Spens set up a bulkhead to make a separate cabin for her, her daughter, and the Maid. Well warned by us, he didn't. She was viciously furious. I learned a phrase or two that I'd never heard from Dad, and treasured them in the hope he would translate them for me sometime. Master Spens promised faithfully that as soon as we were at sea, and his men had the time, the partition would be the first thing to be attended to. She was forced to be satisfied with this, more especially since Bishop Narwe was watching. She had not, perhaps, noticed the saving clause: when the men had the time. Somehow they never did.

We had it all planned to take it in turns to cut her and her daughter off from the Maid, never leaving the wee lass alone with them, but it was unnecessary. The wind and waves were far stronger on this voyage, and most of the land folk fell ill before we were out of the fiord. As soon as she set foot on the ship, young Audfinglas turned as sick as a cat, and her mother scarcely left her side. We wondered nastily what she'd have done if it had been the Maid that was seasick. Even kindly Dame Mathilda, suffering from seasickness for the first time herself, whispered to Lady Grizel that it was worth it, to hold off the Corbie—for the name had stuck. Herr Thore, helplessly shrugging his plump shoulders, stayed on deck with the other unaffected men, away from the messy, smelly cabin. There was no way they could help anyway, and we'd no need of them falling sick in the stink, too.

Audfinglas was sore afflicted. Martha said to me, after seven hours of distressful wailing, "Meg, can you not do anything? Do I not mind your sister giving you a bottle for the seasickness? A wee green bottle. Is that not right? Would you maybe think fit to give the lass a wee droppie—just for the sake o' peace? She's not as bad as her mother, after all."

"Is she not just?" I snapped. "D'you not mind on her in the garden, tug-tugging at the Maid's hair? And grinning when her ma hit me? That bottle's for our princess, not for any nasty wee bizzom with a weak belly. What do I say if the Maid falls sick after? 'I'm sorry, Your Grace, but I've given away all your medicine,' eh? Besides, it fair keeps the Corbie out the wee one's hair."

"Aye, I suppose so," said kindly, soft Martha, frowning, unconvinced. A moan from a pallet sent her running with a basin and cloth.

I'd soon other things to think on. The wee one was neither up nor down with the motion, and I kept her up out of the cabin. As the poppy wore off, she was into everything, trailing that poor popinjay about with her, getting in the sailors' way as they changed back the sail to the plain red one, admiring the archers' bows, and slowly waking up to enjoyment of her freedom. Just before sunset, I was trying to explain why you had to push the tipstave right to turn the ship to the left when Master Spens called to me. I climbed up to him on the fore-castle, the Maid bumping the cage up after me to miss nothing.

"What's that boatie, Meg?" he asked me quietly.

I looked ahead where he pointed, to a brown sail threading confidently through all the thronging knorrs and drakkars, skiffs and shallops and coracles rowing out to wave farewell to their princess. "I can't be sure, sir," I said doubtfully. "It looks like—but no, it can't be. Surely?"

"Aye. Your wee *Petrel*. That's what I thought. What the devil's going on?" His voice rose in annoyance. "As if I hadn't enough to think about! If we run down one o' they damptie boaties, they'll claim more damages than a Genovese banker. Not that they'll get them, mind, but they're a damptie nui-sance!" He gestured to the steersman to head over to starboard, to let the skiff pass on the lee side. It was indeed the *Petrel*, Peem handling the sail, Davie grinning his huge gappy smile up at us and waving as he skilfully swung the wee boat round to come alongside, and Peem threw us up a rope.

I didn't know how I felt. Surprised? Delighted? Appre-hensive? All of them, and more. The Maid beside me was maybe a bit scared at the unexpected excitement. Though as usual she said nothing, her hand clasped mine tightly.

While they were climbing the rope ladder I helped the Maid down from the forecastle, and as we walked towards the group of men in the waist of the ship I looked for my lads. There was Peem, bigger and broader than ever, but where was my wee Davie?

Then he turned round. Wee? My God, I thought, he's near as tall as myself! What's he been eating to sprout like that, in less than three months? I wouldn't have known him, but for his face. We'll not look such an ill-matched pair at the altar now—from the back, at least! I chuckled at the idea. Then I saw their faces, and stopped chuckling. "What's wrong?" I asked anxiously.

Master Spens looked down at the wee lass at my side and smiled, so stiffly it near cracked his face, but she didn't notice. "Nothing at all, lass," he said jovially. "Here's my son Davie thought he'd have a wee adventure, and come to meet us." Davie gulped, and knelt, cap off, blushing and awkward, to kiss the Maid's rather grubby hand. Her manners couldn't be faulted; she gave no sign that she noticed his face, though the side-looks and comments of some of the other passengers annoyed me. I'd get used to it sometime, maybe. She smiled up at Peem, too, and his white grin split his face as he blushed.

"Now," said Master Spens, "will you take this to Bishop Narwe, Your Grace? He's under the sterncastle. I'm thinking he'd maybe have a sweetie for you, if you asked him nice." Her eyes lit up. Carefully taking the useless bit wood he handed her, she staggered across the crowded decks at top speed, bumping the cage as she swayed to the lift of the ship. Everyone smiled as she passed.

Master Spens looked from Davie to Peem. "Well?"

Grins vanishing, the lads glanced at each other, and round at the crowd. Peem spoke for both. "Will ye come up tae the forecastle, sir," he said. "We can't talk here. An' ye, mistress." He couldn't have kept me away with a whip.

Master Spens, smiling determinedly, cleared Sir Michael and Herr Thore off the small upper deck. When there was no one in earshot, the smile vanished. He glared at his son. "Aye?" he said. "I left you in charge o' my affairs, did I not, Davie? What's the reason, then, that makes you leave them to come running over here? I'll warn you now, it had better be serious." He waited grimly.

Davie tried to marshal his words, but as usual when he was excited, his voice went all gobbly, and his father could make out little. I had to translate. "He says there's a plot against the Maid, sir. It's—ach, no, Davie!"

"What?" demanded Master Spens in frustration.

I could scarce say it. "It's my sister, sir. Inge. She's promised her mistress the wee one will never be crowned queen. And Davie says she's made sure o' it."

There was a pause. I tried to control my breath, as ragged nearly as the Maid's. Oh, Inge! And yet I'd known before he said. She'd promised the crown for the de Brus lad, Robert. And she'd have to see he got it.

Master Spens was frowning. "Two questions, then," he said. "What has she done? And how do you know?"

Davie signed to Peem, who squared his shoulders. "She came tae visit the old wife a week back," he said, his voice deep as if dragged out of his boots.

"Asa?" I said. "Aye, she'd aye a soft spot for Asa, though they fought whiles. And Asa fair doted on her."

"Aye, mistress." Peem nodded. "She had little tae say tae the rest o' your family, but she was right close wi' the old one. They was havin' a good gossip at the door, a' by theirsel's, an' I just happened tae catch a word, like. About a maid, it was, an' it crossed my mind it could be the wee princess. So . . ." He paused sheepishly.

"So you just happened to hear? Aye. Well, we'll maybe no whip you too sore," Master Spens said. "Don't be shy, now. Out with it. What did they say?"

"She said she'd set a trap for the Maid, but it was but likely, she said, no certain. An' Asa was tae give her a hand wi' somethin' I couldn't catch, that would be sure. She said she'd seen the Maid dead in her coffin, her father mournin' her. An' now she had tae make her dream come true."

We waited again, for Master Spens to consider. I felt only a dull ache of regret. As if for someone dead a long time.

"And you went and told Davie?" Peem and Davie both nodded. "And you decided you had to come yourselves to tell me?"

"Ye had tae be warned, sir," said Peem warily, "an' there was no other way. An' ye'd telled Davie the way here that often he could near smell it." Davie nodded again, vigorously. "We—we thought it was worth it." They braced themselves for the verdict.

Master Spens paced the deck for a minute, deep in thought; then he turned suddenly to me. "Well, Meg? Do you credit this? You know your sister, and Peem here, better than any. Is it true, think you?"

"Aye, sir," I said quietly, "you can trust Peem's word. He wouldn't lie, not about a thing like this, and he's the memory o' a mule. And Inge would do it. It grieves me to say it, but I know it's true. Don't ask me how I know. But you can believe it."

He eyed me piercingly, but accepted it, and returned to the lads. "And so you just sailed over to fetch me the word, eh?" At his rough tone, their faces stiffened. "You could have been drowned a dozen times over! Or missed us in the dark! Did you never think o' that? You feather-brained, hen-witted, useless, gormless gowks, you! Just a wee jaunt, eh? Like over the ferry to Leith? Just a wee trip across one o' the most dangerous waters in the world, with no rutter, no pilot, no bother, eh? What have I done to deserve you? Beelzebub's bum, lads, I'm—I'm that proud o' you! I wouldn't call the king my uncle!" He threw his arms round them, grinning broadly.

They gaped in disbelief. But the delight in his face as he praised their courage was real. Flushed and stuttering, they grinned and shuffled their feet awkwardly, exchanging glances of relief as much as pleasure, while he hugged and pounded their shoulders. The three of them did a kind of dance, up there on the forecastle, with every eye on deck fixed on them.

It seemed a pity to spoil it, but I had to. "What do we do, then, sir?" I asked. They stopped their circling and their grins faded. "I mean, do we tell folk? Or keep it quiet?"

"Quiet, lass! Quiet as the grave! We must just take thought together, how she could hae planned tae harm the lass. What can she have done?"

Suddenly I knew. "The medicine!" As they stared, I swiftly explained about the bottle for seasickness. "But she'll not get it now! It's safe locked in my chest in the cabin. It'll do no harm there."

"Good lass!" Master Spens puffed out his cheeks, and his beard bristled with satisfaction. "Better pour it away, and that'll be that."

"But what would Mistress Inge want wi' old Asa?" Peem asked.

I remembered the night the king died, and Asa's throat jerking out that great, harsh voice that wasn't hers. "I can't say." I dodged the point.

Davie raised an eyebrow. He knew me too well. "No?" he asked.

"No!" I snapped. But I had to warn them, even if they'd not wholly credit what I said. Even if it was Inge. "I suppose— she might try to raise a storm. She's—she has power, sir. Real power."

They all stared again, but consideringly, and together nodded agreement. Master Spens said, "Aye. That trial—she prayed to her god to save her. But she never said which god. Nor ever said the name o' Jesus. I noticed."

"But ye still saved her, sir?" said Peem.

"Aye. I wasn't sure. She was due her chance."

"Her chance tae kill ye."

"Aye, Peem, maybe so. But maybe not, either. Would she harm her wee sister?" He smiled at me confidently. "Meg here's our warranty o' safety."

But as he reassured them, a string of double meanings slipped a place in my mind and fitted in a new pattern. "Aye would she, sir!" I cried. "I've but just seen it; she thinks I went to the trial on purpose to harm her, to speak against her! She once said if I scratched her, she'd scratch back. And"—my mind ran back over what had seemed an odd twist in Inge's voice—"she thinks you took me there! That we'd planned it together! Sir, oh, sir, I'm feared she's turned my enemy, and yours! Asa aye said the one o' us would kill the other, but we didn't credit it. But now—I'm certain sure she thinks I've tried. And she'll not rest till she's done for us both!"

Slowly, he came round to the idea. It was so clear to me, knowing Inge, I was impatient with him for not accepting it at once. But at last he clapped me on the shoulder like the lads. "Well, lass, forewarned is forearmed, they say. If she raises a storm now, we'll be ready for her!" And he leapt down the ladder to the main deck like a mountain goat in its vigorous prime, shouting into the bustle for his boatswain, his sail-maker, and his carpenter.

I sat down on the deck, hidden by the battlements from the greedy gaze of the folk below us. Davie knelt by me, his arm round my shoulders, supported me as I wept a second time for the loss of my beloved sister, and then lent me his damp sleeve to cool my puffed eyelids, while Peem stood smiling at the head of the ladder and let no one up until I'd control of my face once more.

When at last I could appear without disgracing myself, I

left the lads to see to the boat, which was to be towed behind us all the way to Orkney. I went straight down to lift the key to my box from below my pillow, to get rid of the medicine. But when I set the key in the lock, it was open already. Knowing what I'd find, I reached into the back corner. The wee green bottle was gone.

I turned from the chest and looked round the cabin. It was full of women. Dame Mathilda and her maid, Jean, were in no state to move. Lady Grizel and her younger maid were seeing to three of the priests, and most of the other lasses were lying moaning on their pallets. None of them paid me any attention.

But on the big bed in the far corner lay Audfinglas, her mother and her maid at her side. And by them knelt Martha, carefully not looking at me.

I knew then. Oh, yes, I knew.

I stepped carefully round the mattresses and buckets, to the side of the bed. Audfinglas wasn't the charming pink and cream lass of this morning. Her face was shrunken and wan, greenish even, in the dim light. She whimpered painfully, retching emptily into a bowl her maid held for her. Fru Ingibiorg, a damp cloth in her hand, didn't lift her eyes to me.

"Martha," I said quietly. Martha cast one furtive glance up at me. "Martha. Did you open my chest and take the wee bottle for the lass?"

After a moment's stillness she shook her head, not looking up.

I was puzzled a second. Then I realised. Of course she wouldn't touch anyone else's things. There was but one person here who would. "Then who did?" I asked, to confirm it. "Don't be feared to tell me. I just want to know."

Her eyes turned for an instant to Fru Ingibiorg.

I said nothing. What was there to say? If it was a poison,

either it would work or it would not. What could I do anyway, more than make her sick? And the way the lass was retching already, it might well be that nothing would stay in her long enough to harm her. Or if it wasn't a poison after all, why worry her mother without need?

But even my silence seemed to anger that vile woman. She decided to notice me and reared up, like a snake about to strike. "Did you think, you fool, I would leave my daughter to suffer when my potions could not help her? When this stupid bitch told me there was a medicine here, I would have torn out your eyes to get it, not only opened your silly box." Even those who didn't understand her words turned amazed eyes at the venom in her voice. "Be glad you were not here, or I would have had you whipped for denying it to my child. Now get out of my sight, you cow!"

Audfinglas moaned. Forgetting me immediately, the Corbie turned back to kneel beside her daughter again, gently smoothing the pale hair back from the twisted grey face, and wiping a damp cloth lovingly over the child's forehead.

"Forgive me, Meg," whispered Martha. She was red as sunset.

"It's all right, Martha," I said. "I don't blame you." I turned away rather blindly, praying that whatever was in the bottle was harmless, that I'd mistaken Inge, that Peem had misheard. But in my heart I knew.

That night the ship was fair humming, among those that were fit, with talk of the lads. Master Spens put it about they'd just sailed over for a dare, and opinions varied from the archers' admiration of their skill and courage, to the bishop's condemnation of their foolhardiness. At least no one guessed the real reason. They had to tell the story of their venture time after time.

Audfinglas seemed to get a little better. At least, she

stopped her dreadful dry retching and sank to sleep. Her mother triumphantly sneered at me and lay down beside her, not noticing, as I did, that the child's breathing was slow and uneven. Poppy could do that. Maybe that was truly all it was? Added to whatever her mother had given her?

Audfinglas and the Corbie shared the Maid's grand bed, with its fine embroidered curtains. My pallet was just beside it, to attend her if she woke in the night. It was because of that that the Maid herself was the first to wake when I had a nightmare.

I dreamed that Inge was singing to me. At first it was pleasant, a soothing lullaby I minded from my bairnhood, that aye brought me comfort and sleep. Hush you, it said, fear nothing, there's naught to fright you. Sleep, never fret, calm your foolish worry. It was Inge's voice, friendly, loving.

But something was wrong. The song changed subtly, became no longer soothing, but smothering. I started to struggle against it. Somehow I knew in my dream that if I relaxed, I'd die. I had to stay awake and alert, to fight the hazy warmth that tried to enfold me like a feather bed; or like a spider that wraps its prey in silk, to keep it safe—for eating later. I tossed and heaved, muttering and mumbling.

Suddenly I awoke. The wee Maid was leaning out of her bed over me, shaking my arm. "Wake up, Meg!" she piped in Norse. "Are you all right? Was it a very bad dream?" It was the first time she'd spoken to me. I shook my head to clear away the shreds of the song.

"Get back in here, Maritte!" came the harsh whisper of the Corbie. "At once! Or you will be whipped in the morning."

Obediently she shrank back into the bed. Whipped! Our little princess! And she didn't argue; she was clearly used to it! I watched the long hand gripping her arm painfully to hold her, and wished I could break each elegant finger.

I was quite shocked at myself.

I lay for a long time, remembering Inge in the happy past, listening to the creaking and cracking of the ship's timbers. Was it my imagination, or was the noise louder than before?

Next day Audfinglas was sleepy and didn't want to wake for food, drink, or anything. Her mother said she was tired after her sickness the day before, and with a cutting glare at me gave her another five drops from the bottle of green glass.

I spent all day helping the sick, or with Davie and Peem. The Maid played happily with her popinjay under the after-castle, with the curtain drawn to keep off the wind. We were trying to teach the big grey and red bird to say, "None o' your business!," which we thought would be a fair answer to any question at the English court, but it was slow to learn. Lady Grizel, up for a breath of fresh air, said there were a many folk she knew like that, all fine feathers and no sense. Sir Michael, watching, laughed with the rest, not seeing her eye resting casually on his embroidered velvet. The Maid noticed, and giggled. She seemed brighter this last while.

Master Spens and his crew worked away, reeving extra braces to the sail to help control it in bad weather, doubling the mast stays, frapping ropes at rubbing points, stitching a rope right round the edges of the sail to strengthen it, annoying the passengers by shifting them to get on with the work. He had no time for more than a word with us, but told Peem he'd been ready for a gale before, but now he was ready for ten. And laughed.

As night drew on, I somehow didn't want to go down to the cabin. I lingered on deck as the others settled to bed, shivering, uneasy.

Davie and Peem came up beside me, looking out over the green-black waves with me to the starless dark rising in the east. I turned away from them. "What's wrong, Meg?" Davie asked. I couldn't say. But shrewdly studying my face, he insisted. They'd not take no for an answer.

"I've a queer feeling, lad," I finally admitted. "As if something was about to happen—"

"Something bad?" He surprised me by nodding. "Me too, Meg."

Peem agreed with him. "Aye. An' me. Well, there'll no harm come tae the Maid that we can prevent." The determination in his voice surprised me. Then he looked down at me and winked. "Did ye hear what Lady Grizel said about ye, mistress? Maybe no—ye were that busy wi' the wee lass. She said she's glad ye're wi' us, for that ye're strong for the wee princess, and that's what she needs, no noble blood and coats o' arms. Aye, she said that." I was warmed by her approval— her that had been so stiff at first.

Suddenly the little fair head popped up through the hatch. She was in her night-robe, bare-footed, bundling a mantle untidily about herself and the cage against the cold air. Seeing us at the bulwarks, she pattered across to grip my hand as I curtsied. We smiled at her, as always, but she didn't smile back.

The Corbie's voice called her from the hatchway. "Your Grace!" How did she make it sound like a curse? "Maritte! Return at once to your bed!" As the woman's head rose through the hatch, I stepped aside so that my skirts hid the Maid. The others closed up by me, no word spoken. Fru Ingibiorg glared round. "You! Have you seen the princess come up?"

"Me, mistress?" I said, curtsying again. "If I had, would I

not tell you?" She wasn't sure how to take that, but someone called her from below and she went down again.

"The Maid could be over the side, for all she cares," muttered Davie.

"Aye, maybe," Peem said grimly, and then smiled down at the wee one. "But never fear, Your Grace, we'll see ye come safe tae your throne. Are ye lookin' forward tae bein' in Scotland?"

I translated for the Maid, as usual, for she'd little Scots yet. I think this was the first time anyone had asked her what she thought, instead of simply telling her what was to happen to her. She considered gravely, holding my hand, and then shook her head. Side to side, on and drearily on and on. Her breath began to come heavy.

"It's a grand country. An' ye're tae wed a braw prince, in England. Ye'll be the queen o' the two lands, Your Grace. Will ye no like that?"

The wee lass's head drooped. Concerned, I knelt beside her and found tears running down her face. She was weeping hopelessly, silently, without sobbing or wailing or any other sign of her tears, as if she was well trained in hiding them. Only the gasping betrayed her. I took her in my arms, and slowly, awkwardly, unused to being cuddled, she relaxed against my shoulder. I looked up helplessly at Peem and Davie.

We tried to cheer her, but promises of toys and pets, of maids and games, did nothing to stop the steady flow of tears. At last Peem asked her, "Your Grace, why d'ye no want tae go?"

There was a long pause. The wheezing became worse.

"D'ye no want tae be a queen?" His deep voice was soft.

She shook her head again. We exchanged glances. Poor wee lass!

Peem knelt down on the cluttered deck beside us. "Aye, my dear, it's hard tae be a princess. But it's your duty." His voice was both gentle and firm at once. We joined him in trying to convince her. The tears trickled on steadily.

"You know, my dear," I said, "when you reach your own land, you can send Audfinglas and her mother away if you want to." For a moment there was a pause in the harsh wheezing, and the Maid's head moved on my shoulder, as if this was a new idea to her. "Aye, Your Grace," I said, "you can so. It's hard to leave your home, and your family, and go to a husband and a new life you don't know, just as your father commands. But most women do that some time. I did. See Davie here, he's to be my husband!" But she didn't smile as I'd hoped she would. "And your prince is a fine lad, and will be a great king. And his father, King Edward, will love you, and call you his darling, his sweet angel, and he'll give you everything you ever wanted. Now, isn't that good to look forward to?"

But when we looked, the tears were still rolling down her cheeks.

"What is it, my dear?" I whispered.

And at last she answered. The tiny voice whispered back into the side of my neck, "I'll not be queen. They'll kill me. They all want to kill me. I don't want to die."

I translated quietly, and we all tried to think of something to say.

Now that she'd started, she'd not stop. "I know. I've heard them speaking. My father and his friends. The lords want me dead. They all want to be king. I know it's true. I don't want to be a queen. I don't want to die. I want to go home! I don't want to be a queen! Please! Please don't make me! Please!"

"Oh, Maritte," I started to reassure her, but she burst out at me.

"Don't call me that! She calls me that! Not you—please! Please!" The fear and venom in the whisper were shocking.

It was at least a way of turning her mind from her future. "Just as you command, Your Grace!" I said. As she eyed me in surprise, I nodded, smiling. "Aye, it's as you wish, my pet, for I'm your servant, my wee princess! What do you want me to call you? In private, of course; it must still be 'Your Grace' when there's people about."

She sighed and nodded, diverted from her troubles. "You are called Meg? It couldn't be that, then. A princess can't have the same name as her maid." She frowned, thinking. "Grete, maybe? Or—Marie. Yes. Marie. I like that."

"That's a French name, my pet," I said, and then hurriedly as the big eyes rose stricken to mine again, "but it's a pretty name. Yes, I'll call you Marie. And so will my friends here. Marie." Understanding, they nodded and smiled.

Later, after we'd removed all trace of her tears, at least as far as would be noticed in the lantern-light below deck, I took her down, tucked her in, and held her hand till she slept. Then I came back up.

The lads were still there. Davie sighed. "I can't blame the lass. I'd not wish to be a princess myself; not this one, anyway."

"She's not fit to be a queen, Davie," I said. "She's not well—you've not heard her gasping—this here was nothing—and she's too gentle. If she'd more spirit, more spark . . ."

Peem shook his head. "There's no help for it. Give her a few year, an' she'll like it well enough. If she—" He stopped.

"If she lives?"

"Aye. Poor lass."

Davie echoed him. "Poor wee lass." And they went away forward to find a sleeping space, leaving me sleepless.

THE STORM

◆

*A*ll that night I tossed uneasily. The motion of the ship changed, grew faster, shorter, more violent. The rushing hum of the wind in the rigging rose to a howling shriek, and a terrifying crash—crash—crash started shaking the planking at the stern. My head was splitting.

I knew—oh, I knew. Inge was chanting. Through the creaking and whining of the ship, that dull, monotonous song echoed in my mind, and I could see, almost, the light under Inge's face, the twitching of Asa's throat, smell the leaves singeing. I bit my knuckles fiercely, gripped the little silver cross at my neck, and prayed.

By midnight we were all awake and praying. The din, the pitching and heaving were so furious no one could sleep; except Audfinglas, still as a carving on a tombstone. Someone started to cry, and a dozen joined him.

When Sir David hauled himself up the ladder to find out what was happening, he found the hatch was fastened down on us. He and Sir Michael battered up at it, shouting angrily, clinging and swinging like monkeys as the ship heaved. Bishop Narwe's calls for calm and trust in God were ignored.

Then one of the maids, on her knees weeping and praying in the near dark, screamed that the sea was coming in. When Lady Grizel took over a lantern, we found water running in through the side of the ship, just where the crashing noise was. I suddenly knew what it must be; every time we reached the bottom of a wave, as the *Andrew and Margaret* strained to rise to the next billow, the *Petrel*, towed astern, was charging at the hull. The planks were starting to come apart under the pounding. As we watched, the trickle thickened, gushed.

The ship was sinking! The popinjay, swinging crazily in its cage, joined the hysterical screeching.

As everyone else screamed, prayed, rushed for their treasures, tumbled and fell, bumped and staggered and wailed and splashed and overturned the night buckets, the Maid sat still in the big bed, gazing round with huge blue eyes, smiling slightly. In the dim light from the two lanterns swinging wildly as the ship tossed, the cabin was a panicking, deafening, stinking hell; but the wee lass watched the frantic confusion as if it was an entertainment at her father's court. She was more concerned for her popinjay than anything else.

I balanced on my knees up beside her, out of the crush and the water, while I struggled to dress myself and then her, too, in the warmest clothes I could lay hands on. I paid no heed to the lords banging and shouting at the hatch, or to Fru Ingibiorg on the far side of the bed seizing all the blankets and furs to wrap her daughter. I did notice that the girl still wasn't waking, but her mother had kept pouring Inge's potion into her, glad it kept her quiet. Well, my duty was to the Maid. Let Audfinglas's mother see to her still.

There was a sudden blast of cold fresh air as the hatch

was lifted, and we heard the sailors' shouts outside. The lords burst up to the roaring deck, the priests behind them, and the women started to fight desperately, clawing and punching to follow them up the ladder. One fell back, dragged off by her hair, splashing and screaming, with the crack of a bone breaking. By now there was over a foot of water sloshing around the cabin, some from the side of the hull and more cascading down through the hatch. That was slammed back down from outside, and shrieks rose again as the horn-shielded candles flickered.

"See there, Meg!" the Maid piped. "See the shoes, floating like boats!" She was smiling, and not gasping at all.

I wondered for a second if she'd gone mad. But maybe she just didn't realise the danger. "Come away, pet, Your Grace, I mean!" I cried above the screaming and the howling of the wind, and she giggled.

"Marie!"

"Ach, Marie, then! Don't waste time! Kilt up your skirt! Here, wrap in this!" It was my fine pelican, all draggled. Ach, well. I fastened it round her with a large brooch. "Mind the boxes, now! Will you leave that bird!" But she insisted on lumping the big silver cage with us, to save her beloved pet. We struggled over to the ladder through the wash of water, deep enough now to swirl all the luggage and loose bedding about. Some of the women were away, but Lady Grizel stood at the foot of the ladder with Martha, trying to calm the moaning, hysterical group that remained, and put a sling on the wife with the broken arm.

"She's dressed? Well done, lass!" she shouted in my ear. "I don't know whether it's safer here or on deck, but I'm thinking the deck will be better. If we sink . . . Go up, see can you get out. We'll put her up to you."

I climbed the swaying ladder, clinging desperately as it kicked like a horse under me. As I reached up to the hatch, it opened and a man swung nimbly down. I dropped back to let him by. It was Master Spens's boatswain.

"The Maid!" he yelled at me. "Where is she?"

"Here!" Lady Grizel called back, and he clapped her shoulder.

"Keep her doon here! Dinna let her up on the deck! Stay here, all o' ye!"

"What's happening?" we cried, as he poked about at the leak. The Maid gripped the ladder for support.

"It's that patch yer dad set in—it's givin' way!" This time, I'd no heart to defend Dad. "We'll have tae jam it up wi' anythin' we can find. Start seekin' boxes, bales, yer beds— anythin' that'll support the planks! We'll need tae rig a bucket chain. Stay here! The deck's no safe! I'll put men doon tae ye!"

He turned to climb the ladder, and shouted. We swung round just in time to see the tail of my pelicon trail up the last two steps and onto the deck.

"Fetch her back, Meg!" shouted Lady Grizel. And I left her and Martha and the rest and climbed the ladder again after the boatswain.

Dawn was breaking, dark grey as the sea, just light enough to show the glimmer of white foam marbling the huge combers that roared towards us. The lashing rain and the spume from the wave tops were blown straight across the ship, as she battled up each sixty-foot hill and toppled down the far slope. Every time we reached the hell-shrieking crest of a wave, she tilted far over onto her side and hung a heart-stopping second before she rolled back and slid down into the suffocating trough between the waves, where the bows sank deep before they struggled up, and the heart hesitated again. And again. And again.

The decks were awash. I stopped half-way out of the hatch and clutched the ladder desperately as a wave swept solid along the planking and over me. I was soaked, and another fifty gallons of water poured over the raised coaming into the cabin as I gasped, choking and blinded. Then Peem's hand gripped me. He steadied me out and set my hands on a mast stay. He was aye there when he was needed. "Hang on!" he yelled in my ear. Daft—did he think I'd let go?

Unable to speak against the force of the wind, I had to wait for the next hollow till I could scream, "Where's the Maid? We've lost the Maid!"

He pointed over the far side of the deck. There, crouched among a group of archers, still clutching that daft cage, her hair stuck to her head and face as mine was, the Maid was surrounded by strong arms. She was safe enough for the moment—as safe as anyone on board.

"What's happening?" I yelled, next time the din of the wind in the rigging sank to a screech.

Peem took a fresh grip of the rope, his arms firm and warm round me. He had to bellow, even right into my ear. "Ye know we've a leak? When the boatswain comes back, we'll make a bucket chain. This storm's no right—the waves is headin' straight intae the wind, no followin' it like they should." I knew fine well it wasn't natural. "We've reefed right down, but the waves is still breakin' green ower her. There's three men carried away already, an' two o' the women. What for did they come on deck?"

I just shook my head. How could I make him see the horror of being trapped helpless below decks, in the panicking, screaming dark?

"We're no far off the Orkneys, neither, an' if God's no good tae us we'll be aground. An' in this gale, we'd break up fast. But—"

Suddenly there was a crash, and screaming from the bows. The forecastle had been torn away, its beams smashed by the weight and power of the seas breaking right over it. There had been a group of folk sheltering under it; I watched in terror as they were scattered, some overboard with the planking, some washed helplessly along the deck by the rushing water. One, a great red gash pumping blood from his neck, was swept past us, gaping soundlessly in the howling wind as he was rolled along and then back to the foot of the mast and left stranded round it like seaweed. Two men there, tied on by ropes round their waists, paused in their work to tie him in as well, but as more waves washed over him he didn't raise his head from the water. I shuddered.

"Where's Davie?" I screamed.

"By the *Petrel*. They may have tae cut her away 'fore she sinks us."

I nodded. Poor Davie, losing his boat. I couldn't think, in the din and the fear. I should take the Maid back below, I knew. But all my strength at the moment was needed just to keep myself from being thrown about the deck and carried away. I turned my head into Peem's shoulder and tried to shut out the wind, shrieking death into my ears in Inge's voice. I couldn't.

Cold and noise were numbing me. Do something, I told myself. No—too hard—put it off. "Where are the rest o' the folk?"

"Under the aftercastle. That Fru Ingibiorg, an' her man, useless daftie, an' the lassie. She didna waken. An' Michael Scott. His wife's swept away." Poor little Lady Mathilda. She'd not need to worry any more about her starched linen melting in the rain, I thought stupidly. "An' her maid. One o' the priests as well, an' two archers. Master Spens is in there by the tipstave, tae give the helmsmen a han' if they need it. It takes more than two men tae handle the rudder, whiles. That's where Davie is."

He coughed, and I saw how tired he was. He must have been up all night, as the storm worsened, helping fight it. And he'd not had weeks of rest in Norway, like the other men; he'd only just sailed this water in the other direction. Not in such weather, mind. In the grey light, his face was weary. But he still could grin at me, and I drew courage from his strength.

A deep breath. "Give me a hand, Peem, and I'll see can I get the Maid down below," I called. He nodded.

Judging our moment, as the ship rose up the next wave and the water cleared from the deck, we staggered over to where a dozen archers were huddled against the bulwarks. They stared at us dully, unblinking, no hand out to help us. They weren't cowards; but they'd have faced an army of Turks sooner than this wet, heaving, screaming hell. And at least they'd held the Maid safe.

She didn't want to let go—who could blame her? But I pointed to the poor popinjay, flattened against its bars, its feathers half plucked by the wind, and told her it was being killed up here. I took the cage, and then had to open the archers' fingers myself to free her, for they didn't or couldn't move. Peem lifted her in his strong arms. She was scared now, more scared of the cabin than of the storm. I felt for her, I was scared myself, but we'd be safer below than in the wind and seas scouring the deck. Peem gripped her close while we waited for our moment to run for the hatch.

Suddenly the wind died to almost nothing.

There was a moment's hush. In the unexpected near silence, Master Spens's voice was harsh and shocking, shouting
at the sailors. "Here's our chance! Alec, rouse out the good
sail, and we'll get it out over the bows and back down round
that damned hole! Tam, will you go and start the buckets!
Beelzebub's bum, man, budge your backside! Where's Jeemsie?
Down seeing to jamming the planks? Aye, that's fine. Here,
Johnnie, get two ropes round the sail, and draw it up in the
centre, like goose wings. The reef still leaves us too much
sail, and we must cut it down. We'll just have a wee scoop,
like, at each side, and she'll still have steerage, but she'll
handle far easier! You know what I want? Aye, let's get to it,
then, my lads! Cheerily, now!"

The boatswain charged along the deck, yelling and kicking
at the archers. Reluctantly their eyes came alive. They stiffly
unwound from the ropes where they'd anchored like oysters,
took the buckets he forced into their hands, climbed down as
he shoved them into the hatch, and started to dip out the
water from the cabin. The buckets came up more regularly
and steadily after a minute or two, as the women below helped
and they got into the swing of it, and having work to do
warmed and heartened them.

A gang of sailors hauled out the grand ceremonial sail,
that had been packed away again when we left harbour. Saint
Andrew had a pained look on his painted face as he was shoved
over the bows, to float back under the ship and be tied up
tight to help hold the water out. But then, he was a sailor
himself, so he'd understand. I promised him a four-pound wax
candle, if we lived.

Peem joined the bucket line, emptying the full ones over
the side. I took the Maid from him, over to the hatch, but

then I paused. She didn't want to go down, and neither did I. "We'll wait here, pet—Your Grace—Marie—till the wind starts again. No need to go back till we have to." She gripped my hand, trusting in her fear, and even forced a rather shaky smile. She needed to warm up. I tucked the cage in behind the stays. "Come along, Marie," I said, "we'll help with the buckets." And so we did, passing back the empty ones. The archers, the sailors struggling with the sail, Master Spens, everyone took a second to notice the wee lass, their future queen, helping them, wrestling with the heavy leather and wood tubs. They all grinned, and were cheered by her, and spared time to say, "Weel done, lassie!" And she was happy in their praise, the colour starting to come to her cheeks as she stumped about the deck, my green camlet trailing and torn at her heels, and I didn't care.

The motion of the ship was different. No longer driven, she bobbed like a net float up and down the waves. There was just enough wind to keep her head steady. We were still in danger, of course; the waves racing at us could break over us, and maybe swamp us. But the clean-shaped bows lifted and lifted over them, and the dreadful sharp lurching was less. We were thankful.

A hand gripped my shoulder, swung me round, and my face was slapped so hard I fell back and thumped my head on a rolling bucket. "How dare you!" a sharp voice squawked in Norse past the ringing in my ears. "Is this the way the Scots use their queen? A servant, carrying buckets?" The Corbie's voice rose screeching like the popinjay's. Scolding, poking, she knocked the rope handle out of the Maid's suddenly nerveless hands, and dragged her off aft.

"She—she's to go down to the ca—cabin," I stammered, shaking my head to clear it. But I spoke in Scots, and maybe she didn't understand. She didn't turn, anyway. My head still buzzing, I staggered back to my feet, and followed the pair of them, through the crew's black looks and muttered curses.

With a sigh of relief, I saw Master Spens stepping in front of them as they reached the aftercastle. "Damn you, mistress, I'll not tell you again! Take yourself back down below decks, and get out o' my way!"

She ignored him, pushing the Maid past him towards the shelter. Losing his patience, he grabbed her arm. Suddenly she was screeching and fighting, eyes staring, arms waving, the lords rushing out to help her, or him, all the work halted, every man's attention fully on them both for a fatal minute.

For then a woman screamed and pointed. We looked round. Bearing down on the ship was a mountain of a wave. The greatest wave in the world.

Everything stopped, silent, helpless, as death raced towards us. Nothing seemed to move except that terrifying hill of water. It towered far, far above the mast. The foam at its crest curled, silver-white like Inge's hair. Its depths, the grey-blue and black of her eyes, swirled smoothly up and up over the ship. We rose and rose for a year, faster than a gull flying, tilting helplessly, all other sound lost in the tremendous roar that we heard in our bones, while all our hearts froze and we waited numbly for disaster. And as we reached the peak, the sea reached out and gently, inexorably, plucked off the aftercastle and the folk under and round it, and scattered them adrift on the surface of the water like a lass throwing flowers before a bride.

All the gilded and painted spars split, tossed and jostled, and the spaces between them filled bright with bodies. I knew some of them. There was old Father Constant, face down; and Sir Michael; and the boatswain; and Master Spens. I heard in my mind Inge's voice: "You'll not make old bones." Oh, Inge!

Fru Ingibiorg was screaming faintly above the din. Audfinglas was rolling helplessly down the deck towards us, the rich fur cape tearing off on a cleat, her fair hair floating. Her mother, hurling herself forward to save the child, tripped on a rope, crashing into the bulwarks. But I couldn't see the Maid.

I clung to a stay, my hands rigid. How had I got here? It didn't matter. Nothing mattered. Master Spens was dead. I'd lost the Maid. We were all going to drown. It didn't matter.

Suddenly I saw her, a tiny fair head and a hand glinting not ten feet away from me, on the lee side of the ship, crying silently for help. No, I couldn't—it was too far from any land, and I was afraid! And then under me the ship lurched, and I let go—or did I jump? Anyway, I was in the water heading for her.

Dear God, I thought, if it's not one o' them it's the flaming other. It's a right bad habit to get into.

Then for a while I'd no time for thinking. I grabbed her hair, wound a plait round my left hand, and struggled to stay afloat. The waves were high, but slow now, and the wind, returning with a boom, flattened some of the ripples—and when the ripples were three feet high, and could fall on our heads and choke us, that was a help. And I'd swum in far colder water than this that had been warmed all summer. But where was I heading? How long could I hold on? Would it not be simpler, and kinder, and easier, just to let go and sink? After all the pain, that dark-red door I minded on would be calm and tranquil. No more struggle. Rest, peace, stillness.

Drat that, I thought. And changed my mind: No, this is an emergency; to hell with that! A spar bumped me, one of the carved pillars of the aftercastle, and I shoved it in under my arm between us, to support us both. All the fine gilding was coming off the thistles in the salt water, some of it onto my green overmantle. I started to swear. As I choked and spat, kicked and tore at my kirtle that wrapped itself round my legs, held up the Maid's head till my arm ached as bad as my throat, I was borne up by a furious temper. I cursed the waves for splashing me, the wind for deafening me; I cursed Master Spens for sailing; Dad for the mess he'd let his men make of the repair; King Eric, King Edward, King Alexander; Fru Ingibiorg for holding back our sailing; Lady Grizel for praising my love for the Maid, for I'd not have gone in after her without that encouragement; and Peem for telling me about it; that daft pelican I'd never had the chance to wear, weighing down the lassie; the popinjay, even.

Mistress Spens would be fair shocked at my language, I thought.

But I didn't curse Inge. Somehow, I felt it would draw her attention. And we'd be safe only if she didn't know we were alive.

Safe? Overboard in the middle of the North Sea, in a gale? My God!

Don't think about that. Something in me refused to give in.

The Maid's not swimming with me. She's gone all soft in the water.

Don't think about that either. What were those words Fru Ingibiorg used?

The salt's burning in my mouth and eyes. My arms and legs are like lead. I can't bear to move, nor to breathe. Oh, God, where's Peem? For I'm done . . .

I kept swimming.

Saint Andrew, you'll have to work at it, to win your candle.

O Lord, let now thy servant depart in peace . . .

No. Not yet, dammit! I held on.

But soon . . .

Oddly, it seemed to me as if I was floating above myself, looking down at these two poor lasses bobbing in the mottled green waves; I felt vaguely sorry for them; it was a pity they were drowning, nothing could be done.

God look after Davie, and Peem. And Inge.

"Give us yer hand! Come on, mistress! Meg, waken up, will ye! Yer han'! Reach me yer han'! Pull, man, keep the boatie steady, or we'll lose her! Meg! This way! Here! Meg! Come away up, ye bitch! Yer han'!"

Who was that bothering at me? I knew the voice from somewhere. It was easier to do as it said than argue about it. I held my hand out, no, not that one, that one had the Maid's hair in it, too much bother to untangle it, try the other one, that was better. Something seized my wrist and hauled. It was painful, but it kept my mouth above water. I took three breaths with no sea in them, and started to struggle.

"Goddamn it! Hold still now! Ye'll have the boatie over! Leave off fightin' me, will ye? Hold on there, aye, like that. Thank God we found ye! Now, let me have the wee lass, mistress. Let go, ye bitch! I'll take her. No, Davie, you mind tae yer oars, I'll see tae this end. Keep her head up tae the waves. Now, Meg, mistress, will ye leave go the lassie's hair? Ye'll break her neck—let go—aye, that's it, good lass. Just hold on there, an' I'll have ye out directly."

I clung to the wood above my head. Aye, I knew the voice. I trusted it. If I did what it said I'd be safe. But my fingers started to loosen in spite of me. I tried to speak, to tell this person I was sorry, but I just couldn't hold on as he'd said; but my throat wouldn't work either. And I slipped away.

As the water closed over me, I felt a huge tug at my hair. Ach, not again, I thought. It can't be. Master Spens is drowned dead.

This time, when I woke up, at least I was flat, lying on my side. I gathered, ache by paralysing ache, that I was in the bottom of a boat. The *Petrel*. Davie was steering. Peem was at the sail. I was sore, bumped, and bruised. I was cold and wet. I was alive.

Well, it would do to be going on with.

Dear God! The Maid! Where was she?

I tried to sit up to ask them, and succeeded in moving my head and grunting. However, they noticed.

"Thank God, ye're livin', mistress!" There was no mistaking the sincerity in Peem's voice. Davie joined in, leaning forward from the tiller, the joy on his face clear under the tiredness.

"Where—where . . ." I managed to croak.

"The Maid? She's right in behind ye. Can ye no feel her there?" When I took thought, I could feel a faint warmth tucked nestling into my back. "She's asleep. We got all the water out o' her, well, the most o' it, anyway, an' she'll do fine."

"If we can fetch safe to land," Davie called. He craned down to see under the sail, through the rain and wind. The boat was tossing violently in the waves, and he was having a hard time trying to keep her from turning broadside on to them and overturning.

I realised we weren't out of danger yet. Somehow, now I was with my lads again, it didn't seem so urgent. Maybe I was too tired to care.

"The ship?" I whispered.

"Who knows?" Peem grunted, hauling at a rope. "She drove on past us. Davie'd but just cut the *Petrel* free when the aftercastle was swept away, an' he was knocked intae the sea wi' it. But he'd the devil's own luck, he came up right beside the boatie, an' he pulled himself in. An' then I saw ye an' the Maid bobbin' away, an' Davie floatin' on by, an' I yelled tae him an' dived in an' swam after him, an' he picked me up, an' we came after ye, an' found ye. An' here we are."

"Where's that?" I asked.

Davie grinned. "God knows," he answered. He had a wide scrape down the side of his face, and his nose was trickling watery pink blood onto his wrecked tunic. From when the aftercastle carried away, I supposed.

"No that far off the islands," shouted Peem over the noise of the wind and waves. "Can ye no feel the water?" We could. The boat was jolting about in cross-waves. "Mistress, can ye sit up an' give us a hand? We need tae bail out the boatie. We shipped a right flood when we was breakin' the lashin's on the sail tae start out after ye, an' we've taken in more pullin' ye in. We've done what we can, but I've tae see tae the sail, an' Davie's all he can do wi' the tiller. Come on, or we'll sink yet!"

I've never done a harder thing than moving then. The cold, the weariness—ach well, it had to be done. Nothing handy to bail with. My skirt? Too many holes. I turned and dragged my mantle off the Maid. It was a mercy the brooch had stayed fastened, all she'd been through. Could I use a fold of cloth to dip into the water sploshing about inches-deep in the boat, and scoop it over the side? Aye, it worked. But with the waves breaking all round us, and the rain still lashing down, it took a long time before I saw any good of my labour.

I worried about the Maid. She'd be frozen again, and she should be kept warm. But if I stopped, we might all drown. If only my hair would stay back out of my eyes! And my arms stop aching so . . . and my throat . . .

"I'll ready the oars, Davie!" yelled Peem. "Keep a good look-out! We'll have tae run her ashore, an' hope we find a safe beach."

"But if we hit a rock . . ."

"Aye, mistress, but we must just put our trust in the Lord— an' give Him a wee hand if He needs it." Jokes, in our position! I very near smiled.

Every so often there was a great hooting roar, growing closer all the time. What was it? A sea monster?

"See!" Davie shouted. "Breakers!" He pointed ahead. Peem glanced over and threw the oars into the pegs. "Pull right! Right!" cried Davie, cutting the ropes that held the sail. It flapped free, cracking like a blanket on a washing-line, as he turned the skiff's bows up into the wind.

Peem threw himself back on his bench till the oars bent and twisted in his great hands. "Careful!" Davie warned him, and he nodded, gasping open-mouthed for breath. It was a fair-sized boat for one man to row, and the broken water left him no time or energy for speech.

As I bailed, I knelt up to peer over the side of the skiff. Not that far ahead of us I could make out through the spume a low, treeless shore, a strip of black heather and green grass above a white beach.

"It'll do!" called Davie. He steered to starboard, past a white lather of wild water sucking and swirling round a pile of rocks, and suddenly the roar blasted out of the sea right by us in a spout of foam. I screamed, terrified the Devil was rising to seize us, but Peem heaved us away. We left it slowly behind, and headed into a wide bay. As soon as we entered, the shelter made a difference to the waves, which smoothed into long rollers as they headed for the land. Peem's stroke grew longer as he could judge the water easier. Right up to the end of the inlet Davie steered, to where the waves finally crashed onto a deep curve of sand. We were near safe, thank God.

But not yet. We were too tired to be able to jump out and run the boat up the shore. I knew what would likely happen, and as the *Petrel* ran her keel onto the shore I heaved up the Maid into my arms. The breakers turned the boat sideways on to the beach and, crashing against her sides, tilted her up and over. We were tipped out, floundering in the shallows, our feet tripped from under us by the undertow, our soaking clothes dragging at our exhausted limbs.

After all our effort, we could drown in this last six feet.

I found Davie at my side, helping me up from my knees. Together we tugged at the Maid's arms, for we couldn't lift her, till her head and body were free of the waves, up on the cold, wet sand. But where was Peem?

There he was. So tired he couldn't pull himself up out of the water. He was the strongest of us all; but he'd spent his huge strength on us, on hauling me and the Maid up into the boat, on bailing, heaving, fighting to keep us alive in that last great struggle with the oars. Now he'd nothing left for himself. He was lying back loosely, unjointed, flopping help-less in the foam.

Davie and I staggered along the sand to him, waded in, and seized his wrists. We hauled with the last of our strength, refusing to let the greedy waves tug him back into the tide. And at last he turned lazily in the trough of a swell and came in with a rush that near took us off our feet. The very waves that had tried to drown him cast him right up to the line of seaweed that showed the highest level of the tide. He lay among the pebbles, his eyes shut, barely breathing, but living.

The tide was falling. The water receded. No other waves came as far. Davie and I slipped down to our knees, supporting each other, watching as the *Petrel* caught her sail on a rock and swung as if at anchor, but upside down; as the Maid choked and wailed, shuddering weakly back to life.

We were all alive.

THE ORKNEYS

───◆───

*F*rom the moment the men from Isgarth struggled out against the gale to where we huddled under the broken edge of the turf, where the grass gave way to the pebbles and sand of the shore, I never used the Maid's name. If I had told them, they'd have sent word somehow in spite of the storm to Kirkwall, and within a day or two she'd have had all the care the Earl of Orkney, the bishop, everyone could give her. All my worries would have been over, and myself and the lads well rewarded and famous for saving her. But I didn't.

I called her Marie. I gave our names—Meg, Peem, Davie—said we were from the princess's ship, and left it at that. The lads looked sideways at me when they heard me say "Marie," but didn't argue, and used that name themselves when they spoke to her. Davie could understand well enough the Norse the folk spoke, and translated for poor Peem, who was both dumb and deaf. His grin and hands had to serve as language—and did fine, too.

The thralls and servants who took us in told us the farmer was away with all his family at Kirkwall to greet their princess, and only themselves left, unwilling, to feed and guard the livestock. We'd been very lucky; there were rocks at the entrance to the bay, and all round it, except for the beach at the end where we'd landed. They were hard pushed at first to make up their minds if we should be prisoners or guests, but as we fell asleep before their eyes, they decided to leave it for the farmer to decide; they stripped, dried, and warmed us while we slept, and settled us by the long fires.

I woke late next day, aching, stretching, wondering where I was, only slowly remembering. Had we really been in such danger? What had come to Master Spens? How were Davie and Peem? And—oh, God! I heard the Maid coughing. Not her gasping wheeze, but a choky, dry cough, catching at her throat over and over again, and between the coughs, a snoring noise deep in her chest. I staggered to my feet to see to her. When she coughed, spots of blood appeared at her lips. Her face was burning hot.

The Isgarth wives shook their heads gravely. It was the lung fever, they said. She was sure to die. Would they send for the priest at Marygarth?

I drove them to get me honey, ale, eggs, and oil, and never mind what the mistress would say. Ignoring my own aches, I dripped the warm mixture down the Maid's throat, coaxing her to swallow drop by drop. They'd few herbs, but they had mustard for poultices, and a seaweed that they boiled and smeared all over the bairn. I'd have tried almost anything, and it did seem to help. The folk, once moving, were kindness itself and helped all they could. An old wife had a magic stone she heated red-hot and cooled in milk for the Maid to drink, and chanted spells a whole day. The hair rose on my neck, but I thanked her.

I held the lass, hour after hour, as she screamed and babbled and tried to rise from her bed. I put warm stones to her feet and armpits when she shivered, shaved her head and bathed her with cool water when she burned hot. At times she turned blue, gasping and fighting for breath. For four days and nights I nursed her, while she baked or chilled, struggled weakly, and wept.

Her constant cry was, "No—no—no—I don't want to!" I was terrified she'd finish it, saying she didn't want to be a queen, and the women would hear and guess who she was, but no. She somehow didn't, or wouldn't, say the word. When anyone asked her kindly what she didn't want, she cried out, "I don't want to die!" And of course, they thought they knew what she meant, and reassured her that sure she'd not die. That calmed her.

To my relief, she answered to the name she'd chosen. When I said, "Marie, open your mouth and swallow this," she obeyed. It was one worry less.

I had plenty others. What had happened to the ship? Could Master Spens be safe? And all the rest? And if Master Spens was, God willing, saved, had I the right to keep word of his son from him? Even when the Maid—Marie—lay at peace, I had none. With the worry over Davie and his father and the constant wear of nursing, I had a hard time of it.

One afternoon I started awake. It was how I slept, ten minutes at a stretch, then waking to see to the sick lass. All was hushed. The Maid lay still and silent, the women silent round her. She's gone, I thought numbly.

I reached to touch her forehead and found it running with sweat. The crisis was past, and the child sleeping tranquilly.

Then I saw the women's smiles, and smiled back, and we all cried. We changed the soaking blankets, and I slept right through till next morn.

It was late on that day, when even the old wives had agreed that, barring ill chance, the Maid would mend, that I spoke to the lads. Since they'd recovered, they'd been working with the farm servants, mending the thatch torn in the gale, but now the byres and the main hall were done and they'd paused to rest.

As the Maid was sleeping, I called them out to the shore, taking a needle and thread to darn my tattered dress. The kirtle I was wearing was too tight, and besides, it was the best gown of the lass who'd lent it to me, and I couldn't keep it from her. As the lads walked down, they eased their fingers, cut by the reeds and bramble trails they'd been using, and I promised them a good salve, now I'd the time to make it.

We walked the hundred yards to the beach where the *Petrel* was upturned on the gravel. Her broken mast had been taken out, and her sail, torn by the gale and the rock that had held her, was up at the hall to be mended later. Peem stepped crunching down on the stones towards her, but I stopped him. "No, Peem, leave her be," I said. "There's something we must decide on now."

They looked intrigued. We sat down on the turf edge, and I started my sewing. I found it hard to begin.

"Well, what is it, Meg?" asked Davie.

Peem helped me. "It's the Maid, is it no, mistress?" He aye knew my mind.

"Aye," I said, grateful to him for bringing it out. "I—we can't let her go back." There was a pause, as they saw what I meant, and their breath hissed through their teeth. "She can't go back. She's not fit. She'd die."

"Don't be daft. They'll look after her," said Davie, frowning.

"Will they?" I asked. "Think about it. Soon's we say who

she is, they'll want to carry her back. But she can't travel, not for months and months yet. Can she?" They looked thoughtful. "And if they did agree to leave her here till she was in health, they'd all come to stay here with her. All the grand folk. And the Corbie. Just the life she hated before, stifling her. But you mind how happy she was on board the ship?" They nodded again. "And she'll aye be in danger. She knows it herself. The lords'll try to kill her, like"—it hurt to speak of it—"like this last time, with witchcraft, or maybe poison, or a knife in the dark. Would you put the lassie back into that?"

My dripping tears spotted dark on my lap. I must have been more tired than I knew. They said nothing. Davie's frown was deeper. Peem's mouth was pursed tight. If they weren't agreeing, at least they weren't arguing. I tried again. "It'd drive her from her wits, being held and harassed all ways, with not a soul to trust, not for sure. She's not fit for it. Even if she'd no enemies, she's not fit to be a queen. D'you not mind on her gasping when she spoke on it? It aye happens, and worse than that, every time she's upset. And that happens awful easy. After this lung fever and all, she wouldn't live a year. We can't do that to her."

Davie shook his head. "No, Meg. She's our rightful born queen. It's God's will. You can't gainsay the will o' the Lord!" His tone was doubtful, though.

"Maybe it's God's will that she should escape now," I said. "Here she is with a chance. Nobody knows she's alive. They're all thinking she's drowned dead. Could you live with yourself if you took her back? For I couldn't."

It was Peem who put up the next point. "I've seen ye troubled, mistress, an' I wondered. I'm thinkin' ye're maybe right about the lass's health, but there's more than that tae consider. What o' the crown, mistress? If she's no there, what'll they do? Will there no be war? Wi' all the barons claimin' the throne? Will ye take all the deaths on your shoulders?"

I'd thought long about this. "How should I know what they'll do? Maybe hold a tournament for all the contenders, to let the best man win. Or set up a panel o' judges to decide. Whatever, nothing'll come now that wouldn't come in a month, or a year, when she died anyway, d'you not see that? It'll just be a year early. No difference. Not that much, anyway. Well? I know it's a big thing. An awful big thing. But I've puzzled with it as well as I can, and I swear to you by my hope o' heaven I believe we must keep her hid. What do you think?"

Davie wasn't happy. "We can't! Can we? Can we no ask—"

"Who?" I demanded. I dashed the water angrily from my eyes. "Who can we ask to advise us that wouldn't just give her up if he didn't agree? No, Davie, it's us for it. And it has to be now, for see, there's a ship turning into the bay, likely the master o' the house, and if we don't decide now, we'll have no choice left. You and me, we're her one single hope of life. What do you say?"

I waited. At last they took their eyes off the approaching galley and glanced at each other. I tensed, my teeth tight on my bottom lip, my hands tight on my skirt that I was mending. When I realised that they were nodding in acceptance and agreement, the knot at my heart that had held back my breath suddenly loosened itself, and I near wept again.

"Well, mistress, we're wi' ye that she shouldn't go back, but how do we set about it? What can we do wi' her?" said Peem.

"I don't know," I admitted. "She'll maybe like to be a nun. Or we can say she's a cousin o' mine, and Dad'll take her in, I'm certain sure. Him and his cobbled patch!" I added bitterly. "He can turn a hand to make up for it. Ach, we'll find something for her. Something better than being a queen."

Davie smiled. We stared, and he grinned wider. His shoulders started to twitch. "Better than being a queen!" He lay back on the turf, shaking with his high-pitched lassie's giggle. Peem joined him, but deeper. I was a bit irked until I thought about what I'd said, relaxed into near-hysterical laughter with them, and felt a deal better for it.

We sobered slowly. "They know our names, o' course, but not who we are. Just Marie, Meg, Davie, an' Peem, I've said. I've had nor time nor strength for more," I pointed out. "We'll say she's my wee sister."

"Aye, that's it," Davie agreed. "An' I'm your brother— Meg, dearie!"

"An' we'll all be servants o' poor Dame Mathilda an' Sir Michael that's drowned, so there's none can call us liars."

"Aye, not bad, that, Peem," I said consideringly. Now he'd agreed, he was enjoying the planning. "And there'll be no rush for us to run away home, with them dead. It'd seem right for us to wait for our sister to gain her strength again, and all go back together."

"And no reason to bother the earl," agreed Davie. "Not for servants."

That put me in mind of something. "There's just the one thing, Davie. What about your family? And mine? They'll be thinkin' we're dead. Can you see your way to leave them in that distress?" My conscience bothered me. And should I tell Davie his father might be dead? No. Leave it. I might be wrong.

His bright face sobered. "Well," he said slowly, "there's nothing else we can do, is there? Dad wouldn't be willing to keep it secret. He'd tell, sure as death he'd tell. No, we can't risk it. What do you think, Peem?"

The big lad nodded. "Aye. An' we'll have tae keep quiet here. Your dad'll be seekin' ye, askin' for a lad wi' a split lip. Even when he's away home, if we let folk see ye, word could reach the Earl o' Orkney. An' he'd come for ye, or at the least he'd send word o' ye, an' your dad would come, an' they'd see us an' the Maid, an' it'd all come out. Aye well, we'll just pray nobody here hears the word." He put a great arm round Davie's shoulders, his deep voice soothing the lad's unease, and mine. "An' if they've mourned ye, they'll be the happier tae see ye well."

What would they say? But we'd face that in its turn. One thing at a time. I felt the responsibilities crowding me, tightening round my chest. Well. It was decided. I took a deep breath. The first thing was to get our story accepted, and stay here unknown, till the Maid could travel.

"Come on," I said. "We'll away tell them we think the master's coming."

Half an hour later, Sveyn Sveynsson returned home, noisily. He was small and round and bouncy. We knew that his servants both liked and respected him, and found the tales of his great voice that could carry half-way to Kirkwall were true. Before the knorr grounded on the gravel, not far from where the *Petrel* had overturned, and over the shouts and rattle of the oars lifted and laid together, we heard that the ship bringing the little princess had been overturned. Davie took a grip tight on my hand, and Peem put an arm for comfort round both our shoulders.

The *Andrew and Margaret* was wrecked. We had rowed

north, and were safe on the island of Sanday, but the ship had driven south-west past Stronsay, and on past the entrance to Shapinsay Sound, where she should have turned in to the sheltered harbour at Kirkwall. Instead, she seemed to have tried to enter Scapa Flow, through the narrow channel between Burray and South Ronaldsay. But the currents of tide and wind cast her on the rocks and threw her over. She'd been hauled up now, and beached at Saint Margaret's Hope for repairs.

As Master Sveynsson and his sons splashed ashore, and his wife and daughters were carried in after them, we were pushed forward in an excited babble of welcome and explanation. He looked astonished, delighted, and then sympathetic, and hushed the shouting of his servants. Kindly, he told us that many had been rescued; Davie beside me drew a deep breath of hope. "Lady Grizel, her husband, and one of her maids, fourteen sailors, five archers. You knew about your master and mistress?" he said, and I had just enough sense to nod. "Aye. But Master Spens is gone." Davie gave a great dry sob. Peem, recognising the name, held us both tight, as my knees wavered. "And worst of all, our princess is dead. She was cast ashore alive, but not in her senses, and died within an hour, in the arms of the Bishop of Bergen."

My mind wasn't working. "The princess? The Maid? Came ashore alive?"

His wife nodded. "True, true. Saw her myself, peedie lass. Sad. Not long in the water, but the waves pounded her on the gravel. Badly torn, badly. Died without waking, spite of all they could do. Lovely long fair hair."

Audfinglas! She had been mistaken for the Maid! They were about of a size, and her hair the same colour, and her dress rich; if the face was unrecognisable—but—"Can you tell me, sir, what of Fru Ingibiorg?" I asked.

"Aye, lass, she and her husband are alive, but barely. Their daughter was with them, they say, and lost at sea. The wife is quite demented."

"Sad, sad," said his wife, with no sympathy in her tone.

"They're taking the princess's body back home," said Master Sveynsson. "As if Orkney wasn't good enough for her! But she's to be buried with her mother."

I wondered, with a mad desire to giggle, what the Maid's mother would say to Audfinglas lying by her. Fortunately, the mistress broke in, "Come now, don't be too upset. You're alive!" Her husband frowned at her, but she raised an eyebrow. "True, isn't it?" Satisfied as he shrugged helplessly, she whisked over to the dairy to check what work had been skimped while she was away. Peem and I took Davie away behind the house, where we could grieve in peace.

Master Sveynsson welcomed us warmly. His wife, sharper and meaner, looked sour at me for using her precious oil and honey, but he gathered us into his household as his winter guests with no reservations. For we'd bring news, new songs, new stories, to while away the long dark nights. Of course, we couldn't travel till the peedie lass was well, and if that wasn't till the spring, well, all the better! And he'd see us safe off home whenever we wished. Ludmila, his wife, added, shrewdly smiling, that she was certain we'd not just sit back, but would lend a hand with the work of the house.

We thanked them both with relief. We could have been held as shipwrecked sailors, all our goods and gear claimed by Master Sveynsson, for that was the law. Orkneymen had long made a living out of wrecks. It was our great good fortune that Master Sveynsson was both rich and kind.

It was a long time before we were all recovered from that dreadful day. Davie, in fact, took his father's death easier than I did. He wept for him, and was silent for days, but then returned to his old happy self. But for weeks I couldn't get rid of the feeling I was somehow to blame for Master Spens's death. As if I could have stopped Inge, or told Dad to mend the patch better! And I'd warned him, hadn't I, as well as I could? But my heart aye ruled my head, and I was miserable. Never again to hear him bellow, "Beelzebub's bum, Meg!" Or feel his great hug, or see his warm grin. And all my fault!

One day Peem spoke to me. "Mistress, ye mind that day at Stirling? When ye went tae help your sister?"

"Could I ever forget, Peem?" I sighed. I was making a beaded belt on Mistress Ludmila's lap loom, but could take little interest in it.

"Maister Spens said a queer thing. Ye aye thought the wind couldn't blow wi'out your puffin' it, or somethin' like that. What did he mean?"

My mind went back to that other long day. "He was saying that other folk could make their own decisions, Peem, and I must leave them to do it without my help, for their lives were their responsibility, not mine."

As he thanked me, and wandered off, a glorious feeling of freedom came over me. Master Spens was right. I wasn't responsible for other folk. Nobody was. Inge's deeds were all her own doing, not mine. And Master Spens was a big, strong, clever man; I was no more responsible for his death than for his life. Each single soul was responsible for himself!

A lucky chance, I thought, that Peem should ask just that just then. Then I wondered: Was it chance at all?

But what about the Maid, then? Well, she just couldn't help herself; I'd had to choose for her. Or had I? Oh, well. It was decided now.

She grew slowly stronger. Within her frailness, I knew her spirit was as tough as Davie's, or she'd have withered long since. When I told her what we planned, she took a while to understand what I was saying. "I don't have to be a queen?" When I nodded, she gasped, smiling, her breath whistling. For days, whenever she saw me, her eyes asked me again, and when I nodded, the smile appeared. Gradually, as she accepted it, the tenseness faded from her face.

Queerly, though, her shorn hair grew in white. Not fair; white. Her face relaxed to a child's instead of a wee old wife's, but her hair looked old. I was a bit irked; if anyone's hair showed signs of that day, should it not be mine?

We spent the whole winter in the big steading at Isgarth, so like Dad's, and worked hard for our keep. Master Sveynsson declared he was sick of the thatch being ripped off whenever there was a bit breeze, and he'd re-roof his hall with the huge flat stones from Caithness. He strengthened his rafters to hold them, ready to fetch over the stones when the winds moderated. The gales were fierce; hens, and even sheep, were tethered to stop them blowing away, and at times I had to crawl across the yard on my hands and knees. Peem and Davie worked on both the roof and the ship, a knorr called the *Thin Sow*. Her greedy belly could hold more than you'd ever credit, Master Sveynsson chortled. She was a trading ship, he said half-regretfully. His father Sveyn Asleifsson had summer-raided in the old Viking style, but Magnus, the present Earl of Orkney, had banned it, and was a hard man to cross.

The terrible hooting that had scared us so as we came in to the land was no demon at all. Just as well! On a tiny rocky islet at the entrance to the bay there was a kind of crack in the rocks, and at just the right state of the wind and waves it roared and spouted like the whale.

I spent my time sewing, spinning, knitting, baking, making medicines, telling Master Spens's stories that were new to the folk there, looking after the bairns, and teaching them and the Maid all I knew. Marie learned as fast as any of the Sveynsdotters, her mind slowly stirring to brightness as she recovered from her illness and her fears. We gratefully accepted clothes to replace the ones lost or ruined in the storm, and altered them to fit the lads and myself. I said my poor, battered pelican had belonged to my mistress, and cut it up for a decent kirtle, and the red lining made me a cloak. And though she grumbled about the cloth it took, we made one for Mistress Ludmila to show off with in the kirk at Easter. The dratted thing proved handy at the last.

On my one trip to Kirkwall with Master Sveynsson, I sold my silver cross to pay my candle to Saint Andrew in Saint Magnus's grand kirk there. Just a two-pound one, not four; it was all he was due, for we hadn't all been saved.

"Marie" was everyone's favourite from the start. She was so shy, with the huge blue eyes that widened at any sharp sound, and the sweet, trembling smile; there wasn't a soul in the house that didn't love her, even Ludmila. She was totally spoiled and cosseted, with drinks of warm honeyed milk to bring back her strength—I said milk was dirty, but they insisted, and it did no harm, at least—and bannocks and cream, and a cushion of sheepskin by the fire. She had a kirtle made out of new cloth, and a warm cloak that one of the children had scarce worn. Mistress Ludmila took a real fancy to her. At Yule she was blessed on Helya's night, with the other children. As the oldest wife in the house sang the ancient blessing, I felt my eyes prickle. I wasn't the only one.

We joined in the celebrations with the rest of the household. Peem helped lift the quern-stones on the eve of Yule, to prevent them being run backwards by the trows, the ogres of Orkney, to grind away all the family's luck, and we all prayed together that the trows would not enter the house that night, when despite the danger the door was left ajar and a candle burning to offer shelter for Mary and Joseph, homeless and weary. We each had a Yule-brummie in the happy, relieved morning, a little yellow cake, rayed like the sun that was now returning, and felt at home. But next day when the lads of the island came romping round the steadings to claim food and drink, and a kiss from all the lasses, they didn't seem to want to kiss me. I was queerly disappointed.

In January there was a hard snap, and we were lent ice skates made of ox rib-bones, so that we could go out with the rest to slide on a frozen shallow pond near the house. The crowd round the Maid as she slipped and floundered, and the cries of encouragement and the laughing dismay when she fell in spite of all the hands holding her annoyed me.

"If she's not careful, she'll have Mistress Ludmila down on her for taking all the lads' minds off their work," I grumbled to Davie. We were skating round together, me in the middle, him on one side and Peem on the other. I was a good skater, I knew the colour I got from the exercise suited me, my newly made kirtle and cloak looked fine, and nobody was paying me any attention.

Davie looked across at me. It was still a surprise that he needed to look up no more than an inch. "Putting your neb out o' joint, eh?" he grinned.

I was furious at his nonsense and had my mouth half-open to snarl at him when suddenly I saw it was true. I was used to being the one that all the lads watched, but somehow here everyone was more interested in the Maid. I'd been snippy with her at times, more than was needful, so that the big blue eyes filled with worry, and I now saw why. I was ashamed of myself.

I had to say something. "Aye, Davie," I said, trying to make it a joke, "that's right. I'm all cut and bashed; the lads here won't give me a second look or a whistle, even, let alone a kiss!"

They glanced at each other. Peem looked apprehensive, but Davie, after struggling to keep a straight face, started to giggle. Once started, he couldn't stop; he went on and on until everyone was staring and laughing at or with him. He collapsed in a heaving heap on the ice, honking and snorting, and Peem and I had to drag him off, out of folks' way.

We dumped him by the snow-covered bank, and I glared at him, red-faced with embarrassment. When I glanced up at Peem beside us, it was surprising how red-faced he was himself. He looked as if he was struggling not to laugh, too.

A suspicion came to me. "You lads—what have you been saying about me?" Peem couldn't meet my eye. Davie whooped painfully. As I raised a handful of snow over him, threatening to ram it down his neck, he just shook his head and waggled his hands helplessly. I abandoned the snow. "Well, Peem?" I demanded.

I'd never seen him look so awkward. "Well, mistress—ye see—it was like this—" He stammered to a halt.

"Don't stop there," I said grimly. "What was it like?" Davie honked again.

"We thought—Davie an' me thought—ye'd no like it if all the lads was botherin' ye. An' Davie wouldn't like it neither, see?"

That was true. Both parts, I supposed. "Well?"

"So we—we decided it would be best if we said ye was promised."

"Well?"

"Well—we'd said Davie was your brother. An' it wouldn't

do tae say ye were betrothed tae a lad back in Scotland, for the laddies here can be right wild, an' a—a far-away promise wouldn't hold them off. Ye see?"

"So far. Well? Who did you say—oh."

"Well, there wasn't much choice, mistress," Peem muttered, crimson. "It had tae be me. An' at least I'm big. If anyone was too pushin', I could—"

"Warn them off? Aye." Davie, my betrothed husband, was screaming in purple silence on his back at my feet, unable to get a breath for his laughter. I didn't feel like laughing at all. "Is that how you got that black eye last month? And big what's his name—Thorald, is it?—got his? Aye, m'hm."

I stopped to consider. Davie wheezed faintly. Peem tucked his head down into his wide shoulders for shelter from my temper, biting his lip to keep from smiling. Murder—double murder—would scarcely satisfy me.

Then I took thought to myself. Why let them laugh at me?

I gave Peem a wide smile. "You did quite right, Peem. I'm very grateful. I could have been in a right awkward position, if you'd not been so thoughtful." It pleased me that his jaw dropped and Davie stopped heaving and opened his eyes for the first time in minutes. "Aye," I said consideringly, "you're a braw big lad, Peem. You'd make a fine husband. But if we're promised, we'll need to act liker it. Will you come and skate with me now—my darling?" As his eyes glazed, I slipped my hand inside his elbow and drew him away from the bank. Davie gaped up at us. I gently scooped up another handful of snow and dropped it into his open mouth as Peem and I turned onto the ice again.

Whose nose was out of joint now, eh?

All through till the spring, Peem and I kept up the pretence that we were betrothed. It amused the Maid when I smiled and whispered, but embarrassed Peem something dreadful. Serve him right. Davie didn't seem jealous at all, drat him. He just grinned. Well, he was only thirteen.

We decided we'd better leave in April. The Maid was stronger, I felt, than she'd ever been, for she hadn't a fit of her gasping from October on, but she was afraid of another storm at sea. As were we all, when we thought of it. So we asked Master Sveynsson if we could leave after the March storms were over.

He was generosity itself, first offering to take us back in his own ship, and when we gratefully refused that kindness, helping repair the *Petrel* and giving us stores for the trip. He warned us to take the journey easily, not venturing out if the winds weren't favourable, and we were glad to promise him that, for we'd already planned on it. We'd no wish to be wrecked again.

In the middle of April, then, on a bright morning, we put dried fish, oatmeal, hooks and line, a bundle of blankets, and a firkin of water into the *Petrel* and said our farewells. Ludmila, of the sharp tongue, was sad to lose us. To lose Marie. "Can't you stay a whilie? Just a peedie whilie? The lassie's not right well yet," she begged us, and I was sore tempted to leave the Maid with her. She'd be loved and cared for, but among Norse speakers, so close to Norway, she'd surely be discovered. I couldn't risk it.

I kissed her hand. "Mistress Ludmila," I said, "we must thank you and your man for all your kindness to us. The longer we stayed, the harder it would be to drag ourselves away. But we beg you to accept this, as a token of our gratitude." And I gave her the great silver brooch I'd pinned the Maid's cloak with, the night of the shipwreck. We'd found it wedged under a thwart in the *Petrel*. It was a fine thing, a curvy triangle near as big as my hand, a swirl of dragons, their eyes gleaming red garnets. It pleased us all to be able to give her such a noble parting-gift.

She wept again, and pressed her lips to the Maid's cheek. She and her daughters gave us gifts in their turn, a sharp new eating knife each, with a horn handle, to hang at our belts. The Maid herself was in tears.

Then it was the turn of the men. Peem and Davie had found a huge tree-root cast up on the shore and had spent all their spare time for the last two months hiding in a byre, carving it into a new figurehead for the knorr in the shape of a pig's head. When he saw it, Sveyn roared with delight. "A pig's head for my *Pig*, eh? See the peedie eyes, so greedy, just like my *Piggie*, eh? A touch of red paint and there will be no ship as fine in all the North." He couldn't praise it enough. He, too, gave us a farewell gift, of ten pennies to buy shelter on the way.

We called Marie from Ludmila's clinging arms, and at last, after near as much fussing as when we'd left Inverkeithing, we set sail down the bay for home.

HOMEWARD

◆

*A*s we'd been advised, we took our time on our
journey home. Though we knew we must end up
at Inverkeithing or Dunfermline, thinking on the trouble
awaiting us we were in no hurry.

Peem was worth his weight in cloves, for he turned out
to be expert with the sling. Not being a freeman, he'd not
been taught the bow, like Davie, but with a thong, a scrap
of leather, and a three-ounce pebble he could do near as much
damage. "It's no much use against armour, no havin' a point,"
he said, "but for huntin' it's a sight cheaper than a thirty-
shillin' bow an' arrows at two shillin' each—an' no fear o'
your bowstring stretchin' in the rain neither." Though at first
he grumbled he'd lost his eye, and got only one oyster-catcher
or gull in a score of shots, he soon regained it, and we ate
well, fish and sea-birds—tasting equally fishy, but we were so
hungry each day, we'd eat anything. Once we found a pack
of seven or eight wolves at a dead seal lying on the shore. A
few well-slung stones thumping off their sides drove them away
to a safe distance off the carcase, which was fairly fresh, and

the next two nights Peem ate himself a sore belly on roasted seal steaks.

Another time we were stranded by a sharp gust of wind that drove us onto the edge of a huge pebble bank at the mouth of a river in the Firth of Moray, and horsemen came at us with spears. There was no shortage of stones there, and Peem held the horses off till we could heave the boat back in the water, and then he and Davie fair lifted the skiff out into the bay.

In the main, though, we sailed just when the wind was right, twenty or thirty miles in a day, landing near lonely fisher cots down the coast. We were usually welcomed as a novelty to talk about for weeks after, and fed on eggs, fish, and bere bannocks. Our hosts wouldn't take a penny for our food, for the guest was a sacred trust. We were driven off only once, near Macduff, as pirates. We told folk we were from Thurso, going down to an uncle in Berwick, as our father had died. It was likely enough, and never questioned. Going gently and carefully, not every day or even every second day sometimes, stopping for the Maid to rest and recover, it took us a month to reach Fife.

We didn't go into Saint Andrews or Crail for fear of meeting a friend of Master Spens. Davie's face was too recognisable, and if he was seen, there would be questions and the Maid maybe found. There was aye a risk that some fisherman or sailor might recognise him, or the *Petrel*, though we'd painted her black, and her sail was worn and patched now, but what could we do?

We stopped for the night at Wemyss and hauled the boat up out of the tide just by the great caves. It was a busy shore, that, with the fishing, and the sea-coal dredgers raking the water at low tide. The caves were full of gear, baskets, nets, boats up for repair, barrels, piles of coals, wood, rope, creels, stuff of all kinds. And among it all, not a few families of homeless folk, scraping a living working and stealing as they could.

A servant came down from the castle, perched away above the cliff-head, to check the strange boat, but when we told our usual tale he only taxed us a farthing and went off to report that we were harmless. We borrowed a hot coal to start our fire of gathered driftwood, and settled down in a corner near the mouth of the most northerly cave, where we could keep an eye on the boat.

"Well, so far so good, Meg," Peem said. "But what now? Where do we head for, the morn? Inverkeithing to find your dad?"

I was laying out the wee haddock we'd caught that day, flat on the hot stones by the fire Davie had built up, while the Maid spread out our blankets. It was a routine by now. She looked up. "I'm feared, Meg," she said. Her Scots was fine now, and she was talking freely. "Are you sure he'll take me in?"

We'd been over this a dozen times. "Certain sure, pettie," I reassured her cheerfully, though I'd been feeling more and more uneasy about it myself. "But I'd be mortal glad to know just how things stand at home."

"There's maybe somebody about here can say. I'll try can I no find out," said Peem. "Give us a shout when the fish is ready." He rose, stretched tall to ease his stiffness from the boat, and wandered out into the twilight.

He returned not five minutes later, a woman at his side. "Here, Meg, here's somebody ye know," he said, grinning. Somebody we knew! How could he betray us like that? I peered at her in the firelight, but the thin face was strange to me.

"Aye, ye do so," he insisted. "Mind that time we pulled a wifie out from below the horses? In the snow? This is her."

I still didn't recognise her, but of course I remembered the event. "Good e'en, my lady," she said. Her voice was rough, and she sniffed constantly and rubbed at her red-raw nose, but her teeth gleamed yellow in her narrow smile. "I'm thinkin' ye'll no want folk told ye're here, eh? An' sma' blame tae ye, wi' what Jeemsie Macduff o' Donibristle says he'll dae tae ony Spens he catches—an' yer big callant here that he'd sooner hang than eat his dinner. Aye, a long memory he's got, eh? Ye needna fear for me givin' ye awa'. There's some would dae it, but no me. If I've my wee laddie by the fire this night, it's thanks tae you an' yer man here. I'll no forget ye, my lady, an' you riskin' yer life for me. What way can I aid ye?" She spread her ragged shawl to the fire's heat.

Though the beggar wife's words and smile were friendly, I somehow felt uneasy still. I thanked her and asked did she know how my father was.

Her eyes flicked from one to the other of us. "I've bad news for ye, my lady, that I'm sore at heart for ye, an' ye sae lang frae hame. Yer dad's . . ."

"Dead?" I asked, as she paused. The Maid and Davie stared, silent.

"Aye, mistress. This six-seven month now." The black eyes never blinked in her brown face as she sniffed juicily, crouched by the flames for warmth. "Mind yer haddies there, mistress," she warned me. As I sat rigid, she turned over the wee fish roasting by the fire, and somehow a large piece fell off one. "There noo, see, I'm a' thumbs!" she apologised. The fallen bit, ash, sand, and all, was carried stealthily to her mouth in one broken-nailed hand.

"What happened?" asked Peem. I couldn't speak. Davie

slid his hand into mine, and I clutched it desperately. I'd known something was wrong. It had been heavy on me for long days past.

"Weel, when news came how that the wee princess was drownded, an' Maister Spens an' his son, an' ye as weel, the word wis that the ship sinked because o' a patch that Maister Rolf hadna right mended. So the Council sent for him. An' when the spearmen came tae the house, he wisna weel, but he rose frae his bed, an' went oot tae them, tall as a king." I could imagine it. "An' then he jist clutched sudden-like at his heart an' fell like a tree, an' was deid when they turned him ower." Oh, Dad! "An' then the folk was that ragin' that the wee lassie wis deid, an' the land no settled after a' this time, they came that night in a rabble wi' torches an' burnted the shipyaird, an' the house, an' the auld witch as lived inby the fire there. All yer sisters an' their men wis awa' safe hours before, but she wouldna leave. She stood at the heid o' the great table as they shoved in the door, an' cursed her ain folk for leavin' her, an' the burghers as came for tae burn the hoose. She said they wouldna lie safe in their beds theirsel's if they burned her oot. But they done it anyway. An' yer folks is scattered a' ower the land. I heard as how some went tae the youngest ane, Birgget is it, as lives doon Berwick way, I'm no certain sure. But there's but ash left o' hoose an' yard."

Another bit of fish lifted to her mouth. I couldn't move. Why had I never dreamed of this, that Dad would be blamed for the ship's loss? And the princess? For of course it would happen. Dad was gone. And Asa. And the house.

I'd known something was wrong. For long enough I'd known. And my fault.

"I'm sorry tae gie ye the news!" she apologised again. I remembered to breathe, and drew a deep sobbing gasp. Her eyes kept returning to the fish. Without a word, I pushed two of them over to her. I couldn't have eaten them anyway. Her eyes rose, black and wide, and she snatched up the hot meat silently and vanished into the dark.

After a long time, Davie moved first. "Ach, Meg!" he said. He put an arm round my shoulders. "I'm—I'm that sorry!"

The Maid came to the other side. "Me too, Meg," she murmured.

There was a great aching empty hole inside me. Out of my own hurt, I turned on them spitefully. "Are you sure you want to be seen with me now, Davie Spens? The daughter o' a ruined man that they say killed your own dad? A traitor, who murdered his queen! And sister to a witch! Your mother'll not want me in her family now! And I don't blame her! I wouldn't care for me myself. I've brought my dad to his death! And yours! I might murder you some day! Never fear, Master Spens, sir, I'll not hold you to your promise! I can aye wed Peem—if he'll condescend to have me!"

I started to laugh and cry together. A part of me watched the two young ones draw together in horror at me, and listened to the bitter, hateful words pouring out. I was ashamed of myself, going on as if I couldn't trust them, as if I hated them, but I couldn't stop speaking, shouting, screaming—

Peem's hand cracked across my face, stunning me into silence. "Stop that, Meg!" he snapped at me. "This is no way tae mind on your dad! He was a good man in his day! Mind what Master Spens said—ye're no responsible for the world's actions! He'd be black ashamed o' ye, carryin' on like this. An' so would your dad! They deserve better o' ye. An' so does Davie!"

My madness dissolved into simple tears. I clutched at him,

and Davie and the Maid as they drew near, sobbing sorely. The Maid patted me gently.

After a while, as my tears hiccuped into stillness, I felt Davie stir. He drew off a bit, and looked sideways at me. "D'you not want to wed me, then, Meg?" he asked. "I like you. But—do you not like me? I thought you did."

He sounded so sad that even in my misery my heart went out to him. I took a grip of myself. "Aye, Davie, I do so like ye," I assured him. "I like you fine." I wouldn't embarrass him by saying I loved him, though it was true.

He smiled waveringly, and his chin firmed. "Aye, well, then, we'll be wed this summer like we planned, and my mother'll just have to like it or lump it," he announced. Then he stopped for thought. "Unless—how long should you mourn your dad, think you, Meg? It's just as you like yourself."

The tears near started again, at this strangely adult consideration. "No, Davie," I said. "We'll do just as you say." As his smile grew again, I made myself straighten away from Peem's shoulder. There were things to do. If I let myself think about it, I'd cry again, and we'd no time just now. We were in too much trouble. I shrugged away from their comforting, weakening arms. "Well, what do we do now, then?" I asked them, sniffing and blowing my nose hard. "Where can we go? Can we take the lass to Mother Alison? Davie?"

He accepted the change of subject, but shook his head regretfully. "No, Meg. She'd not likely help, and if she did, she never could keep it a secret. Not with Mary and Anna there. They've too many gossiping friends."

I quite agreed, but he had to be the one to say it. "Your brothers, then?"

Again he rejected the idea. "They'd be scared, Meg," he said in irritation.

There was a pause. "Well, who would help?" I said wearily. It was about time somebody else had an idea. The Maid's hand in mine was icy cold.

Peem coughed, rather apologetically. "It seems tae me, mistress, that if there's no secure place for her here wi' either your dad or Davie's family, she'd be better out o' Scotland altogether. Would that be right?"

The Maid nodded vigorously. "Aye, Meg, away from all the men that would kill me!" she chirped eagerly. "Can I not go back to Norroway, to my own dad?"

"He'd just send you right back to be wed to Prince Edward," I said, though I longed to agree. "Are you certain sure you'll not do that? It would be far the easiest."

They looked at me as if I'd gone daft. "Meg!" Davie cried. "What are you at?" He started to get angry. "It was you started all this carry-on! Now you want to send her back!" Then he remembered my father, and looked conscience-stricken, as if somehow he shouldn't argue with me. It irked me.

"No, I don't!" I snapped. "I but want to be sure!"

"I am sure, Meg," the wee lass said anxiously. "I don't want to be a queen, not ever. But—but if you say it's best—"

"Hold your wheesht, Marie!" Davie told her. "We're not stoppin' now! What was in your mind, Peem?"

The big lad, who'd been waiting patiently for us to finish, reached out first and pulled the fish back from the heat. "Eat up while we're speakin', then," he said, and as they turned to the food the tempers lowered. "Well," he went on, licking his fingers, "there's but the one man I can call tae mind who might give us a hand. Master Grossmeyer."

"Master Grossmeyer? The apothecary?" Davie voiced the surprise that I felt. "What for would he help?"

Peem looked uncomfortable. "He's from one o' the Hansa League towns, Davie, round the top o' Germany. They want tae keep the trade in the North Sea an' the Baltic all in their own ships. They don't want tae see Scotland an' England an' Norroway a' joined together, tradin' among theirselves, an' takin' cargoes away from the League. So they'll maybe help us, just tae stop this marriage. An' Master Grossmeyer, he's a good man, he'd no let them just kill the wee lass, like some might. If we asked him, he'd likely put her across tae Flanders or Saxony. She'd be safe there." As we gazed at him, he flushed. "It's the best I can think on, mistress," he muttered.

When I could close my jaw, "Peem Jackson!" I said. "When did you get to be an expert on international affairs?" He ducked his head shyly. "You—you're a constant source o' wonder, Peem. To look at you, a body'd think you'd not sense enough to come in out o' the rain, specially when you're grinning, but here you are with the exact right answer to the problem, same as aye!"

Davie was nodding and smiling, nearly cheering him. He flushed even more at our praise. The Maid wasn't so happy; but it offered safety, and she'd pick up the tongue quickly, we assured her; see how well she'd done with Scots!

We were still talking about it when the beggar woman came creeping back to our hearth. Two laddies, as thin as herself, slunk after her.

"My lady, this is my bairns, Tam an' Joe. Mak' yer courtesy, then, see!" The wee lads knelt awkwardly in the sand as she cuffed their heads lightly. It was clear that they were her reason for life, from the way her eyes clung to them as she spoke. "It wis Tam I had that day in Dunfermline, my lady."

"Oh, aye?" I said. I knew why she'd brought them into

the cave. Well, we'd fish left. "Come up to the fire, wife, and eat with us. Come away, laddies. Mind your fingers, now, the fish is hot!"

We watched as they tore at the fish, scarce waiting for them to cook or to cool before bolting them, for all three were clearly near starving. I stopped them after a while, to let their bellies settle, and as the lads sucked the fish-heads, their mother paid us with the other news.

We knew already that there had nearly been a war during the winter between de Brus on one side and the Balliol and the Comyns on the other. But the woman told us that now it was all being settled by law. The Guardians of Scotland—those that were left—had agreed to ask Edward of England, as brother-in-law of the late King Alexander the Third, to judge among the various claimants. All the nobles of Scotland had been summoned to a meeting on the Border in a few days' time, and were buzzing about like bees, she said, gathering in their kinsfolk to support them.

"It seems like the best thing, eh, Your Gra—Marie?" I said. Drattit, I'd not called her that for ages. Why now? The beggar looked slyly interested, and I knew I'd slipped up there. "No fighting, anyway." Davie was frowning. "What do you say, Peem?" I asked, trying to cover up.

He shook his head. "I'm mindin' the tale o' the two mice that asked the cat for help, mistress," he said slowly. "They'd a wee scrap cheese they baith claimed, an' cried on Tibbie the cat tae be the judge."

The lads grinned. "Whit happened, then, maister?" asked one.

"Tibbie ate the cheese, an' the mice as well," said Peem grimly. As they laughed, he pursed his lips and shook his head. "Aye well, we'll just hope these mousies has more sense,

• 229 •

or more strength, than them in the story. For Scotland's a fine tasty skelp o' cheese. An' King Edward's like tae be a hard cat tae handle."

I scarce heard what he said. I was thinking of the lad calling him "master." It was wrong, of course, a bit of beggar flattery like the wife calling me "my lady"; he was just a poor cottar's lad, not the master of a household or a learned clerk that was due the title. But he was a fine man now, and no blame to the boy for the word. Aye, I thought, if a man's as fine and strong—aye, and kind and clever—as Peem, he's more claim to the name than some that's just born to it. I felt a cheerful glow of pride in him. Again.

We gave the beggar family some more fish, and the mother was full of thanks. "An' I'll no tell any ye're here, mistress, nor any o' ye. Though the lad's face there's as good's a label who he is, eh? An' naebody'll ken frae me about the wee lassie. Marie, eh? Aye. However much siller they offers. It's no me would tell on ye. Naw!" She smiled slyly and confidently.

"That's good o' you, wife." I beamed at her. I gave her a silver penny, of the four we had left, and they left, gushing blessings on us.

Davie scratched his head. "Do you trust her, Meg?" he said.

"Aye, son, near as far as I'd trust a stoat," I replied. Peem was already folding our blankets. "Slip out after them, Davie," I said, "and see where they go. If they settle to sleep in one o' the other caves, or in a tent, we can maybe relax." But he came back after a few minutes, saying he'd lost them.

"I'm sorry—" Peem started, but I cut him short.

"No, Peem. Any normal wife would keep silent. How could you know? Come on, then, lassie," I told the Maid.

"We must find another place for the night. Davie, make up the fire, and heap nets or something to look like folk sleeping. We'll slip down to the boatie and push off. Come down quiet when you hear Peem whistle. She may leave telling about us till the morn, thinking we think we've bought her off, and we'll be far by then. And whoever seeks us can do without."

The Maid was looking worried, as well she might, for if we were found by one of the claimants to the throne, or their supporters, they weren't likely to let her live. Nor us neither, come to that. I was glad to hear her breath still clear. She'd her own courage, the wee one.

We sailed for an hour to one of our old haunts, a wee burn foot near the Bell Rock. Rolled in our blankets, we huddled together for warmth in the bottom of the boat, and slept till the bell ringing for Prime across the bay in Inchcolm Monastery wakened us. At least, the others slept. I had time, now the shock had passed, to mourn for Dad. Why did he have to die? Was it my fault for hiding the Maid? Did Inge mean it to happen? Where were the rest of my family? Oh, Dad, Dad! And Master Spens, and all the rest! I tried to hold myself still, but often that night Peem reached over the wee ones and held my hand tight, while I shuddered silently and the tears ran free down my cheeks.

At first light, as we yawned and shivered, "What now, mistress?" he asked.

I pulled myself together. Mourn again later. "Well," I said, "this is a safe place enough for Marie and Davie to stay hidden while we go in to the town to speak to Master Grossmeyer." He frowned. "D'you not think so?"

He hesitated. "Aye, maybe, mistress. If they keep their-selves quiet. But . . ."

"But what?"

"I'm thinkin' it would be better if I went in myself. Alone. You're well known, mistress, like Davie there. See your hair, wi' the white streak? There's too many folk would recognise ye. Better just me on my own."

We looked at him, reassessing him again. A cottar's lad, to organise the rescue of a princess? But he was clever, that was for sure. "Aye, well, maybe," said Davie.

"Aye," I agreed, "Master Grossmeyer'll listen to you as well as to myself—maybe better even, you bein' older, an' a man." It had aye irked me, that, but you just had to accept it. And I was so tired!

Marie nodded, but Davie was worried. "But, Peem, have you no friends yourself that'd know you?" I'd not thought about that.

As Peem frowned, the Maid suddenly giggled. "He could shave off his beard?" she suggested wickedly.

He flushed scarlet, a hand going protectively to his fine, curly gold chin. "No, no, Marie," he protested urgently. "That'd not help!"

I studied him more carefully. "No, lassie, you're wrong. It's his beard will hide him. For it's grown since last year, and he looks older and more—more mature." True enough, under that mat, it was hard to see what age he was. "Aye, Peem, I'm thinkin' you're right again. Aye. On you go, and we'll rest here. It's about six mile to Dunfermline. You'll be back by noon, if you hurry. Aye, an' to hide my white streak in my hair, buy me a cloth for my head. Here's a penny. If we've to go among folk, I'll disguise myself as an old married wife." As the Maid started to giggle again, I frowned at her. "What's wrong with you, lass? That's what I'll be, come summer, with my man Davie here!"

Peem stood up quickly. "I'd best be away, mistress," he

said, and we wished him God speed, kissed him, and waved as he scrambled off up the brae.

As he waved back and disappeared, we turned to hide the boat. She was in among rocks, and we lowered her mast over her stern, draped the patched brown sail over her, and huddled back into our blankets to wait.

It was cold, that early May dawning. The mosses on the rocks were damp. I felt chilled and uneasy, and had to fight back the tears. The young ones were depressed, too, by the dreary greyness, and the dew and mist seeped through the coverings and right into our bones. I tried to cheer them, saying it wouldn't be long now, Peem would be straight back and bring us good news.

"Will he bring us a hot pie, eh, Meg, like he did at Crail?"

"Six mile? It's not likely to stay warm, Davie," I had to admit.

"Well, can we not make a fire?" he suggested. "See, there's mussels on the rock there we could roast, and get the chill off ourselves."

I considered it carefully. "Well. We're at least eight mile from where the poor wife saw us. Even if she went straight to the laird at Wemyss, he'd yet to rouse his men, send them down seeking us, and then put out the word. And maybe he didn't believe her at all, when we weren't there." I cheered up a bit. "Maybe she's had a whipping to learn her not to tell lies, eh?" They grinned. "Aye, we'd best still be careful, but if we hide the fire well, I think we might risk it. The mist'll hide the smoke, and for sure we're needing the heat."

The Maid and I clambered out of the skiff and up the bank, gathering dry twigs and branches, while Davie splashed along the shore for the mussels. We found a tiny clear hollow, well hidden by rocks and trees all round, about a hundred yards in from the shore, and I started a fire with my knife and a stone. When Davie brought up his tunic full of shellfish, the flames had died to a wee bed of coals all ready for them. Warming our hands luxuriously, we watched them slowly gaping, dribbled salty water on the sweet orange meat inside, and happily scorched our fingers and lips on the hot shells.

As we sat back at last, content for the moment, tucking yet more in round the hot ash, the sun finally burned through the mist and into the sheltered hollow. It was warm and comfortable, and the sweet, heavy scent of the may blossom humming with bees all round us hung like incense. The bairns' eyes were blinking drowsily; so were mine. The boat hadn't been the softest of beds.

"Run down to the boatie, Davie, and fetch us up the blankets," I said. "We'll just wait up here, where it's warmer." He roused reluctantly, stretching and grinning, and moved away to the gap down to the beach. The Maid picked up another mussel, looked at it for a minute, shook her head with a sigh, and put it back. "Full?" I asked her, and she nodded with a sleepy murmur and smile. Lucky to forget that easy! I wished I could. But I'd not spoil it for her.

Suddenly Davie raced back through the broom bushes. We sat up, alarmed, hearing for the first time the sound of horses and men down by the water.

"It's him!" hissed Davie. "Macduff o' Donibristle!"

I couldn't believe it. "How?" I asked. "How did he—"

"Sh!" he gestured fiercely. "How should I know? But he's found the boat. The beggar wife's with him! And they'll find where we climbed the brae—I slipped as I was coming up with the mussels, and there's a clear trace! Run!"

We were already running, up the far side of the hollow and away through the trees. The Maid was gasping a bit, but with fullness, not the old distress. Luckily, we were on the edge of the great forest that had once run nearly right across Fife, and there was plenty of it left: trees, bushes, hillocks, and dips to hide an army. The old bracken rustled under our feet, and the brambles hidden under it tripped us, but if we could get far enough in, we were safe.

Unless we met an outlaw band. Or a sounder of wild boar. Or a pack of wolves—no, that wasn't likely. I hoped.

But now how could we warn Peem? Or even find him?

As we ran, Davie and I gave Marie a hand. She was stronger than she had been, but still not as fit as we were. She had her pride, though, and tugged herself free except clambering over fallen tree-trunks or leaping burns. There was a confused din behind us, but when I paused for a second to look back I could see only leaves. Luckily, we were all in colours easy to hide; my kirtle was green, the Maid's dark blue, Davie's tunic brown. After a bit, we eased our pace and stopped behind a clump of whins.

"Had they hounds with them, Davie?" I panted.

"No, Meg, thank God. They were all archers on horseback that I saw, about a dozen. And that beggar wife sitting like a lady up behind one o' them. What for would she do a thing like that, after we helped save her and her bairn?"

I shook my head. "Did you not see how thin they all were? Just a handful o' bones. If my child was starving, I might be tempted myself to win some silver, even this way." Davie wasn't convinced and growled deep in his throat, but said no more, and I turned to the Maid. "How's it with you, pet? All right?"

She nodded, bent double and heaving for breath, but found energy for a quick smile. "Right enough, Meg!" she whispered, and I was proud of her.

"Well, what now, Meg?"

I could have seen Davie far enough. It was aye me to decide! "We can't go back to the boat. And we'd best move on, in case he can get dogs from a house nearby. But which way?" I looked round, trying to think. Which way? The sun was half up—it must be in the south-east. "We'll head that way—west. It'll take us that bit closer to Peem's road back. I don't know the paths here, but that's the way to Dunfermline, I'm thinking. Watch out for folk, and keep your ears open!" And never mention the kind of men, or animals, we might meet.

They nodded, getting their second wind with the brief pause. "Aye," said Davie, "and we'll walk in water whenever we can, just to be sure no hound can follow us." That was good thinking.

It was hard going except where we found a stand of beeches, that kill everything beneath them, and could trot on the even brown mat below them. We splashed along several burns, in and out of pools and bogs, wide around fields by a wee loch, and away up a burn that trickled down the foot of a long slope. It ran the way we wanted, and we scrambled up it among the brambles and alders, the flowering may, whin, and broom, our faces and arms scratched as bad as our legs with the jagged branches. But then the burn turned alongside a road, quite a good track, likely to the farm we'd carefully avoided by the loch, and we made better time. I carried the Maid a good bit of the way.

At last I called a halt. "We must be near half-way to Dunfermline now, I'm sure," I panted. "And dogs'll never track us the way we've come. We're safe for a while. I'm fair beat." I collapsed on the bank of the burn, where it had cut deep down beside a huge beech tree. "I don't know about you bairns, but—"

"Who's a bairn?" demanded Davie in mock anger. He wasn't much out of breath—he'd been scouting ahead, not carrying the lass—and rather excited than scared by the adventure. He grinned at me and the Maid. "I'm fine."

"So'm I," piped up the lassie's voice where her knees wavered by the tree. "But if you need a rest, Meg, you sit and we'll wait for you."

We were forced to laugh. "Aye, well, pettie," I told her, "if you're that fresh, you can go up the brae with Davie and look out for Peem, as well as for Sir James." They sobered at once, glancing round the dense green around us.

Davie took the wee lass's hand. "Come on, Marie," he said. "I'll climb a tree for a better view." He winked at me. "You can give me a punt up, eh?" As they scrambled off, her voice breathlessly demanding what a punt up was, I sank back with a sigh into the hollow between two great roots, leaned back on the smooth grey bark, and in spite of the danger, in spite of my dad and how I should be crying for him—a tear slipped out, but only one—in spite of my worries over Peem and outlaws and Sir James and wild beasts, I fell sound asleep.

When I awoke with a start, Inge was looking down at me.

DEATH OF A MAID

◆

I sat up with a gasp of surprise. There were others with her: the Lady of Carrick, an older man, and a younger, a right dandy, and a body of servants in the yellow and red de Brus livery. But Inge filled my eyes.

She no longer looked like a girl. She was a woman now, strong and confident, needing no bright colours, furs, or embroidery to draw the eye. Her robes were practical for travelling, plain dark grey like a nun's gown, but her silver-gold hair was held in a gold net, not a coif, to show she was a maid, not a bride of Christ, and the gold and pearl brooch glowing at the neck of her cloak would have bought three books for any convent. Her warm lips smiled at me. Her cold eyes did not.

"Aye, Meg. I'm glad to see you well," she murmured in that singing, gentle voice I remembered—but now I sensed the granite strength behind it. "I knew somehow you weren't drowned. I was sure I'd have felt it, and I didn't. It's good to find I was right, eh?" That was why she was glad; not my health.

The Lady of Carrick leaned forward from her seat high on a great chestnut horse, holding her groom's belt to steady herself. "Is that girl the reason you insisted we come round all this way, Inge? Who is she?" Her voice was still just as keen and haughty as her face, and the odd half-French accent was as clear as I minded it.

Inge turned her head slightly, but not her eyes. "Madame, pray allow me to introduce my sister to you. Margaret, rise and show courtesy to my mistress." As I struggled to my feet and curtsied, the more clumsily in comparison with her elegance, she didn't offer to help me. I wondered where were—no! She could aye tell what was in my mind. I must get her away from here as fast as I could—and not let her know I'd anything at all to hide. Pray my face wouldn't betray me! Think on something else—not—

"You're here all alone, Meg?" Inge's voice was a touch sharper. "I heard your laddie with the—mischancy face was drowned? There's been no word o' him since the death o' his ill-fated father." She glanced up at the nobles. "I foretold Master Spens's death years before it happened. Did I not, Meg?"

The break in her stare at me had given me time to gather my wits. "Aye, you did that, Inge. I'm that pleased to meet up with you! I'm promised now to wed the lad that saved me from the shipwreck. You maybe mind on him—Peem."

I could see her thinking back. "Peem? Oh, aye. That's the lad helped save your life at the whale, isn't it? But a cottar laddie—what a sore come-down for you! And it might reflect bad on me; maybe I should forbid it. He's saved her twice, it seems," she explained to her mistress, who was fidgeting.

More than that, did she but know, I thought.

But the nobleman was restless, too. "What for are we

wasting time, Inge? We've not that long to gain the Border."

She smiled at him, and he quietened. "Patience, Lord Robert, patience. Do I often waste your time?" She turned back to me, and the dark blue-grey eyes were piercing and deep. "Where have you been this half-year past, Meg?"

Tell the truth when you can. And don't look her in the eyes. "An island in the Orkneys. We were cast up on it, and the folk there took us in."

"We? Who, exactly?" The tone was cutting.

"Me and Peem." Don't think on—

She wasn't quite happy. "No one else? Hm. Did you see the Maid drowned?"

A trick one, this, I thought. "No. We weren't on board then. The sea took us off when the aftercastle was swept away. But we heard the Maid was cast ashore dead after the shipwreck." I had to get her off this, before I made a mistake. "Was that not the word you had yourself?"

"Aye . . . and something about a popinjay that was blown ashore, and for that it could speak they thought it was an angel and brought it to the bishop." The Maid would be glad to know what became of it, I thought with a daft giggle I clamped hard down inside me. Asa used say your mouth could shut tight to stop your thoughts getting out. Typical Asa. No time for that now—keep your mind on Inge! "Where's your man, then, Meg? Not a very loving callant, to leave you alone like this."

"He's away to"—what could I say?—"to see can he find a garron for me. For I've hurted my"—better not say my ankle, she might take a look at it—besides, I've already stood up without wincing—telling lies is awful difficult—cough to cover the hesitation—"my back, not that bad, but I can't walk far. I fell yesterday."

"Aye? A sore thing, that. How did it happen?"

Make her think little of me. "I tripped running from a cow and her calf." How long could I keep it up? I wasn't blushing, thank the Lord. Yet. How long would she keep prying? How long would the nobles stay at peace?

Not long, it seemed. The young dandy, ages with Peem, his great white horse sidling and tossing its head till the air sang with its bridle bells, interrupted us. "Father, we've to be at Edinburgh the night. Come away, Inge, you've seen your sister. If you're concerned, put word down to Inverkeithing as we go past, an' they'll send someone out for her. We must be on our road."

Not your husband—your son. Then this must be Robert, the future King of Scots; this young callant, impatient, hard, and arrogantly selfish.

His mother nodded, smiling, but his father looked at him with dislike. "Mind what you're at with that beast!" he snapped testily as the powerful stallion bumped his own less fine gelding and nipped viciously at it. "He's wild as a fox! Where you find the gold for all your gear—that velvet's far too good for a travelling coat—I've told you till I'm sick and tired—"

"You're not the only one that's tired! I'm fair deafened with you!" This must be a familiar quarrel. Why could they not carry it on far from me? They pulled round to ride on, and Inge, with a last sharp glance, beckoned her own groom to come over and help her mount. Had I managed to get away with it? To hide—the people I mustn't think about? It looked like it. I bit my tongue to stop myself smiling. Thank God the—they'd had the sense to stay hid.

Make it look right. Whine, that would put her off. "Inge, will you not stop and help me? Take me up behind you! Pray you, do!" Pray she didn't.

The cold eyes above the charming smile slid back to me.

"But your man will be back soon, no doubt, my dear, and you'd not want to miss him," she was murmuring sweetly, when there was a thudding of hooves down the track. The youth shouted to the servants and sent his horse caracoling to the front, drawing his sword with a scrape and a cheer. No coward, then.

A troop of mounted archers charged along the path. At their head thundered Sir James. The beggar wife clung behind one. And trailing at the rear, his hands tied to a stirrup leather, ran Peem, his tunic and hose torn and the blood running down his shins where he'd fallen and dragged.

They drew rein hard when they saw the group awaiting them, weapons poised. For a few seconds there was no noise but the trampling of the horses, and then Sir James saw me. "There she's! That's the kitty I'm seekin'! Let's have a hold o' her! The bizzom's mine!" His bull bellow sent the horses rearing.

The youth forced his beast down with an ungentle hand and stood his ground. "Who, sir? And who the devil are you, that claims her?"

There was a minute of confusion while they sorted out who was who, and who wanted to arrest whom. During it, Inge kept her eye on me. As I tried to run to Peem, she gripped my arm. "No, no, wee sister," she breathed in my ear maliciously, "just you stay here. There's no hurry." As I struggled, she twisted my wrist and held me still. Her delicate hands were amazingly strong.

"Peem!" I called in distress, and his face turned towards me, swollen and bruised. His eyes were half-shut, and he hung on the rope, dropping to his bleeding knees by the horse's side, his mouth hanging open, panting heavily.

Suddenly the nobles were round me. Sir James gripped my

chin in biting fingers, and jerked my head up to look at him. "Where are they?" he demanded. "The lad and the lass? I found your callant there down the way a bittie, seeking you, and I could have hanged him there and then, but I'm that soft-hearted!" He looked round, and as his men laughed, he grinned like a rat-trap. "He says he doesn't know what I mean, but you know what, my kitty? I don't believe him. Is that not a strange thing? And me so simple!" Another guffaw. His smile vanished, but not his teeth. "I could get it out o' him, aye could I, but I'm thinking I'll be quicker asking you. Where are they, hizzy? Tell me, my bonny bird, or I'll claw out your fine billy's guts with my own hands before your face, so I will!"

I cried out as he squeezed and shook my jaw violently. I couldn't have answered even if I'd known what to say.

Help came unexpectedly. "Lass and lad? What folk are these, sir?" Inge snapped at him.

He turned and eyed her insolently. "My, my, here's another bonny bird!" He grinned. "What's your interest in them, eh?" As she stood still, unsmiling, unafraid, awaiting his reply, his grin faded, and when Sir Robert and Lady Marjory chimed in to repeat the question, he frowned. "They came with her and her callant there, in their boatie," he explained. "A wee lass and a laddie with a split lip. He's the Spens laddie, and I've a wee bit business to attend to with him, since his father's dead. But the lassie—why, d'you know her?"

The eyes of the two women had met in sudden comprehension. "I knew it!" exclaimed Inge. "I knew there was more to this day than just— Meg! Tell me now, where are they? Tell me, Meg!" She faced me, and her dark eyes held mine. Her voice was soft and hypnotic. "Tell me, Meg!" This was my sister that I still loved in spite of all. She gently stroked my cheek. "Tell me, my dear."

Oddly, it was Sir James who stopped me from speaking. "Who the hell are you, you bitch, and what the devil have you to do with my prisoner?" She startled and swung round, turning angry eyes on him, releasing me.

For one second I was free, and no eyes on me. I slipped among them and ran over to Peem. After a brief snatch after me they left me alone for the moment, seeing I couldn't escape among all the mounted archers and servants. While they argued behind me I knelt beside him. "Oh, Peem, Peem!" I whispered. It near broke my heart to see him so beaten.

Something about him puzzled me, even as he sagged against my arm. His shoulders were maybe not quite as drooping as they might be. As I took his head gently in my hands, I caught a glimpse of his eyes, alive and alert behind the huge violet swellings, glancing a brief warning at me. My heart leapt. I held him to me, my head bowed over his. The faintest whisper came to me. "Knife." What? A knife? Of course— my wee eating knife, in its sheath at my belt, its dull horn handle hidden in the folds of my kirtle.

Carefully, quickly, shielding my movements between our shoulders, I drew the short blade and slipped the hilt into his bound hands. "Away!" he whispered, but I was already moving. Now I had to move aside, to draw all eyes from him, give him a chance to free himself. Then—maybe . . .

Maybe what? Against two dozen armed servants and archers? Who did I think he was—the Archangel Michael?

As I turned aside, I saw the poor wife watching us. Had she seen? She said nothing, didn't move. She couldn't have. Could she?

I stepped away from Peem to meet their combined attack. "No, sirs, I don't know where the lad and lass are, they're nothing to us, they just shared our fire. The lad having a harelip was pure chance." They didn't believe me.

They hit me. Several teeth slackened. Sir James used his whip. I cried, and said the same thing again. At least, with the beating, my face had a good reason for being red. After a while, when my legs were sagging, they stopped and looked at one another, and Sir Robert shrugged and nodded. The next I knew, Sir James was holding me before him, my two wrists tight behind me in his left fist, while his right hand held a dagger at my throat. I couldn't struggle. He swung me round in a circle, and shouted to the forest. "Listen to me! D'you hear me, my bonny bairns? Come out o' that, you wee devils, or I'll cut her throat here and now! D'you want to see her blood? Come on, come away out!"

Inge for some reason was frowning. My head ringing, I was near fainting, and just thinking dully that it wouldn't be a bad idea if the knife point wasn't right under my chin, when there was a stir among the folk. A small figure had appeared among the trees.

"It's her! The Maid!" Lady Marjory whispered.

"No!" I cried, as loud as I could. "No!" But no one heeded the whisper.

The little figure clambered stolidly down the bank, to stop only a few feet away from us, the white cap over her cropped white hair glowing in the dappled sunlight. She curtsied. A lovely curtsy on the brown beech mould, her head high, back straight as an arrow, and her breath gasping only slightly. "Here I'm, sir," she said. "What do you want with me? Leave go o' Meg. She's done you no harm." Oh, dear God! Marie!

"And where's the laddie, then?" he asked, grinning at her tiny stateliness.

"He's run away," she said, with such assurance I could near have believed it, if I'd not known Davie better. "Leave Meg go free," she repeated.

With a bellow of laughter, he dropped my wrists and

shoved me forward so that I tripped and fell at her feet. "Your servant to command, Your Majesty!" he said with an over-elaborate bow.

He was jesting, but the words seemed to send the Lady Marjory into a fit. Suddenly she screamed like a woman de-mented. "No! I'll not allow it! You will not have it, you! It is not yours! No! Never!" Shrieking, "Never!" she snatched her son's sword from his scabbard and leapt at the Maid, who ducked in fear.

Inge cried, "No, stop!" The young man tried to catch his mother's arm. I reached up to hold her off, but I had no chance. The wild woman swung hard over my head at the lass shrinking before her, but the Maid dodged under that sweep of the blade, and the next, as the menfolk stood dumbfounded. But the third time, just as Inge caught at her free wrist, the woman thrust straight for the lass's breast. The Maid cried out, a choked scream, twisted, and fell. She crashed down into the bracken not three feet from me, the sword sticking out from the side of her chest, dragging it from Lady Marjory's hand. She kicked and moaned just once, and lay still.

Sir James laughed and clapped, and his archers cheered. Inge let go and turned away.

As the rest of us gaped, stilled by the sudden horror, Sir James stepped forward, bent, and pulled the sword with a jerk from the Maid's body. There was blood on the blade. "Aye, well, my lady," he grunted, "you know I could arraign ye for murder? For this isn't your land. There's but me has the right o' pit and gallows here." We didn't move. He laughed again, eyeing her with a sneer. "But I'll not, see, for it's a long while since I've seen a better blow! I wouldn't have expected it o' you, my lady! Not a fine court lady like yourself!"

He offered her the sword. She didn't look at it, or him, but stared in an unblinking trance at the tiny body in the bracken by her feet. Suddenly she rubbed her hands on the sides of her skirt as if to clean them, though there was no blood staining them. She shook her head angrily and turned to her son. "Robert, get me away from here," she commanded in a dry whisper. He beckoned a man to bring up the horses and took his sword from Sir James, carefully wiping the blade in the bracken, his mouth twisted.

His mother lifted a foot to the hand of the groom ready to help her mount, but suddenly changed her mind. Like a weasel she spun on Inge. "You, how dared you try to stop me?" she demanded.

Inge was looking down at the little body among the crushed green fronds. "That wasn't necessary," she murmured. "She'd never have been—"

"Be silent!" snarled Lady Marjory, her lips snapping tight shut. She glared bitterly. "You said she was dead!"

Inge raised a dark gaze to her. "It was the other lass I saw. I know that now," she murmured slowly. Then her mood flared to a matching anger. "I promised you," she said clearly, "that I would clear the way for your family to claim the crown o' Scotland." The young man was staring at her, his jaw dropped. "I had done so. That bairn was no threat to you." She looked sick.

I added my word to hers. "No, my lady," I said bitterly. "She just wanted to go away and be an ordinary wee lassie, and it was all settled, that's what she was going to do. She wasn't going to claim the crown. You'd no need to slay her. Oh, Marie, Marie!" I sat by the body, too tired to weep.

Inge looked at me oddly. "You love her that much, Meg?"

"Near as much as I love you!" I said, bitter again. "And

see where it's got me! And all o' us—Dad, and Asa, and the rest o' them!"

"Believe me," she said softly, "I never meant that. If I'd known that would happen, I'd—I'd never have started." Her eyes were blue. I did believe her.

"Is that true, Mother?" the young man was asking. "That's why Inge's been with us these years? I aye wondered why . . . You wanted to be queen!"

The lady stiffened, and tugged her wrist out of his urgent hand. "No!" she said. "I wanted you to be king! King of Scots! And so you will be, my son!"

He swung away, and up to his saddle. "Over a bairn's body!" he snarled.

She faced him out. "Over a thousand, if need be! Over anything!"

But when he turned raging down at her, she flinched. "Did I ask you? You'd have me eat the bairn's heart if you thought it would help me! Well, I'm for no more! Get rid o' that witch! I never want to set eyes on her again!" Or on you, his eyes shouted, but he didn't speak it out loud.

She stammered, "What? What?" recoiling from his fury. "But all I do is for you, my Robert!" As he reined his horse back, she trailed after it, her face working, her hands raised beseechingly. "Robert? Robert!"

Suddenly her husband, that she had totally ignored, grasped her arm and spun her round to face him. "And what about me, then?" he demanded. "Your other Robert! What had ye planned for your husband? I'm in his road, am I not? What poison did ye have ready for me? What witchcraft?" Her eyes didn't sink before his. He was afraid, and the more spitefully angry for it. "Well, lady," he snapped at her, "I'll remove myself from danger—and from you! Robert!" The young man, speaking to his grooms, ignored him. His head snapped round, though, when his father shouted so that the forest rang, "I hereby renounce my claim, and my father's, to the crown of Scotland! Let my son Robert claim it in my place, if he dares—and may it bring him no good fortune!"

He grabbed the reins from his groom, pulled himself into his saddle, and leaned down to his wife. "Let that satisfy you, wife! I never wanted this crazy claim; it was my daft father and you were so hot for it! Now I'll be off to England, to my estates there, and I'll assure Edward o' my loyalty and live in peace and comfort. If I see you again at the Day o' Judgement, wife, it'll be too soon! You understand me?" He jerked his horse's head round and galloped off down the track, his servants flocking excited behind.

The future king gaped like an idiot for a second, and then, with a dawning grin, struck in his spurs and galloped after, with no glance to his mother nor to the wee lass on whose death his claim was based.

The woman stared after them. Her shoulders drooped a moment, till she took a deep breath and reared her head again. Her eyes rested a long second on Inge; then she turned deliberately to Sir James, standing enjoying the show.

"Sir, you understand I would be most displeased if anyone spread word about this, no?" she said with dignity. It was as if the screeching harridan who had stabbed the poor Maid was a different person. She never lowered her eyes to the body or me, but ignored us. So did Sir James.

He leered at her. "I take your meaning, my lady." He nodded jovially. "Aye, aye. None o' my men'll say a word if I forbid it."

"Nor mine," she agreed. "It will be worth your while, my lord. Well worth." And went on smoothly, "They are not the only ones here."

An eyebrow rose, but not in surprise. "No," he grinned

admiringly. "Jock, lad"—he turned to his men—"put a blade through that—what! Where is he?"

The rope that had tied Peem's wrists dangled empty by the horse's side.

The huge man turned puce with rage. "How the devil did he get out o' that? It's cut! Who gave him a knife? Who was supposed to be watching him?" There was, naturally, no answer. "Get out, you eyeless, useless devils! Find him, or I'll hang you instead o' him! And all your misbegotten kinsfolk alongside o' you! Move, you clods, before I skin you!" His whip whistled to spur his men on. They scattered angrily and anxiously into the forest, some afoot, some still mounted, searching the thickets for Peem, while their master stood in the path and shouted at them. He seemed to have forgotten Davie for the moment.

At last he turned back and caught sight of me, still collapsed nerveless in the ferns by the Maid's body, my bruised face and jaw throbbing, my legs like jelly. He looked at me consideringly for a second and glanced across at Lady Marjory for her nod. "Dod, what a waste!" His eyes gleamed, admiring but regretful. "But if you want silence, my lady, we can't take the chance. Donal, spit that wee hizzy!" he shouted. A stocky man left the horses that he'd been holding and started towards me, a broad hand going to the hilt of his knife.

Lady Marjory's face beside Sir James was totally calm. Her sharp voice cut through the men's shouts around us. "I said anyone, sir. Anyone at all."

His eyes lit up with sheer pleasure in destruction. "Right you are, my lady!" he shouted, laughing again. "Take them both, Donal!"

The man grinned and saluted obligingly, and the long knife glinted.

I staggered up. "No!" I tried to say. "Stop it! I'll not let you . . ." I stepped foolishly in front of Inge, spreading my arms out to keep him off her.

I heard her draw in her breath hard behind me, and, ignoring the man's approach, she turned me to face her. "You'd save me? Why?" Suddenly her whole face changed, melted, looked as if she was going to laugh and weep together. She drew a long, shuddering breath. "O-oh! My God—how could I be so blind? That old hell-cat—I should have known better! Meg, my dear!"

Her eyes were bluer than I'd ever seen them. Behind me, Donal's feet scuffed the leaves. I swung despairingly round to face him as he came towards us and reached for my shoulder, drawing back his knife.

Inge's firm hand pushed me violently, knocking me sideways away from the man's grasp, across the beech roots, out of immediate danger. She stepped between me and the burly archer, she now sheltering me, showing no fear. As he stepped towards us, she lifted a hand as if to bless—or curse. "Touch me, man, and you'll not see the sunset!" she warned him. He hesitated a second, but Sir James behind him laughed even louder, and it spurred him on. Slowly, it seemed, he reached out, gripped her raised wrist, and pulled her forward.

She made no sound but a little click in her throat. Her eyes and mouth opened, it seemed more in surprise at his daring to touch her than at the hurt, and as the blade drew out, she sank gently to sit as if resting at the foot of the beech tree. Sir James's roars of laughter echoed emptily in my skull.

She tugged urgently at my skirt. "Run, Meg!" she whispered.

Movement came back to me. I scuttled blindly where she pointed, across the track under the nose of Lady Marjory's horse that reared and knocked Sir James aside as he grabbed for me, and away in among the trees. But I was stiff and tired, and the footsteps of Donal and his master thudded closer.

The beggar wife leapt out in front of me. I yelped with terror as she yelled, "I've got her, my lord!" But as she reached for me, her arms were far too high, and I ducked under them, catching a glimpse of her grinning as she fell with a screech to trip the first pursuer into the brambles. Then I was past, only one man behind me. The burn turned here, deep and muddy. I splashed down into it, and as my feet were slowed, I threw myself forward into the water away from a swinging blade and a shout of triumph.

A pair of boots splashed in beside me. A voice yelled, "Right, hizzy, I've got you now!" A hand gripped and hauled at my hair, but suddenly there was a shout and a crack, and a scream of pain, surprise, anger. A sword fell splash beside me. I was dropped, and rolled over to see Sir James, astride my legs, screeching and holding his right elbow, while his hand hung limp and twisted.

Peem! Peem and his sling! Oh, thank God!

Donal leapt down into the bed of the burn beside his master, his long knife drawn back. There was a twang and a softer thud. He folded down into the water by my side, an arrow sticking out of his chest. Hurt as he was, he started to push himself up. I tried to crab away, but Sir James was standing on my skirt. Moaning and cursing, Donal stabbed over at me.

Davie came sliding down the bank, holding a bow, and swung it so that its tip knocked the archer's wrist. He dropped his knife and had to spend a moment hunting it. Davie tried to pull me away, but he slipped in the mud. Donal grappled with him, and Sir James kicked the lad's feet from under him and trampled him. The archer grimly heaved his knife up again. Both the men were hurt, weakened, and Davie was agile and wiry, struggling for his very life, but he had no chance. I screamed for Peem, but he was dodging through the trees, fending off the knives of two of the other archers with a rough branch. He couldn't help this time.

Suddenly I came to my senses. Why was I sitting useless, while Davie was in danger? I groped desperately in the peaty mud round me till at last my knuckles scraped on something long and straight, hard and heavy. It was Sir James's sword. I was holding it by the blade, but quickly changed my grip to the hilt, and as Donal stabbed again with his long knife, so did I with the sword. I felt the point hit him and slide in, I don't know where, for my eyes had shut tight, but he yelled, splashed with a choking sigh into the mud by me, and lay still.

I opened my eyes on Sir James, squinting down at me, clutching his elbow that was shattered by Peem's slingshot. He kicked forward at me, but as I struggled to rise to my feet, the sword blood-stained in my trembling hand, yelling desperately with all my remaining breath, wild as any madwoman and dripping water-weed and mud, he changed his mind. Painfully he stumbled up the bank towards where he'd left his horses, shouting for his men to rally round him.

Lady Marjory screamed at him to finish us off, and as he paid her no heed, she grabbed and shook his arm. The hurt one. With a bellow he struck her across the face with his other fist, knocking her to the ground. Her groom lifted her over to her horse, gaping and gobbling with shock. As the man hoisted her to the saddle and sprang up before her, Davie's bow sounded again. The arrow pierced Lady Marjory's skirt and saddle. The horse reared, and the lady near fell off. She screeched and kicked wildly across the crupper of the beast, mantle flying, her man having to hold her on with one hand while with the other he tugged vainly at the reins of the bolting animal. Davie cheered gaily as they vanished down the track.

He was enjoying himself, dodging about among the trees near the hazel bushes where I was now hiding. His bow was too big for him and kept getting caught in the branches. I never knew he could curse like that. Where had he got the bow? From one of the archers, of course. But how? Peem, most like, who had disappeared. So had his opponents—no, one was lying still. I didn't dare shout for him, in case one of the searching archers found me. I'd done all I could. I crouched dripping in under the leaves, clutching the sword, praying Peem and Davie would be safe. Why had my eyes shut as I struck? I hadn't meant them to. I wondered had the poor wife meant to catch me, in truth, or let me by? She was well away; I'd never know now. Was that man dead that I'd hit? I hoped so. Or did I? Think about it later.

Davie cheered again. His archery practice was proving worthwhile at last. Thuds and yells among the trees showed where Peem's slingshots were landing. He must be well yet. Thank God.

At last Sir James and his archers ran—those that could. Eight of his troop as well as himself were hurt, and three bodies were slung over their horses as they galloped off, cursing us and shouting threats. "I know you, Davie Spens!" Sir James's voice sounded thin down the track. "I'll find you, never fear it! I'll destroy you, you and your family both! And that brown bitch . . ." It faded with the hoofbeats.

We came out cautiously onto the path and looked at each other. Slowly it sank in. "Beelzebub's bum! We've won!" Davie cheered, waving his bow in triumph.

Then he looked across where the Maid lay, and his wide grin faded away.

BETTER THAN A QUEEN

◆

"I never thought we could live," said Peem soberly. His swollen, bruised face was sad.

"Nor me, Peem," I whispered.

He put an arm round my damp shoulders as I trembled and sagged, for I'd small strength left now. "Davie lad," he said, "go down the road a bit an' watch that they don't come back, eh?"

Davie looked briefly as if he was going to obey without argument, but then he saw Inge. His face tightened, and he cried, "Eh, look there! Damn her to hell! It was her did all this! Killed my dad! And poor wee Marie! And all the rest! I'll—" He stopped. What more could he do to her?

"Leave her be, lad," Peem's deep voice advised. And Davie struggled uselessly for a second to find fitting words or deeds, and went limp. He gave one great sob and, without another word, went off up the track, head down, slashing his bow at the unoffending bracken.

Peem left me by my sister and clambered down to where

the burn ran into a tiny pool just beyond the roots of the beech tree where Inge lay. Stiffly I knelt down by her.

She leaned back against the grey bark, her cloak just a shade darker, supported by the two roots where I had slept such a little time before. Her skirts and cloak were spread elegantly even now. She smiled up at me, the shadow clear gone from her eyes, gentle blue and rather rueful. "I'm sorry, Meg," she murmured. "I never dreamed I'd want to hurt you."

"Did ye no?" said Peem, wincing as he washed his cuts and bruises in the cold water by our feet. "Well, mistress, ye made a damn good try at it."

"Oh, wheesht, Peem," I said. I'd no tears. "I aye loved you, Inge. I never stopped loving you, I think, even when I hated you."

"Well, lass, it looks like Asa was right." Her speech was slipping back to the broad, gentle tones of the old times. "Old bitch. The one o' us has been the death o' the other, right enough. If she hadn't said it, maybe . . . But . . ."

"You saved my life, Inge," I said. "You did. And you died for me."

"Ach, she was bound to kill me anyway, sooner or later," she murmured. Her voice was growing weaker. "There's another bitch, eh? After all I'd done for her . . . And her son . . . Ach, well. Mind it wasn't just me helped you."

"Aye," I said. "Peem. He's saved me that often, I think he could do it in his sleep."

Peem shook his head as he climbed back up the bank to stand beside me. "If Meg hadn't contrived tae slip me her knife, I couldn't have done nothin'," he said. A tiny warmth glowed deep down beneath my misery.

She smiled again. "An' Davie." I nodded. "Tell him I'm sorry for what I did to him as well. His father was a good man. It's been—ach, well." She sighed again, deeply, and seemed to gather her mind again with some difficulty. "And you owe the wee lass there. She came out to save you. You've a great gift, lass. A gift o' love, for we all did it for love o' you."

"Love o' me?" I couldn't understand. "What for should they love me?"

"You don't know?" I shook my head. "That's why." At my puzzled expression, she started to chuckle. Then she coughed, her hand tightened briefly on mine, and she winced for the first time. Her eyes lifted up to the sunlight glinting through the gauzy greens above us. "I don't want to die. But I should have known. I saw this place once long past, in the red of the fire. The beeches and the burn. I should have known it. But . . ." Her voice faded as one shoulder half-shrugged.

I looked up at Peem. "Run for a priest!" I whispered.

He shook his head. "There's no time, mistress," he said.

She'd heard us, and gripped my hand tight again for a second. "No priest." Her breath was rasping a little now. "I have lived by the law. My master's law. To wish, to dare, to obey, to keep silent. He'll not forget me." Whose law was that, I wondered; none I knew. Her master? The Devil? Surely not! Her soul would burn in hell-fire for ever! But sure she wasn't all bad! As I started to pray for her, she smiled at me. "Never fear for me, lass. I chose my own way long ago. But you mind and keep clear, like I said. You've a touch o' the Sight yourself, but not the art to control it."

"The Sight?"

"Aye. How often do you know what's to be, eh?"

I thought back. I did seem to know things sometimes before they happened. Did she mean . . . "Am I a witch then, Inge?"

She smiled hazily. "No, lass. You could have been, if Asa

hadn't taken against you so sore. She taught me, and she might have taught you. But she wouldn't. Now mind, you must never . . . never . . ."

Her voice failed and she lay still for a minute. Then her hand shook mine lightly. "Take this, Meg. You'll have more need on it than me." The long, white fingers of her free hand fumbled with the brooch at her throat, and as the clasp gave, I caught it. The great pearls gleamed. She nodded, the faintest dip of her head. "Aye, that's it. Fishes' tears, they say. But they'll bring you no harm. It's yours now. And the gold net from my hair."

As her eyes wandered dreamily to the blossoming bushes all round us, she nodded again. "It's bonny here. Bonny. Aye. Bury me here, Meg lass. No consecrated ground." Her lips twitched slightly. "All the good pious souls would spin like tops if I was laid alongside o' them."

The joke took its toll of her. She coughed again, and a speck of blood rose scarlet at her lip. I wiped it away, and there was a pause, as she gathered her strength anew. Her hand pressed mine, her eyes were anxious. "You still love me?"

"For ever, Inge. I aye loved you." It seemed to reassure her.

"And I love you too. I know it now. I'm sorry. I've done my best for you, Meg. To make up for . . . It's the last o' it. See?" She gestured, a hand twitch to the side, but I'd no time to look. Slowly her smile faded. Her grip on my hand slackened. A soft breath whispered, "No tears, now . . . nor mourning. Be happy." I could just make it out. "Love . . ." Her eyes lost their focus. Oh, Inge!

She was dead. And the Maid was dead. It had all gone wrong. And all my fault, interfering as usual. I just sat, holding Inge's slack hand, wishing I was dead too.

Peem gripped my shoulder sore and shook me slightly. And again. I looked up, irritated, to see what was bothering him.

Over where Inge had been trying to point, there was a stir in the bracken. Just where the Maid had fallen.

I screamed. Davie came running back, bow ready. Then he tossed it aside, shouting, and leapt forward to help the wee lass up to the path.

She had a torn gash in her kirtle on the left side of her chest, and a great dark red stain all round it of drying blood. But she was alive. I could scarce bring myself to touch her, even as Peem lifted her in his strong arms and set her where she'd not see Inge.

She was boasting. "See, Meg?" pointing proudly. "I've a cut right round from here to here, and oh, it was sore! But I didn't move!" As I said nothing, she looked doubtful. "So they wouldn't know I was still on life! Was that not right?"

"Right?" I finally managed to speak. "Aye—aye, lass. But how—"

"How did it not kill me?" She grinned and showed us, wincing. "See there!" Inside her gown, pinned to the seam at the high waist, was the great triangular brooch we'd given to Mistress Ludmila on Sanday. "She gave it back to me, while you were all looking at the figurehead. She said to keep it hid, so you'd not be insulted by thinking she didn't value your gift. But she wanted me to have it, for she said it was worth a deal o' silver, and would maybe save me some day. And it has, hasn't it?"

"Aye, Marie, it has that," said Davie, fingering the deep dent the blade had made in the silver. The garnet dragons' eyes were like drops of blood. He was the only one of us that still had his voice. Peem and I were speechless.

"And I did just what you said."

"What was that, lass?" asked Davie as we stared yet.

"When that lady stabbed me. She hit me with the sword, and it knocked me down, and my new gown tore. And then I heard you, clear as anything, Meg, saying, 'Keep still! They'll kill you if you move!' So I did it. What you said. My side hurted sore, but I lay still and didn't stir. Whenever I wanted to move, I heard you tell me to be still. But I felt awful fuzzy-headed for a whilie there. Your voice sounded strange—not like you, not really. And then I heard you talking, and I knew it was safe to come out." As I still didn't respond, her triumphant smile wavered. "What's wrong, Meg? Did I not do it right?"

Seeing her worried, I untangled my wits. "Nothing's wrong, lass, you did fine. Fine. Better than any o' us could have guessed. We're—we're surprised, that's all. Aye. And pleased." It was the best I could manage, with Peem and Davie gazing from me to Inge, lying there in the grass. They knew I'd said nothing. So whose voice had she heard?

At last I pulled myself together enough to tear a strip of my kirtle and put a bandage on the Maid's cut. It was nasty, not very deep, but long and ragged, torn by the edge of the brooch, and hard to bind, being right round by her ribs. It was clean enough, but when she tried to walk her legs gave under her, and we sat her down to rest while we buried Inge.

A good bit up from the track, where we'd not likely be seen, a great tree had been thrown down by a gale, with a hole where its roots had torn out of the ground. We carried Inge's body up to it, and the lads started clearing away the soft, broken earth to deepen the hole, while I washed, rinsed out our filthy clothes in the burn, and gathered leaves and flowers.

As they worked, with hands and a split branch, Peem told us his news.

Master Grossmeyer had been most helpful. He had a sister in Flanders, her own children all grown and away from home, who he said would be glad to take in the orphaned daughter of a friend of his, and ask no awkward questions. "A good soul, and kindly; das little mädchen will happy with her be. And we will nothing about Norroway or kings say to nobody, ya? And you will tell her to keep her silence absolute about it also. Absolute, ya! She will with a friend of mine go, whose ship Inverkeithing for Oostende will leave with coals on dis same evening's tide. I a letter to him will write, and to mine sister also. It is for you der mädchen to bring to der harbour in good time. Mine friend with a good man will send her on to Bruges. And I all charges will pay, for memory of mine good friend Patrick Spens. Ya, it will all be well."

Peem imitating the strange accent made the wee lass laugh, a hand pressed to her sore side where she sat wrapped in Inge's cloak on the fallen trunk. "So ye've tae be down at the quay at sunset the day, Marie," he went on, "an' we'll just slip ye aboard quiet-like with nobody seein' nothin'." We looked at the sun. "No, never fear, there's a fair bittie time left, an' no that far tae go."

"And then we'll need to be off to Dunfermline, eh?" said Davie. He didn't sound over-enthusiastic.

It didn't surprise me that the Maid's face fell, for I knew she'd not want to leave us, but strangely, Peem's face was even longer. "What is it, Peem?" I asked anxiously, setting down my bundle of golden broom. "What's wrong?"

Davie glanced at him, stopped his digging, and straightened his back. He was standing by Peem, a fine lad now and I never heeded his mouth, brave and confident, nearly tall, lively, good-natured, and helpful, aye ready to give me a hand if I needed it.

I suddenly knew I'd rather have Peem's hand. It wasn't

that I didn't love Davie; I did. But more like a younger brother. He'd grow into a fine man, but I wanted a man now, not in five or ten years. It was Peem's arms I wanted round me, and had done for long enough, though I hadn't known why. I wanted, I needed, his strength, his comfort.

But I was promised to Davie.

A promise could be broken.

A solemn oath before God?

Our fathers' promise, not ours.

But it would hurt Davie sore, to be rejected, wouldn't it? Could I do that to him, when I liked and loved him so well?

Dear God, what should I do?

If I chose Peem, I couldn't go back to Mother Alison with Davie. I'd maybe never see him again, for he'd not want to see me, that was for sure, when I'd shamed him before all his family and friends. And Dad was dead—we'd nowhere else to go. What could we do? But if I chose Davie, how could I bear having Peem by me? I'd have to send him away. But how could I bear that?

My thoughts had only taken a second, but in my confusion, I'd a hard time catching up with what Peem was saying. "Ye can't go tae Dunfermline, Davie." We all gaped at him. "For your mother's no there, she's at her brother's house in Dumbarton. An' if she was here, ye couldn't go near her."

"Why not, Peem?" Davie asked, as I tried to find my breath.

"I'm sorry, Davie, but it seems she's gone a bittie daft. She blames Mistress Meg for everythin' as has come on her—the loss o' her man an' her youngest son, an' her place in the town."

"What?" I sat down by the Maid with a bump.

"Aye. Now her man's dead, she's no the wife o' the greatest

merchant in the town. An' she'll no let nobody have anything tae do wi' her, for shame that her man didn't bring back the Maid. An' Master Grossmeyer says now she's clean off her head about ye, mistress. I'm that sorry, Davie. She runs about wi' a kitchen knife seekin' ye, Meg, tae kill ye. Ye wouldn't be safe in the same town wi' her, leave alone the same house."

Davie was horrified. "Will she no get better?" The poor lad sounded scared.

"Ach, she's fine, Davie, except when she thinks on Meg. Master Grossmeyer said she'll likely calm down in a year or so. Ye mind she was aye—aye nervous. Wi' her turns. Aye ready tae be hurt or upset, eh? Aye."

"I must go to her!" He set a hand on the edge of the hole, as if to leap out and go right away.

"Just as ye think right yoursel', lad," Peem said doubtfully, "but there's no need, I'm thinkin', no right the now, anyway. She's her daughters an' her brother's family tae mind her. An' if she doesn't mend, they've spoken tae the convent there, an' they'll take her in as a boarder, an' tend tae her there. Seein' you might even make her worse, Master Grossmeyer was sayin'." After a pause, Davie nodded, accepting it. Peem looked round at us all. "Aye. But what do we do now?"

We blinked round at each other blankly. The Maid's hand, cold in mine, tugged hard. "Can you not come with me, Meg, then? I'm—I'm feared to go on my own. All that way, to strangers. Please, Meg!" Her lip trembled and she bit it to steady it, her big eyes pleading.

I was shaking my head when Davie spoke. "Why not? It's perfect! We'll all go!" As we all stared, he flushed with excitement. "Think on it! Look, Meg!" His hands danced on the edge of the hole as he sputtered in his rush to get the words out. "Here's me with Sir James threatening murder to me and all my family. And the way we dealt with him, you can't blame him, eh? It's been worrying me. But Ma and my sisters are far away from him now, and like to stay far, so she's safe if I'm not about to draw his eye. My big brothers can look after theirselves. And here's you that Ma can't take in, and Peem's not got a place neither. We're all three homeless. The one thing that's sure is that Marie here wants you and needs you—she's hurted, and—d'you not see? We can all go together!" He ran out of breath, his eyes eagerly searching our faces.

The Maid's smile lit up all her face. "Aye, Meg, aye!" she breathed, and bit her lip again, but to hold back her joy.

Peem's head was down, shaking slowly in absolute refusal. Davie started to argue, beating out his message urgently on Peem's arm, and the Maid knelt down by the edge of the hole to join her pleading to his. Their voices echoed round my head as on the day of Inge's trial. I looked over at her, lying there quietly under the hazels, and as if she'd spoken to me I knew what I had to do. This was the time of all times for honesty.

"Stop! Stop it! Listen to me!" I said. Whatever they'd been saying, they stopped and stared. "Davie," I said gently, "I've something to tell you. I love you. I'd be proud and happy to wed you, whether your mother wished it or no—but I love Peem as well." I didn't look up to see how they reacted. I clasped my hands between my knees and forced myself to go on. "Peem, I've but just discovered this the day. Just this minute, even. I love Davie like a brother. But it's you I want to wed. Now"—I paused painfully, and had to breathe deeply and swallow before I went on—"that's how I feel. I love you both, but I'd rather wed Peem. But I don't want to lose either one o' you. I'd like it if we could all go together. That's what I want. Now it's for you to say what you want."

I waited, my head down, pleating my dress between my fingers. It was near dry now. A lass shouldn't go about telling lads she loved them. It might put them both right off me. What would they do?

Somebody took my hand. I looked at the sleeve. It was Davie.

"Meg, are you saying you hope to wed Peem, but if he doesn't want you you'll take me as a kind o' second-best? I can't say I'm flattered—"

Just as I was about to protest that that wasn't what I'd meant, Peem interrupted. "Ach, be quiet, ye wee devil!" My heart stopped, almost. He leapt out of the hole, and his huge fist took my hand from the lad's, pulling me to my feet. "Meg— Mistress Meg—d'ye mean that? That ye'd rather wed me?" I nodded blindly. "I've loved ye this three year. Are ye sure ye love me?" I nodded again. "Look at me, mistress. I'm just a cottar's lad. Are ye certain?"

I lifted my head. "I'm but a craftsman's daughter myself, Peem," I said. "And I'm not that pretty—not the now, anyway!"

But as I put my free hand up to my swollen face with its split lip and bruises turning as blue as his own, Peem took hold of it and shook his head. "The bonniest lassie in the whole world," he murmured. As he leaned towards me, I tilted my face up to meet his gentle kiss, and the earth at the edge of the hole caved in under us.

We crashed down on our backsides in the soft soil on top of Davie, all three yelling with surprise.

Davie and the Maid near split themselves laughing. "Ah, true romance!" spluttered Davie as we disentangled our-selves.

With a sigh, Peem hoisted me back to firm ground. "We'll get away from these bairns sometime," he promised me. "But,

Meg, my dear, I'm that glad! Ye don't know what it's been like. You near drownin', an' then flirtin' wi' me up at Sanday, an' then comin' down in that wee boatie, an' all the time I couldn't let on anythin' o' how I felt—" He bit at the back of his hand to hide his face and his feelings.

My heart was so full of happiness I could scarce breathe. Then I thought about my other lad. "What about you, Davie?" I asked. "You—you don't mind?"

He grinned wide. "Ach, Meg, I knew he loved you before he did! I'm not daft. He was all washy-eyed about you, mooning round like a motherless calf—" I clouted his head lightly. "Aye, it's well seen you're not going to be my wife now, or you'd have more respect for me!" He seemed to be falling into another fit of his disastrous giggles.

"Be serious, you gowk!" I snapped at him—but I couldn't help grinning myself. Part of my mind said, "Your sister's dead this day, and not yet buried! And your dad! And you've maybe killed a man!" but I shut it up. Time for that later. And Inge had told me herself to be happy. "Davie, I don't want to hurt you."

"Ach away, Meg!" he snapped back. "If you hurt me, I'll let you know!"

I eyed him a bit doubtfully, because I felt there was more there than he was saying, but—well, if he didn't want to say it, it wasn't for me to insist. Specially not just now. There was something bothering me, more urgent than that. "But, Davie," I said, "have you thought what you can do to support yourself? Marie's going into the household o' Master Grossmeyer's sister, but the rest o' us can't expect the goodwife to take us all in as well. Peem can aye find work, as a porter or something—"

Davie interrupted me briskly. "Porter? Don't be daft, Meg,

we'll do far better than that!" His voice was firm, and clearer, somehow. "I've it all thought out! Here's what we'll do."

"Aye, Master Spens, sir?" Peem's tone was ironic.

The lad reddened slightly, but grinned. "Aye, and you can just take that smirk off your face, Peem Jackson. I can read and write a fair handful o' tongues, more than most clerks. And we're not penniless. Don't forget we've that great gold brooch o' Inge's, and the silver one, to give us a good start."

"A start in what?" I didn't know what he was talking about.

"In trade!" He was surprised that I'd not understood. "I've helped keep my dad's books this two year past, and with me to count and cipher, and Peem to travel, we could start a good line in fancy dyestuffs and leathers. There's a man just setting up trade in Bruges has the clearest colours Dad had ever seen. And I know the men that'll buy them in London and Lisbon. Not quantity, you understand, but the finest quality. That's where the money is. In a year or two we'll make a good living, with a wee bit luck, God willing, and you'll have a house o' your own, Meg, and Marie can even come and live with us if she wants." From her face, she surely wanted. He realised he'd not asked what we thought, and looked at us enquiringly. "Well? I'm not saying it's certain, no trade is, but it's a good chance."

Peem thoughtfully raised an eyebrow at me. "What do you say, Peem?" I asked him.

"I think aye, sure he can do it," Marie butted in, wide-eyed and enthusiastic, and Davie flashed her a smile.

"No," Peem said firmly. "We can all do it together."

I nodded agreement, thinking hard. I didn't want to hurt Davie again—not today, anyway—but I had some doubts. After all, Davie was but thirteen, and I knew what daft tricks he could get up to, none better. Master Spens had thought a lot of him, but let Davie get the idea that he was the main partner in this venture and he'd run wild. But suddenly I saw how to put a rein on him. "There's just the one wee thing you've forgotten, Davie."

"What's that?" he asked, frowning.

"It's not your brooches. They're mine—mine and Marie's."

He was taken flat aback for a second, and Marie giggled again at his face, but he shrugged obligingly. "Well, we'd all be partners, anyway," he said. "That's fair, isn't it, Peem? The women put in the silver, and the men put in the work."

"Aye, fair enough," my big lad—my big man said.

"You don't think running a house for you is work as well?" I asked. "Would you care to try it?"

They raised eyebrows at me. "Do you want a bigger share, then?" Davie asked.

Well . . . But we all owed each other too much to be petty. I thought better to shake my head. Peem grinned again. "It's maybe as well," he said. "It's no just ye lasses has siller. I've a fair wee bit mysel'."

"What!" I said, astonished. "How?"

He grinned his wide grin, still innocent-looking in spite of the bruises stiffening his face. "The archers. Just lyin' about, some o' them, no doin' nothin'. An' if I found I'd a minute tae spare, I just had a wee keek in their pouches. Terrible thieves, they were. More siller than an honest man could come by in a year. It wasn't right that they should keep it, was it, now?" He reached into his pouch, drew out a good handful of coins, and poured them from one hand to the other in satisfaction at our surprise. "It'll pay our way tae Bruges, at least!"

Davie, Marie, and I eyed the coins, and one another, and started to laugh. "Peem!" I said. "You're a disgrace! I never thought to see you steal!"

"Ach away, Meg," scolded Davie. "We'll put it to better use than they would! An'—er—he's no the only one." Proud and rather shamefaced together, he reached into his own wallet and showed us a half-handful of silver. "Not as much as you got, Peem, but better than a slap in the face with a wet haddie, eh?" As we all started to laugh, he laughed joyously with us.

But he was the first to sober, and draw a deep breath. "Aye. Later. Come on, Peem, let's get done here. Or are you wanting to kick down more earth yet?"

They were soon finished their digging. We all cleaned ourselves in a clear runnel, and the lads put on their tunics. Still damp, but they'd dry on them. We spread the bottom of the hole with fresh green branches. We laid Inge's cloak out on them, and then herself. There was almost no mark on her gown; she lay there as if she was asleep, with even a tiny quirk on her lips like a smile.

I covered her with all the flowers I had gathered. May, creamy and scented like her skin; broom, yellower but no brighter than her silver-gilt hair; bluebells scarce as deep as her eyes; speedwell and cherry, daisy and ramson, wild plum and the first pink buds of the roses. The others helped, with sprays of beech and bracken, till at last there was nothing to see but a great heap of leaf and blossom. Then we gently shovelled back the spilled earth, and all was hidden. I planted a tiny birch seedling, to grow as slender and graceful, silver and gold and beautiful, as Inge herself. It was all the mark she'd have wanted.

We knelt to pray by the side of the grave. But we didn't weep for her.

I glanced sideways at the patchy remains of the great dark stain I couldn't rinse completely out of the Maid's kirtle. How could such a thrust not have killed her?

Was that what you meant, Inge, that you'd done your best for us? That you'd turned aside the sword point? Or was it you who warned the wee one to be still? Or—you couldn't have brought her back, could you? Surely never! Or when you bade me run, did you give me the power to move again, for I couldn't have done it the minute before? Oh, my dear! Thank you! Whatever it was, thank you! God bless you!

All she'd done before was washed clear away by this, the proof of her love for me, beyond and in spite of all.

Then Peem took Marie up in a piggy-back and set off, Davie scouting ahead. I checked on the brooches pinned inside the neck of my kirtle, tucked into my pouch the lock of gleaming, fine hair I'd cut, that I'd treasure always in its net of gold, and hesitated, sore of heart as of body. I was afraid.

"Come away, Meg," Peem called. "We've a ship tae catch, mind." He grinned up at me and held out his strong hand. My heart rose, and I ran down the hill towards him and the Maid.

No, not the Maid now; just an ordinary maid. Better than a queen.

Glossary

———◆———

a' — all
ain — own
ane — one
Arbroath smokie
  smoked haddock, spe-
  ciality of town of
  Arbroath
auld — old
aye — always *or* yes

bailie — magistrate, town
  councillor
bairn — child
bannock — oatcake; flat
  scone
Beltane — May Day
bere — medieval type of
  black-grained barley, no
  longer grown

bizzom — girl (insulting)
bothy — hut
brae — hillside
braw — fine
breeks — short pants with
  separate legs usually tied
  at the waist, worn under
  a tunic
burn — brook
burthen — burden, to
  measure size of a ship

callant — young man
capuchon — hood
clashmaclavers — gossip
corbie — carrion crow
cote-hardie — tight over-
  tunic with sleeves
cottar — poor farm worker

dae — do
daft — stupid, mad
damptie — damned, dratted
dollies — thick woollen pads on bell ropes for handholds
drakkar — long, low Viking-style dragon ship

firkin — small barrel
firlot — wooden bucket
firth — estuary
frae — from

garde-corps — loose over-tunic, coat
garron — pony
gie — give
gowk — fool

hame — home
Hansa League — trading confederation of merchant towns in North Germany
hizzy — hussy
Holy Rude — Holy Cross (Holy Rood)

kirk — church
kirtle — dress

knorr — broad-beamed Viking-style trading ship

lang — long

marchpane — marzipan
mind on — pay heed to, remember
mumpit mowdiewarp stupid mole

noo — now

ower — over
oyster-catcher — wading bird of the sea shore

peedie — small (Orkney)
popinjay — parrot

rutter — book of maps

sae — so
sair — sore
saltire — diagonal X-shaped cross
shift — underdress (worn only by the well-off)
skelp — chunk
sort — put right
souter — cobbler

tae — to

tipstave — early form of
rudder; vertical pole used
instead of ship's wheel

vair — squirrel fur

whins — gorse

wisnae — was not